D1010959

THE UNSTOPPABLE

BRIDGET
BLOOM

THE UNSTOPPABLE

BRIDGET BLOOM

Allison L. Bitz

HARPER TEEN

An Imprint of HarperCollinsPublishers

HarperTeen is an imprint of HarperCollins Publishers.

Library of Congress Cataloging-in-Publication Data
Names: Bitz, Allison L., author.
Title: The unstoppable Bridget Bloom / by Allison L. Bitz.
Description: First edition. | New York : HarperTeen, [2023] | Audience:
Ages 13 up. | Audience: Grades 10-12. | Summary: Sixteen-year-old
Bridget Bloom has to find a new way to shine when she is challenged not
to sing for an entire year by her prestigious Broadway-pipeline boarding
school's dean.
Identifiers: LCCN 2022029534 | ISBN 9780063266704 (hardcover)
Subjects: CYAC: Singing—Fiction. | Humility—Fiction. | Boarding
schools—Fiction. | Schools—Fiction.
Classification: LCC PZ7.1.B5623 Un 2023 | DDC [Fic]—dc23
LC record available at https://lccn.loc.gov/2022029534

Typography by Laura Mock
23 24 25 26 27 LBC 5 4 3 2 1
First Edition

To my grandparents, including the OG Socks and June

ONE

TWO THINGS ARE IMMEDIATELY APPARENT: dorm rooms bear a remarkable resemblance to jail cells, and they smell like Grandma Evelyn's basement but with zero homey nostalgic vibes. I flip-flop into the middle of the joint, doing a full one-eighty.

"Bridget? What's wrong?" Dad snakes a suntanned arm across my shoulders and hugs me to him.

My long lashes are fanning away, working hard to keep my eyes from overflowing. "It's, um. Small."

Dodge, my other dad, chuckles. Which makes sense. The system with my parents is that Dad comforts me, Dodge toughens me. "C'mon, kiddo. You knew this was the size of the room."

"Reading on a website that a shared room is fifteen-by-fifteen and then seeing it in person are two very different things."

The cinder-block walls are a god-awful shade of light blue, like

1

someone threw a bad Insta filter over a perfectly fine cloudless sky. There's a gross tile abomination underfoot, and the trim is black *rubber* of some kind, I think. All of this is a far cry from my comfy farmhouse room back in Lynch, with its gleaming wood floors, original oak trim, and massive picture windows. Dad is an antique-loving contractor, and our house is his second baby (I'm number one, of course).

The state of this room is confusing, really, because Richard James Academy in Chicago is the boarding school of my dreams. It's extremely prestigious. Rigorous. Everyone who goes here is effing brilliant, so I'll fit right in. Best of all, it's very, very far away from my backward rural hometown in Nebraska, where I have always stuck out like a glittering emerald in a sea of shale. But I suppose I forgot to account for the fact that it's also *old*, and old doesn't always mean "cool vintage vibe." Sometimes old just means shabby—hence, this dorm room.

Just as I'm about to throw myself onto my unmade mattress in despair, I'm hit with inspiration—a Bridget Bloom specialty. This room isn't at all like my bedroom, but it *is* like Lynch. Drab and dingy and too small for the likes of me. I'll do to it what I've been doing to my hometown for the entirety of my sixteen years—I'll make it fabulous. I grab the garment bag I'd slung over the school-provided desk chair, unzipping with gusto, but not *too* much gusto. Its innards are sacred. Carefully, I draw out a prized possession: my mermaid costume.

My dads fought me on bringing this. "Why in the world would you need that at boarding school, B?" said Dodge, ever the practical

2

dad. But I knew—just *knew* from some deep place in my soul—that I needed it by my side. A talisman, maybe. A reminder of who I am. A Halloween costume, if worse comes to worst.

And, in the case of this shit dorm room—wall decor.

"Help me. I'm hanging this up," I say.

"I'm confident in your ability to wield a clothes hanger. On your own," says Dodge, shaking his head.

"No, I mean—I'm hanging this up *here*. Over my bed. Like a mural." Because it's perfect. It's green and purple and iridescent, and unequivocally *mine* and *me*. Dad made it for me a few months ago, when I landed the role of Ariel in the school musical. The school had its own mermaid costume, but the thing was a clear no-go for me. I couldn't get the fin up past my hips, and those shells covered up only about 30 percent of the girls. And not even the most important 30 percent. Given Lynch Public Schools has zero budget for the arts and was threatening to recast a smaller but far less talented Ariel for that reason, Dad stepped in and saved the day. He'd whipped up my size-eighteen mer-miracle at home with just his sewing machine, a whole lot of shiny fabric, and his imagination.

I'd looked absolutely killer in my custom fin-and-shells, and I'd also killed the role. No kidding, I was a tremendous Ariel. I hit every line, every note. I was so *on* for opening night that I turned "Under the Sea" into an impromptu duet. I'm just that good.

So good that no one else in the musical even thought to invite me to the cast party after the show. I intimidate Lynch kids with my many talents. It's been like that for years now. One of the many, many reasons I needed to get out of that town.

3

In any case, my beautiful, sparkling mermaid costume is a symbol of me and of my dads' unwavering love. What better thing to brighten up my new home away from home in Chicago, five-hundred-plus miles away from the place I've lived my whole life?

Dad stares at me blankly. "You sure? I mean—"

"Yes, I'm sure. Where are the Command hooks?"

Five minutes later it's up, a smudge of chaos in the midst of monotony. Just like me. "I love it," I say, standing back to take it in. "But it's not enough."

I'd optimistically brought about twenty mirrors from my antique mirror collection, which covered the walls of my bedroom at home. Now that I see the room, though, I realize I'll be lucky if there's space for half of them. No matter—the cell block needs all the help it can get, and I put us to work faster than you can say *extreme dorm makeover*.

We hang mirrors until the whole right half of the room is covered, but it's *still* missing something. Panache. Appeal. Feng shui. *Something*. In desperation I say, "Put the shell one up over there," pointing to a blank piece of wall near the door.

Dodge purses his lips. "Isn't that Ruby's side of the room?"

Ruby Deterding is my roommate. She's from Maryland. She's also a first-year student, but she's a sophomore, whereas I'm a junior. Like me, she's going to be in the music focus program (MFP) here at Richard James. We've chatted a couple of times via an app the academy uses to match roommates, but that's it. Essentially, she's a stranger, and one who *has* to like me.

I shrug. "Won't I be doing her a favor? Adding *this* much class to our dungeon of a room?" I suppose the washed-out blue paint is meant to be neutral and soothing, but honestly, it's the color of despair.

Dodge seems dubious, but Dad elbows him in the ribs and they do as I say. The shell mirror goes up and about six others with it. In the end, seventeen mirrors find homes on the sad blue walls of my cell.

After the bed is dressed and my clothes are put away, a framed picture of me and my dads finds a place of honor on top of my dresser—a shot from an amusement park, our collective winter-white faces smattered with early spring's freckles. "It's perfect," I say, surveying our work.

"Just like you," says Dad, bopping my nose.

I shove at his shoulder but let the cheesy compliment ride. I'm probably not perfect, but I *am* pretty great. And about to get greater.

Dodge fishes a stack of bills out of his wallet. "Now, here. This should cover some beginning-of-the-year groceries and things. Like we talked about, we'll put some money into your account every month, but you need to pay attention to your spending, okay? No antiquing on this student budget." He grins, but there's a pinch around his eyes that sends a twinge of anxiety through me. Only once did I check on the tuition and boarding costs of this place, and the figure was enough to make me choke on my dollar-store seltzer. But my dads don't talk money around me, and they assured me we could afford this. Still, I did some research on my own. According to a Reddit thread I found, r/RealTalkRJAcademy, most of the MFP musical theater kids are sponsored by old Broadway-obsessed donors—meaning I'm a shoo-in. Some rich lady will choose me, after she sees me perform. I can feel it in my bones. (I made sure to forward that thread to the dads. Just in case.) If everything goes to plan, I'll be all set with a sponsorship by next semester.

"I'll be frugal," I promise. "And no antiquing." Which, for a Bloom, is a *big* concession.

After that we start our goodbyes—and I say "start" because boy, do they take a minute. I had a feeling it would be a little torturous for all of us, even though I've been antsy to get out of town for months upon months. My breaking point with Lynch was at the end of my freshman year, when Derek Czerny pelted me in the head with a spitball for the umpteenth time. And not the fun, "I'm just kidding around" kind—the huge, wet, "I really mean this" kind of spitball. Bridget Venus Bloom cannot deal with that sort of indignity, and it was about then I started begging to move, to transfer schools, to *anything*. And then, *Eureka*! An ad for Richard James Academy in Chicago popped up on YouTube. The prep boarding school is known for churning out the likes of future senators and surgeons, the Hollywood beloved and pop stars— the latter of which usually come out of the academy's music focus program. MFP students are basically guaranteed acceptance to any college music conservatory or a pipeline straight to the stage.

Case in point, Duke Ericson, current Richard James senior and poster child for the academy. Duke is originally from Kansas City, Missouri, is six feet even, Afro-Latinx and white, loves pizza, rides a motorcycle, and prefers women without tattoos. At least, that's what his Wikipedia page says. He went viral on YouTube last year when he put up a video of himself singing an original song with Blythe Rosen, a mega–pop star, and now he has a whole channel of uploads. He's an inspiration. Also, he's melt-your-underwear hot.

And Duke is just one of many shiny examples.

In sum, the more I read, the more I realized Richard James was the *only* place for me to finish my junior and senior years of high school (as it was too late to audition for my sophomore year). A ticket out of Lynch *and* the key to my destiny of Broadway stardom? Check and check. I've never wanted anything more, except maybe The Spotlight generally.

Still, my dads and I are all we've got, now that Grandma Evelyn has died. We're in the midst of group hugging when the door cracks open, and Ruby Deterding steps hesitantly through the threshold.

After much observation over the years, I've determined there are two distinct types of music-loving kids. First, there are the musical theater mavens, who are shouty, wear bright clothes, and are known to wave their arms in a dramatic fashion when feeling something deeply.

The other type—the instrumentalists, I call them—are more reserved, aloof, and either frumpy or plain clothed. They inherently possess a snobbery about not calling music written in the Romantic or Baroque periods "Classical."

I am of the former group. Obviously.

It appears my roommate is of the latter. Her brown-and-blond pixie cut *could* be edgy but isn't, and she wears jeans and a Pink Floyd T-shirt. But the real giveaway is the cello case she hefts along with her, which is bigger than she is. She's flanked by two stuffy-looking middle-aged white people. The man's in a suit, and the woman sports a cardigan that's almost exactly the sickening color of our cinder blocks.

But it's my solemn duty to become best friends with my roommate, even if she *is* an instrumentalist. That's just how this stuff works.

"Hi," I say, jutting a hand out to Ruby. "I'm Bridget Bloom."

Ruby shakes limply, smiling in a Target cashier kind of way. Courteous, but fake. "Hi. I'm Rub—"

She's interrupted by Dad. "Bring it in, kiddo," he says, and though her eyes are wide and incredulous, she steps into his open arms. "Welcome to the Bloom family, Ruby. And don't mind us—we're huggers," he says before letting go. Then Dodge takes over, squeezing her again.

For a flash, Ruby's smile brightens, but then an obnoxious throat clear draws our collective attention to Ruby's parents. They wear twin looks, a hybrid of polite and judgy, something that only the super-rich seem to know how to pull off. Neither offers a hand out to me or my dads. Possibly because their arms are full of suitcase handles and boxes and comforter sets. Possibly not. Hard to tell.

Meanwhile, Dad blows right past the pompous faces and wraps his arms around each of the Deterdings in turn, suitcases and all. "So nice to meet you," he says.

I remember my manners. "This is Chad, aka Dad," I say, pointing to my blond-haired, sunshiny parent. "And this is my Dodge," I add, presenting my mahogany-haired, stoic dad with a flourish, because it's not like he's going to do this for himself.

"Your . . . Dodge?" says Ruby, looking confused.

"Oh, it's the *cutest* story," gushes Dad. This is the kind of thing that horrifies most kids my age, but honestly, it *is* the cutest story, and so on-brand. "We adopted B when she was almost two. Her mom, Carol, was Dodge's younger sister. Unfortunately Carol died in a car accident, and B's bio dad was never in the picture to begin with."

All eyes look to Dodge at this point, as always, and he issues a sad, soft smile. "I'll miss my little sister forever, but she left us the best gift of all—the daughter I would've never otherwise had. And Carol lives on in her, another gift."

Dad barrels on with the story. He's kind of immune to the big feels of it, since he's told it so many times. "At first we tried to get Bridget to call him Daddy, but she was already talking by then and called him Dodge—and *everyone* in town calls him that, after his truck," adds Dad, rolling his eyes. "We'd say, 'B, you understand Dodge is your daddy, right?' and she'd say—"

"He's Dodge. But now he's *my* Dodge," I say, finishing the story in a baby voice, as I always do. I've got the imitation of past me down to a science. Of course, I was too young to remember any of this myself—I remember nothing of my mother, beyond what I've been told and seen in home movies—but I've seen the video of this moment so many times that I *feel* like I must remember it.

"And I'm still her Dodge," says my pickup-truck-driving farmer dad, grinning.

I'm grateful as hell for both of my dads, though I sometimes wonder what life would have been like if my mom had stayed alive.

9

By all reports, I'm a lot like she was. Redheaded, stubborn, scary bright, and talented. She was headed for bigger things, until one icy patch of road took her life.

And so I'm headed to those bigger things in honor of her. I'll do what she didn't get to.

The room remains silent in the wake of our family origin story. Dodge fills the space. "My actual name is Mike," he offers.

"Oh, how lovely," says Mrs. Deterding, finally, without one speck of warmth. She may as well have said, "Can you *please* shut up, you baboons."

My dads finally seem to notice the frosty awkwardness rolling off the Deterdings. "Well, Chad. I guess we should head out and give Ruby and her family some space," says Dodge.

I let Dad and Dodge hug me for an egregious amount of time before pulling away. I assure them I'm fine now, going to be fine, will call them if I need anything, will try not to stray too far from campus alone, etc. They shove a box of condoms and a package of dental dams into my hands and make me promise if I'm going to have sex, I'll have safe sex. (Out of my periphery I see Mr. Deterding's eyes boring into the prophylactics like they are the Devil's Work.)

Finally, their need for squeezing me to death is satiated and they make their tearful departure, managing to *not* hug Ruby or her parents as they go. I assume I'm going to be relieved with two fewer bodies in the room, but as soon as they're gone, my rib cage starts feeling a little tight. Like there's something big growing in there. I take a seat on my extra-long, not-super-comfy, creaky twin bed, rubbing my palms against the satiny lavender bedspread we'd selected at Target last week. I think I'm fine. Am I fine?

Now with more space to maneuver about, Ruby can fully take in the splendor that is my eye for home interiors. She steps away from her parents and moves from mirror to mirror, stopping to observe each one. "Oookkkaay. Let's talk about this, um, decor," says Ruby.

"Yes! Let's." If I had a tail, it'd be wagging. Our first roommate discussion! The mirrors could be a total bonding moment. Each one has a story.

"What in the world *is* that?" Ruby sneers up at my radiant mermaid costume–turned–art like it's autographed clown portraiture. She homes in on the shell-encrusted mirror, my favorite. "I thought . . . wow, I thought the rooms would be blank slates. Did the academy provide all this hideous stuff?" She pulls at the mirror, and I gasp in alarm as my body moves involuntarily toward it. You can't handle a mirror *by its shells*.

"Um, no. That's mine. They all are. I thought . . . well, you know what they say about mirrors making a room look bigger."

The three of them ogle me like pretentious guppies. Finally, Ruby's mom clears her throat. "Thank you for trying to . . . freshen up the room, Bridget. I'm sure you and Ruby will find a way to make the decorating work for both of you." She digs an elbow into Ruby's arm.

Ruby massacres what some might call a smile. "Sure. Yeah. Of course. Thanks, Bridget."

With the three of them now walking all over the room and all over my enthusiasm, and no dad barriers to shore me up, I'm starting to feel claustrophobic. "I'm going to let you settle in. It was nice to meet you, Mr. and Mrs. Deterding."

"Oh, it's Deeeeeterding, dear," says Ruby's mom, laying one of her many bags on Ruby's bed.

"Gotcha. Okay, well, until next time, then," I say, hastily removing myself and shutting the door behind me. Once in the hallway I inhale deeply, then go in for another gulp of sweet, sweet oxygen. The Deterding family had sucked the life right out of my dorm room.

Kids and parents swarm, carrying boxes, piles of clothes, rolled-up posters. One dad hauls in a wooden apparatus that's possibly a bunk bed. Impressive. I try to catch someone's eye, anyone's, desperate to have my second first meeting go better than my attempt with Ruby and her parents, Mr. and Mrs. Fakey McFakerton. But everyone is too busy to notice me.

Suddenly very aware of my solitude, I lean back against the outside of my door and flick on my phone. There's a text from Dad.

Dad: Remember—we won't text until you do! Even the most prolific plants need space to grow and BLOOM. Go be the star you already are. We love you, precious girl.

My feels overflow, and my eyes get soggier than I've let them get all day.

"Hi!" says a voice at point-blank range, scaring my tears right back into their ducts. A tall woman with long beachy-blond waves and impossibly dark blue eyes stands in my personal space.

I'd take a step back if I could, but there's nowhere to go. "Hi?"

12

She clasps my upper arm, her sun-kissed skin several shades darker than mine, though we're both white. "Are you Ruby?"

"No." Thank God. No taste in decor, if I were. "I'm Bridget."

Something flitters across her face—nervousness?—but it's gone in a blink, replaced by a twinkling smile. "Ah, Bridget Bloom. What a name! I couldn't forget it once I saw it on my roster. I'm Piper, your hall counselor."

"Hall counselor?"

"I'm here to help you figure things out. I can guide you to your classrooms. Point you to other school resources. Help you talk through difficulties you might run into. You know, all that good stuff."

"Wow. Um, thanks?"

Piper moves in close and cups her hand over her mouth, like she's telling me a secret—but doesn't whisper. And it's a good thing: it's as loud as the New York Philharmonic in this hallway. "Hey, can you come with me for a minute? To a quieter place? There's something I need to talk with you about."

Even though that sounds ominous as hell, it's *still* better than going back into the cloying discomfort of my own damn room. "Sure."

I follow Piper until we reach a huge, heavy wood door with fancy carvings—the kind of thing Dad would drool over. Behind it is a room that's maybe an office, maybe a fortune-teller's haven; it's hard to say. Floor-to-ceiling bookshelves, dark wood panels, a big oak table, and fluffy armchairs with ottomans—this is the vibe. When Piper flips the wall switch, several floor lamps come on, but they're dim, because they're all covered with gauzy fabric.

"What *is* this place?" I say as Piper gestures me into a mauve wing chair.

"I call it the comfort library. It's generally where I meet with students who need to chat in private."

"Oh. Well, the room is nice." *But what the hell are we doing in it?*

I don't need to speak the question for Piper to hear it. "So, Bridget. We need to talk about your placement score. And the music focus program."

Here's how Richard James works: first, you apply with essays, grades, standardized test scores, and letters of recommendation—a lot like a college application. It's highly selective, but I'm an ace student with a knack for selling myself in writing. Obviously I got in. Once you're admitted, you can apply for a focus program. Music is one, but there's also visual arts, journalism and creative writing, science and engineering, history and pre-politics, and math. My audition for the MFP—which I came to Chicago to complete last month—involved singing a prepared solo and playing a piece of music you've never seen before on the spot, otherwise known as sight-reading.

I sight-read like a boss, and the panel judges for my prepared solo were thrilled with me. One of them shouted, "Brava!" as I left the stage. I'd brought down the house just as hard as I always do, maybe even harder. There's literally no way I didn't get in.

Piper continues, her face squeezing in a concerned-adult kind of way. "You didn't get in."

TWO

THERE IS A KIND OF pause that books often refer to as "pregnant." I super-hate that description, partially because ew, but also because I'd never experienced one.

But now I have. This silence is long and heavy and *loud*.

"Excuse me?" I finally manage to say, praying to whoever's out there that I've just got an earwax problem.

"I'm so sorry. You weren't admitted to the MFP. There was a computer glitch with the scoring of the theory tests, and we just got it all sorted late last night. Your test score was . . . really bad. There's no tactful way to say it," says Piper, grimacing like she's in physical pain.

An anvil plummets into my gut, landing with a dull thud, and promptly my hands and feet break out into a clammy, anxious sweat. I'd forgotten all about the theory test—more like blocked it out, that's how awful it was. All music focus students took it online last week. My understanding was that they were just placement tests, though, not *admission* deciders. Holy shit. This is very bad.

I mean, of course my theory test score was low. It's not like Lynch or anywhere within driving distance has theory courses. The only music theory I know I learned from Grandma Evelyn (aka Grams), and she's been gone for almost two years now. My knowledge is neither fresh nor vast in that area, but I thought it was enough and they'd teach me more here. Isn't that the *point* of a music program? To teach me music stuff?

"I. Um. Wow." For once in my life, I have no words, only a very vomity feeling in my stomach.

"I know this must be shocking," Piper replies sympathetically. "Octavia wanted me to discuss your options with you."

Octavia Lawless is the chair of the MFP *and* the dean of students. "My . . . options?"

"Yes. We know you might have come to Richard James specifically for the MFP. A lot of students do. So if you want to withdraw from school entirely, you still can, at no financial penalty."

Couldn't they have let me know all of this when we were still back in Lynch, before all of my clothes were hanging in my sardine can of a dorm room closet and my mirrors were disrespected by my cringey roommate and my dads were headed home? Piper must read the anger on my face, because she says, "I'm really sorry you're so late in finding out. We tried to call this morning but couldn't get ahold of anyone."

"Really? What number were you trying?"

Piper spouts the ten digits off the sheet with my test scores, and I realize what happened.

"Our home phone." A relic in the era of mobile to even have such a thing, but Dodge insists on having a landline.

There's a ball consisting of every painful emotion imaginable welling in my throat. My vision goes hazy around the edges, like I'm dreaming—wait, maybe I *am* dreaming. Nightmaring. I pinch myself, hoping I won't feel it . . . but no. It hurts. Not as bad as my heart hurts, but the pinch leaves a mark.

And Piper's looking at me expectantly. I need a plan. Now. Lordy. "What happens to me if I decide to stay?"

"You'd be a gen ed student, which obviously still provides a really, really great college-prep education. And you can try out for a focus program again for your senior year."

I sigh. Richard James *is* a great school, there's no doubt about that. It's also not Lynch, which is a huge bonus.

"Octavia also wanted you to know you are welcome to take any of the music courses that are available to gen ed students. You can load your schedule up with those. She encourages you to sign up for Theory One if you want to try again for music focus next year."

I perk up a little at that. "So I can sort of . . . create my own music focus program for this year?"

"As long as you're taking the required core academic courses, the sky's the limit. You can even take piano lessons!"

Okay, so this is going to be fine. I'll be in spirit what everyone else *officially* is, no big deal. My chest has just started to depressurize itself when Piper adds, "The only thing you can't do is perform."

All the happy thoughts leave my body. I am the opposite of Peter Pan going airborne. I'm crashing into the ground, my life vision going up in a Bloom bonfire.

And Piper says it so blithely, with the delivery with which one might say, "And tonight's dinner is chicken strips." As if it isn't the absolute dream crusher of all time. *Anything but perform.* Performance is my life. It's embedded in my DNA. It's my destiny. Taking it away from me is like ripping off my right arm. Hell, maybe both arms.

Not to mention dashing those sponsorship hopes—no donor can choose me if they can't see or hear me. But I can't even deal with that right now. The financial part of my worry will have to wait for another day.

I nod reluctantly and Piper relaxes back into her armchair. As she crosses one Birkenstock over another, I notice her perfect, blue-toenailed feet. Literally, I had no idea anyone's feet could be so graceful. Try as I might to make them pretty, mine are long and boatlike. Good thing I'm more of an Ariel than a Cinderella. Flippers over slippers, that's what I always say.

Though I wouldn't say no to a fairy godmother right about now. "What's your take on Octavia?" I ask Piper.

Piper's gentle smile freezes. "Octavia is . . . complicated."

"Complicated?"

Piper pierces me with her midnight-blue peepers. "My best piece of advice when it comes to Octavia is to lie low. You stay out of her way, and she'll more than likely stay out of yours."

"And . . . if I don't stay out of her way?"

"I would compare it to kicking a hornet's nest." I wince. Octavia sounds more evil stepmother than fairy godmother.

Piper barrels straight back to the original topic. "Anyway, what do you think about joining us as a gen ed student? I really am sorry to spring this all on you. Feel free to call your parents if you need to discuss it."

I shake my head, because if I call my dads, I *will* cry and they *will* come swoop me up and haul me back to stupid Lynch, and I can't think of anything more humiliating than that. I've been talking up Richard James to anybody at my old school who would listen, and often to people who were clearly doing their best to *not* listen. Derek Czerny and his spitballs, and Emma Shafer, who used to be my best friend until for some reason in eighth grade she wasn't, and Lizzie Papik, who rolled her eyes anytime I spoke in class or sang in the halls or *anything* that made me *me*—I need for *all* of them to see what I'm made of. I am Richard James material. I am too much for Lynch.

I'm not going back. I'm just going to have to find a way to make this work.

"I'll stay," I say finally.

"Oh, good! I'm glad. Now, let's talk about your living situation. You chose a music learning community floor. You can stay put, or we can move you to a different floor."

"Are there . . . are there any others like me? Kids who are doing a lot of music but who aren't in the MFP?"

Piper's face scrunches sympathetically. "Not on your floor."

My teeth grind as I consider. Living here among the people who were living the life I wanted would definitely be a very special brand of hell. And yet. I'd still be having classes with a lot of these folx. And even if I wasn't technically one of them, I think my best shot at fitting in anywhere is with other kids who love music like I do.

And did I really want to move all my mirrors again?

"I'll stay in my room. But would it be okay if we kept my non-admittance to the music program between you and me?"

"Sure thing. No reason to shout it from the rooftops," says Piper.

"Thanks." I'm considering heading outside for a nice, long, wallowing cry when inspiration hits. As it does, when you're me. Yes, this whole MFP situation sucks to the nth degree, but so did my dorm room, and look what I'd achieved in there. I'm unstoppable. It's kind of my thing.

When a door closes, a window opens. It was one of many Grandma Evelyn–isms, stated with a repetition that was annoying until she wasn't there to say it anymore. Her face swirls so clearly into my mind just then, her sweet wrinkly eyes slightly taunting. *Since when did you ever back down from a challenge, little miss?*

I just need to find my window.

It's been forty minutes since I made like a library and booked it out of my room. Maybe it's okay to go back.

I stop at my door, pondering the etiquette of entering a room one shares with someone else. Do you just walk in? Knock? Maybe roommates typically have a signal, like a three-toned whistle or maybe some Morse code tapping? Finally, I rap lightly before letting myself in.

Ruby sits atop her plain-but-pristine white bedspread, magazine open in her lap. There are no signs of Mr. and Mrs. Suit and Sweater—a small mercy. A new-looking Apple laptop sits on Ruby's desk, flanked by a pair of fancy speakers, and a few framed pictures adorn her dresser and bedside table. It's all very classy, very chic, and I have one startling, shocking moment of feeling *less than*.

Which I hastily throw out the dorm window, which Ruby has cracked just a tad, despite the swamp-like Chicago summer heat. I cross the room and wind it shut.

Seven mirrors lie in a neat pile on my bed.

"I ended up not needing those," she says as I examine the discarded decorations.

I grab handfuls of Bubble Wrap out of the trash can under my desk and start to wrap each mirror. I don't dare put these precious pieces in the mail, but I'm also not sure where we're going to keep them in this matchbox of a room. My top teeth crush into my bottom lip, an attempt to keep it from trembling, and I turn my back to Ruby so she can't see my glassy eyes.

Today is a lot. That's all there is to it.

"I think they'll fit in the closet, on the top shelf," she says. She's as intuitive as she is cruel, folx.

"Thanks, that should work fine." The words come out of me thicker than I'd intended. I clear my throat. "Did your mom and dad get going?"

"They had a couple of things they wanted to shop for while

they're still in town, but they'll be back to take me out for dinner. One last hurrah."

Of *course* they're going shopping. Because clearly, this is a family that needs even more expensive things.

But the family dinner part was a good idea. A send-off meal with my dads might've been nice. I'd thought I was ready to say goodbye before, but I think really I'd just been tired of being smooshed in the car with all my stuff and NPR. A pang of loss slices through my chest, and I finger my phone, considering calling to see if they're still in the city. Then I set it down on my desk and walk away, busying myself again with the Bubble Wrap. Calling them now would *not* be a good idea, for reasons upon reasons, the biggest one being that I don't plan to tell them I'm not admitted to the MFP. Not yet, anyway.

Ruby fills the silence between us. "My theory placement score *just* hit my in-box. Nothing like waiting for the last minute! Did you get yours?"

My molars chomp down toward each other so fast that I clip one side of my tongue, releasing a surge of metallic blood into my mouth. I should hate the feeling, because it effing hurts, but the pain feels oddly good. Sorta right. And it gives me a different kind of pain to focus on, something that isn't Ruby the Privileged bragging about her theory score.

"Yeah. I'm in the basic class." It's only sort of a lie. Tonight I'll log on to the Richard James registration program and sign up for as many music classes as I can, including the ultra-beginner-level theory Octavia suggested.

"Ah. Cool. I'm in intermediate."

"Cool," I say, though nothing about any of this is cool. It is all shit.

But Ruby isn't done torturing me. "Did your parents take off already? Like, leave Chicago completely?"

I lean down to fiddle with my perfectly tied double-knotted shoes so she can't see the tear pricks that come immediately surging back. "Yeah."

"You could come to dinner with us, if you want."

A whole evening with the Stuffies? "Thanks, but I already have plans."

"Really?" She's eyebrowing and frowning like she's surprised. She must think it's *so hard* for me to make friends. I'll show her.

But for now, I will lie. "Um, yeah. I met some kids while I was out exploring the dorm. We're going to eat in the dining hall."

"Oh. Well, enjoy."

"You too."

I carefully place the wrapped mirrors on the top shelf of the closet, then stay in there, acting like I'm organizing my stuff (which is already perfectly organized). Ruby makes me twitchy—the exact opposite of what I'd expected in a roommate. So much for the easygoing girl-talk, witty banter, and giggling that are the hallmarks of bunkmates, per TV shows and movies everywhere.

When I finally exit the closet, Ruby's got her face in her phone, so I grab mine and do the same. Maybe it's just me, but it feels like there are about fourteen rotund elephants in the room.

A gross, slimy chunk of feeling starts in my head and drops into my stomach. Rather than dissolve in the acid, it stays there, steadfast, a brick in my gut.

Dread may be the densest of the feelings, but nothing, *nothing*, can douse ambition. I fill my head with plans for the next day—my first real day as a Richard James student!—and something like hope, and like determination, fills the space where the dread was, nearly washing it out.

My newfound emotional space gives me room for plotting, and a plan cracks through. I have all the right skills for persuasion—fast talking, a certain amount of charm, loads of moxie. Not to mention my raw musical talent. I can still get in the music program for the year, I *know* it. Piper's advice to steer clear of Octavia rattles through my noggin, but I find myself able to dismiss it, word by word. Lying low might have worked for Piper, but it's not my thing. I'm about the least subtle person I know.

I hope Octavia's ready when I kick her hornet's nest.

THREE

I WAKE TO THE SONG that's served as my alarm for the last several months ("Firework" by Katy Perry, because it's so *me*), but everything else is unfamiliar. The bed's lumpy in weird places, my arm's hanging off the side. The light in the room's all wrong. Window position is off. My heart thuds in my ears with near panic confusion: *Where am I? What day is it?*

Lavender calm washes over me as I remember I'm at Richard James, and today is the first day of classes. Baby, I *am* a firework, and it's time to put on a show.

Hope surges yellow and I spring out of bed. I linger in the shower, breathing deeply, letting the steam massage my vocal cords. After today, I intend to be able to use these magic cords for more than sucking vapors and making stupid small talk with Ruby. I'm unstoppable. Octavia Lawless won't know what hit her

25

once I visit her office to remind her of my exceptional talent. It'd be a disservice to the school to not let me perform.

I make my damp way back to the room and find Ruby isn't up yet. How in the world is she going to be ready and to class by eight? My making-a-public-appearance routine takes about eighty minutes, and I assume that's gotta be about the industry standard for people with a strong sense of personal aesthetic.

The hair dryer and the lamp on my dresser have been on for about a minute when Ruby sits up in bed, hair sticking in every direction. "What time is it?"

"Six thirty-five!" I shout over the hair dryer.

"Ugh, so early," she says, lying back down and folding a pillow over her face. Two minutes later, she rears up again, face red. "How much longer do you think that'll take?"

"Um, probably at least another five minutes. I've got a lot of hair," I explain, holding one thick strand out to demonstrate.

"Could you maybe run the dryer somewhere else?"

Entitled much? "Well, I guess, but don't you think you should probably get up anyway?"

"I can be ready in ten minutes flat. I've got until at least seven fifteen."

"But what about breakfast?"

"How long do you think it's gonna take me to eat, Bridget?"

Well, hell if I know. I always try to give myself plenty of time so I'm not late for anything. Feeling prepared helps me with nerves. Not that I'm going to explain all this to Righteous Ruby. "I'll just finish up in the bathroom."

"Thanks. I appreciate that." She burrows back into her cocoon of blankets and pillows.

By 7:17 a.m., I'm dressed and leaving the room, and she's just barely up and moving. Yeah, we'll see whose stress management strategy pans out better. (Spoiler alert: Mine. It'll clearly be mine.)

As soon as I walk into the cafeteria—known as "the Rot" by Richard James students—I wish the friends I told Ruby about were a little less fictional. Sure would be nice to have some people to sit with right about now. Would've been nice last night, too, instead of eating granola bars alone in my room while Ruby was out with her parents.

I need to look cool, laid-back, like the kind of girl a person would want to chat with over avocado toast and coffee. Like my insides are not trapped in one long, horror-movie-worthy scream. I dig my phone out of the side pocket of my bag and unlock it, because nothing says "I've got this" like checking your phone while you stand awkwardly at the threshold of a bustling room. No important notifications await. My dads have honored their commitment to not text until they hear from me.

I jam the phone into my back pocket and gaze back out into the crowded cafeteria. Duos and trios of students sit together, spread out across long rows of table. But they're all strangers to me.

All but one.

I almost go into cardiac arrest when I see him. Duke Ericson's there. Like, *right there*. After months of seeing him on my phone screen only, the experience is surreal. His straight, dazzling teeth stand out against his medium reddish-brown skin, and his toned

27

biceps strain the sleeves of his fitted T-shirt. Do I *actually* go to school where this absolute dish of a human being goes? Hot damn, the only way my life could possibly get any sweeter is if I can get him to fall head over Converse for me. His head's thrown back in a laugh, and the gaggle of students flanking him are busting up, too.

All but one.

A mahogany-haired kid with an intense smattering of freckles and a T-shirt emblazoned with Freddie Mercury's hot face sits on the fringe of the group, and I wonder if he is my *in*. But honestly, it's also hard to tell if he's a part of the Duke Fan Club or not. His position at the table would say yes. His face would beg to differ.

Only one way to find out. I grip my tray tighter as I make my way toward my fellow Freddie fan, as nonchalantly as possible. As my tray clinks the table, plastic meeting plastic, I raise my eyes from my scrambled eggs in greeting.

"I like your freckles," I say.

His eyes, which are lashy and already on the big side, open even wider. They're light brown, but with a flower of yellow around the pupils. Mesmerizing, really. "You're one to talk," he says, one side of his mouth hitching up. "But for the record, I like yours, too."

We grin at each other and an eggbeater starts churning in my chest. Maybe because of his sunflower eyes, but maybe because this could be my key to meeting Duke. I *knew* I could make friends here. I'll show those Lynch losers what they were missing out on when I come home for Christmas with an entourage of talented friends.

"I'm Max Griffin," he says.

"Bridget Bloom."

"Wow, an alliterative name."

My smile is growing wider by the second. "Wow, what a nerdy thing to say. Please take that in the most complimentary way possible."

"I will. Nerds run the world." He's also still smiling, but his freckles disappear under the blood that's rushed to his cheeks, and I can't help but feel a little proud of myself for making a boy blush. "You're new," he says. A statement, not a question.

"Yeah. It's my first year. Must not be yours?"

"Nah, it's my fourth year here."

"Wow. You like it?"

He sips at what's left of his orange juice. "I do. Richard James is a better fit for what I'm good at than normal high school."

"And what are you good at?"

"Music," he says. "I'm in the focus program."

"Me too!" The words slip out—I meant to agree that I'm good at music. But now I don't really know how to correct myself. And I don't really want to.

"Awesome! Hey, wanna exchange numbers? It's good for us music kids to stick together."

Us music kids. My first actual, non-sucky-roommate friend at Richard James. There's no turning back now. "Of course," I say, handing my phone to him. I lean back in my chair, considering him as he studiously enters his number. "I think I'll put you into my phone as Freddie, in honor of that magnificent shirt."

He snorts. "For the record, it *is* a magnificent shirt."

"Oh, I'm being serious. Big Queen fan over here."

"Well, then by all means," he says, handing back my phone.

"So glad I have your permission, sir, because ten bucks says my big mouth slips and calls you Freddie in person, at least once."

His eyes land on my mouth then. "Are you that forgetful, Bridget Bloom?" He's got this look on his face I can't quite figure out, but something about the curve of his lips tells me he's enjoying this.

"I think it's more like impulsive. I've been known to speak without thinking. Act without thinking. Sing without thinking."

"Oh, you're one of those singer types?"

I nod enthusiastically. "I'm a pianist, too. You?"

"Used to be one of those singer types, too, but I'm here for guitar. And theory."

"Who comes to Richard James for *theory*?"

"Only the coolest nerds. You'll find us in room 313 at nine a.m., AP music theory."

I make the face of "oh hell, no" and Max snickers, then pops a grape into his mouth. "So, are all the girls from wherever you're from as confident as you are?"

I scoff. "Nebraska, and no. Bunch of lemmings, for the most part."

"Yeesh. No lost love for home sweet home?"

"Not really. Where are you from?

"Kansas City."

"Really? Do you know Duke Ericson?" Same home city, same breakfast table . . . it stands to reason, right?

His gaze falls south, into his mostly eaten oatmeal. "Yeah, I know him."

"That's so cool!"

"Yeah. So cool." Except his frown says it's the least cool thing ever.

"What, don't you like him?"

Max shrugs. "No, he's fine." He stands without finishing his food, picking his tray up. "Anyway, I've gotta go. See you around, Bridget."

"See ya, Max."

He rushes off like he's got a flight to catch. What the hell just happened? I ponder this while methodically chewing bites of egg, but no answers come. I do an internal shrug and write it off. There are more pressing matters at hand—such as, *the* Duke Ericson is still mere feet away. Would it be weird to slide over and join him and his group, midmeal? I take a ferocious slurp of my coffee and cringe—bitter, too black. *Buck up, Chicago girl*, my mind says, and this time my slug is big enough to leave berry lip stain on the white ceramic mug.

Okay, you've got this. I grab my tray and lift out of my seat, almost to standing when Duke's entire group vacates the table. They float off toward the exit in a flock, echoes of laughter trailing behind them as they go.

Knees suddenly weak, I sit back down, hard. What was I thinking? I'd just walk up, introduce myself to Duke, and that'd be it? We'd be history in the making?

Well, yeah.

Fortunately, I'll have more opportunities to catch his eye. I'm goddamn Bridget Bloom, and I make shit happen. As I glance down at my cell phone clock and realize it's almost time for my very first Richard James class, my Duke-inspired adrenaline rush catches a second wind. Isn't it weird how excitement and nervousness do the exact same things to your body? Same song, but with a key change. I gather my things, all ready to go, when a tray hits the table in front of me.

"Oh. Hey," I say as Ruby spreads her napkin across her lap.

"Hi. Your friends already leave?" She doesn't make eye contact, and I can't tell if she's being sincere or snide. I suppose it doesn't matter, really—just the sight of her makes me feel sick and sad and like an outsider at the school I'm trying to make a home out of. Away from Ruby is always the best place to be.

"Yeah, just a second ago. I'm headed off, too."

"Okay. Guess I'll see you later," she says. She takes a bite of her bagel as she scrolls a social media feed on her phone. Never looks up.

And as I stride away, I don't look back.

FOUR

MY FIRST COURSE OF THE day is uneventful, dare I say anti-climactic. Notable details include the following: I've learned that caricatures of humans *can* be found in the wild, as evidenced by Dr. Burns, our English prof. He's old, white, wearing a tweed jacket, and nondescript enough to be the sage "challenger of status quo thinking" in any teen movie.

But my heart rate skyrockets as I walk through the door of my second class, because it's theory. Theory 1, to be exact, aka Theory for Dummies. Piper said that the MFP students who only barely passed their theory exams are also in this level, along with gen ed students who want to take it as an elective. (*Who* in the actual hell would volunteer for that?) It's a useless subject, but it stands between me and everything I want. And *that* thought is making me sweaty, and I don't want to leave with swamp ass, so I try a silent

Bridget Bloom Booster Talk (copyright pending). *How bad can it be? It's the introductory course. You're a boss and you've got this.*

The seats toward the back are almost all taken (shocker), but there's one left, way back in the farthest corner. I hustle toward it, moving as fast as I can without my boobs nailing my chin. Once I've claimed my spot, I stretch out in my chair and heave a cleansing sigh, knowing I've at least minimized my chances of being called on.

A tiny brown-haired Black woman in a gray sheath dress calls the class to order and introduces herself as Dr. Milhouse. Her voice is a cross between a news anchor's and a kindergarten teacher's, and I find myself tuning in, even though I struggle to understand the words coming out of her mouth. Inversions, incidentals, diminished minors? At least it sounds pretty.

The girl sitting to my right appears to be taking detailed notes. I look down at my blank notebook and feel a shock of inadequacy.

Without turning my head, I glance over at her notebook to see what I've been missing. What's there is a rainbow, a unicorn, and a decent rendering of Dr. Milhouse. My shoulders sag with relief as I jot on the corner of my own notebook.

"Nice pictures," I write, then slide the notebook next to hers.

She sees it and her eyes dart up to meet mine. With the tiniest of smiles, she scrawls something on the page opposite her doodles and pushes it over to me. "Thanks. Tryna stay sane. Not easy in here."

The unicorn doodles and her admission of near insanity make me feel not quite so alone. And so I take a risk and write:

34

I suck at theory.

She writes back.

Me too.

I guess if we were any good, we wouldn't be in here.

Right?

Woe is us. We are the sad.

We go on like this throughout the class, though to our credit, we do stop and take some actual notes when Dr. Milhouse starts writing stuff on the board. I've just shoved another note over to the girl asking what class she has next when my name rings out, sounding like a song in Dr. Milhouse's gentle timbre. Maybe she was a Disney princess in a former life. Or maybe *for real* on Broadway a few years back, who knows?

"Bridget? Ms. Bloom?" she says again, craning her neck around the room.

I raise my hand. "Here."

"Oh, there you are, way in the back. Bridget, what's the next note in the sequence?"

I look at the notes she's written into the staff on the board. I know the notes, I could *play* the notes, but I don't know what note completes a second inversion triad in C major. I'm opening my mouth to embarrass myself by saying "I don't know" when the girl's notebook slides under my hand.

"E. The top note is E," I say with much more confidence than I feel.

"Very good, Ms. Bloom." Dr. Milhouse goes on to explain how inverting the chord again brings the triad to its root position.

Which, for the record, does *not* seem like theory for beginners. What in the world have I gotten myself into?

I shoot the girl a look of gratitude as I write on her notebook.

You sure you suck at theory?

She shrugs as she smiles down at the page, where she's begun doodling some flowers and hearts around my words.

When the class finally ends, I turn to the girl immediately. "I'm Bridget."

"Liza."

"Like Liza Minnelli?"

A droll smirk. "My namesake."

"For real?"

"Wish I was kidding."

Now that I'm looking at her head-on, I'm struck with how stunning she is. Long, straight, shiny black hair, the kind you could hide your face behind if you used it like a curtain, but Liza's is tied half back. The clear bronze skin underneath glows. I bet she exfoliates daily. Her dark eyes are rimmed with thick black eyeliner, and she wears lipstick that's so dark purple, it's almost black, too. But she's the kind of girl who would be just as pretty with a bare face, and for a split second I feel dumpy and fake compared to her. And then I recover myself and remember I'm Bridget Venus Bloom, destined for the Big Time, and awesome in my own curvy, redheaded right.

"Where you headed next?"

She slings her bag over her shoulder. "Lunch. Want to join?"

"Definitely."

And just like that, I have a real friend to sit with in the Rot.

It's almost as if I never lied to Ruby. In fact, after a half hour of the kind of witty banter I'd hoped to have with my roommate, I already feel like I've known Liza for years.

Ruby walks into the Rot as Liza and I are walking out, deep into an exploration of whether the Beatles or the Rolling Stones were the superior boy band of the sixties. I wave at Ruby as we leave and note, out of the corner of my eye, that her head turns to watch us.

Look at me, having something Ruby doesn't.

After lunch I've got some free time before I'm due in another class. I wander the halls of the Anderson building, which houses the Rot, a few classrooms, the school auditorium, and the offices of most professors.

I stop short when I realize I'm standing in front of just the office I need to visit today, if I'm going to bring my inspired plan into fruition. "Octavia Lawless, Dean of Students, MFP Chair," reads the plaque on the door. The piece of paper tacked to the nearby bulletin board states her office hours are "11 to 1, MWF," and lo and behold, it's twelve thirty on a Monday. The door's ever so slightly ajar.

I take a deep breath and knock three times. Once to announce my arrival, once to ask for permission to be let in. The third one is all swagger.

"Come in," says a voice I know is hers by sound alone. I've seen Octavia on a few of Grams's VHS recordings and once in person, when she was in an off-Broadway production of *Chicago*.

And I've watched numerous online videos of her promoting Richard James.

I push the door open and the Key to My Fate sits behind a massive black desk. I hold back a gasp, because *wow*, I'm *sharing space with Octavia Lawless*. She's as striking in person as she is onstage, though she looks older without her stage makeup. There are subtle but definitely there streaks of white in her chestnut hair and lines around her mouth and eyes. But her slim, graceful hands—the subject of more than a few art review write-ups, the way actor Octavia speaks with her hands—are the same as I've always seen them. Her signature bloodred fingernails hover above paperwork.

"Can I help you?"

"Maybe," I say breathlessly. I can't believe I'm *meeting Octavia Lawless*. "I loved you in *My Fair Lady*."

Her flawlessly proportioned face, which I'm used to seeing lit up with a huge smile and open mouth, sits blank, almost bored. "I had mono for most of the duration of *that* particular musical."

"The Tony committee didn't seem to notice!"

She blinks at me, face still mum. "I fail to see how a discussion of my performance accolades is helpful to you, dear."

"Oh. Yes, sorry. I'm Bridget Bloom."

Her eyes graze me from my hair to my toes, then up again. I'm not sure whether she's checking me out in an "I like your outfit" way or in a "monkey at the zoo" kind of way. "Yes, I remember your audition."

Heat rushes to my cheeks. "I'm glad it was memorable. Actually, that's what I came to talk with you about."

I get another full eye graze, this one definitely more of the zoo animal variety, which punctures a hole through the hopeful balloon swelling in my chest.

"What do you want to discuss?"

"The music focus program."

"Ah. What about it?" Octavia's red nails begin tapping, one by one, across the top of her shiny desk.

"Um, well. I understand why I didn't get in. But I need to perform. This year."

Her brows come up. "Performance is reserved for MFP students only, and I'm afraid that's not an option for you. You failed your theory exam. Spectacularly."

Man, does everyone and everything at this school *love* to remind me of how badly I suck at theory.

I take a deep breath and soldier on. "I'm aware. I'm working on theory. In the meantime, could you make an exception? I'll do anything to perform. I *need* music in my life. It's like . . . it's a soul thing."

"You can build music into your life every single day at Richard James, even if you're not in the MFP."

I huff, indignation hovering dangerously close to the surface of my face. "It's not the same."

"I suppose not." She pauses and we study each other. I think she's waiting for me to back down, but I can't. Won't. "You'll do anything?" she asks finally.

"Anything."

"Fine. I'll allow you to join the Advanced Solo Performance Seminar—"

My head inflates so quickly I think it might explode, and the whirring of my ears is so loud I almost miss the last part of Octavia's offer.

"—as an accompanist. Our regulars within the program are quite busy preparing solo pieces for auditions, and we need one for that class."

I deflate. I try not to let it show on my face, because Octavia is watching me. Intensely.

"Your piano skills, most notably your sight-reading and chording, were more than adequate. I'm sure you would make an excellent student accompanist for our MFP students. It may represent another constraint on your time, so I really need you to think about—"

"I'll do it." Because of course I'll do it. I said I'd do anything and I meant it. "But for the record, I'm good enough to *really* perform here. Front and center, singing and dancing. I know I am."

Octavia sighs and rubs the bridge of her nose, her nails stop-sign red against her bisque skin. "Ms. Bloom. Your talent was not in question. Your ability to handle the rigor of the music program *is*, however."

"But my grades, my piano skills, my singing, *everything* but theory is good!"

"I read your file many, many times, believe me. Our decision not to admit you to the program wasn't made lightly. But we can't set you loose on being a front-and-center performer until we're sure you have a firm grasp on the foundation of music—theory. It's how we do things here at Richard James."

"But—"

"Our decision stands." She stares at me, unyielding. I'm not sure she's blinked this entire time.

My shoulders slump as the life force drains out of me. My face drops toward her dark plank floors. I won't give her the pleasure of seeing me cry.

"Okay," I choke out as I turn to leave.

"I'll change your schedule to reflect that you're now in Advanced Solo Seminar. As an accompanist."

"Thank you," I say woodenly.

I'm halfway through the door when her voice halts me. "Ms. Bloom?"

"Yes?"

"You might consider working on your humility."

Her words catch me like an open hand across the cheek. As if it's not enough that she's taken my wheelhouse from me and rubbed my face in my poor theory skills, now she's going to tell me to be *more humble*? Hasn't she already humbled me enough?

"My humility. Okay?" I can't stop one saucy eyebrow from yanking up toward my hairline.

"No matter how badly you crave the spotlight—and I realize this may be a significant craving—drawing attention to yourself with your voice will only distract from the work you need to be doing in the classroom."

"Noted." My voice shakes only a little, which is a miracle, given how hopping mad I am.

"I do hope so, because I must admit—I fear you aren't made

of the right material to manage the challenges you will face this year." Though she waves a hand around in her trademark graceful-nonchalant way, her eyes bore into me like lasers, like she can see all the way into the middle of me.

She has no idea what I'm made of.

My throat is tight and I'm swallowing tears, but I thrust my chin in her direction. "Watch me," I say as I turn on my heel. I may be leaving my dreams in the stark office behind me, but I'll be damned if I let Octavia Lawless take my pride.

FIVE

MONDAY NIGHT SLIPS INTO TUESDAY morning as I toss and turn under my still-stiff comforter. Dad washed it before packing it, and it smells like home. Like them. I miss them, even if they do live in the worst town ever. I soak my clean bedspread with salty tears.

My dads aren't the only thing I'm grieving. I'm mourning *me*. I'm one whole day into the Richard James experience, and already, I'm unsure of who I'm supposed to be. My run-in with Octavia spins on a loop in my head, probably leaving permanent divots in the gray matter. *You might consider working on your humility.* My humility? I don't get it. Did *she* climb to her level of prestige by blushing and dismissing compliments and letting others take lead roles, while she watched? Doubtful. And for the love of Judy Garland, I can *sing* even if I don't know which sharps or flats a B-major scale has.

When the clock rolls over into five a.m., I give up on bed. I need comfort more than I need sleep. I grab my book bag and head straight out to the quad before I can talk myself out of it.

Back in Lynch, one of my go-to activities for mending a broken spirit was driving alone out to an abandoned country road, lying on the hood of my dad's (vintage, lime-green, effing awesome) VW Beetle, and taking in the stars. They were a reminder of two things: 1) In the scheme of things, my problems are actually very small; and 2) I shine like the cosmos, too, when I'm not sad. Somehow, nature's light show and the soothing heat of the metal under my back have never failed me.

But Chicago isn't Lynch. The quad is peaceful enough in the dusky not-yet-dawn, sleepy darkness still settled over its carefully curated landscaping and pristine grass. But the wood picnic table I lower my PJ-clad body onto isn't warm, and when I turn my face toward the sky, there are no distinct stars, only a milky sheen over black sky. I hadn't realized the lights of downtown Chicago would be enough to obscure the entire panorama of cosmic wonder.

Talk about a metaphor.

I lie there and lie there, thinking about my dads. And home. And how the hell I'm going to make it here without being an MFP student. I lie so long that the sun starts peeking out between the trees.

"Wow, you really *do* have freckles."

My body quakes and I ratchet up like a Bridget-in-the-box. "Jesus," I say, one hand over my heart.

"No, just Max," he says. "May I join you?"

I lurch from the tabletop to sit on the bench like a normal

44

human, and he plunks himself across from me. He's already dressed for the day in jeans, sneakers, and yet another T-shirt that features Freddie Mercury's epic mustache. Also unlike me, he's clearly taken a shower—Clean Boy scent pours off him in spicy waves. There's a part of me that wants to be self-conscious, out here in my white pants and camisole with cutesy rainbows strewn all over them, no makeup, messy bun. But Max seems as at ease as Max can be, so I play it cool, too. "What're you doing out here so early?"

"You were the one sprawled out on the table like it's a bed. Did you *sleep* out here?"

I sigh. "No. I didn't sleep much at all last night."

"Why's that?"

Because life as I know it is over. Because I'm not allowed to do the thing I came here to do. But I can't say that, so I say, "A lot on my mind."

"Wanna share?" He peels open a banana and hands me half.

"You talking about your food or my misery?"

"Either. Both."

I chomp the banana and consider. "What would you do if you couldn't get someone to *see* you the way you want to be seen? No matter what you said."

Max chokes on his mouthful. "I might have some experience," he sputters, reaching for his water bottle.

"You do?"

He nods as he drinks, and while his face is mild, the sunflowers in his eyes are burning. Like what we're talking about is something very important in a way I can't even grasp.

"Well? What did you say?" I prod.

45

Water and banana down, he's quiet. Gazing-off-into-the-distance-level thoughtful. Finally, he comes back, yellow-brown eyes crashing into my hazel in a way that makes me squirm. "I think maybe it's less about what you say. More about what you do."

Huh. So, if I used the wisdom of one Max Griffin, words would have less weight with Octavia than actions. And if *that's* accurate . . .

Banana churns in my stomach as the answer hits me at my own middle C.

I don't like this new idea. In fact, I hate it. But still, it rings with rightness and, more than that, with *righteousness*. Octavia wants me to be *humble*, and she made it clear that if I'm singing at all, she'll see it as an attention grab. She doesn't think I can do Richard James without singing. She doesn't think I can be *humble*.

I'll show her humble.

I won't sing, at least not in front of anyone. And it's going to suck. Hard-core *suck*.

Singing is my signature spice, my comfort blanket. It's so tangled up in me that I'm honestly not sure where it ends and I begin. Worst of all, when I'm not singing, I'm just like everyone else. Plain, boring, fading in like a copper penny on a hardwood floor. Forgettable.

Silencing my voice will hurt like tearing out a piece of my soul. But endgame, it'll hurt less than proving Octavia right.

"Hey. Where'd you go?" Max says, lightly brushing my forearm. His hand is balmy and makes me realize I'm a little cold.

I pull on the hoodie I was using as a pillow. "I'm back," I say as my head pops through. "Just had a major life epiphany, no big deal. Thanks for the advice."

He smiles, but it's a distant one. Despite not moving an inch, he's so much further away. And then he *is* moving, and his book bag lands with such a heavy thud that my whole side of the table bounces up like a seesaw.

"Holy shit, what do you have in that thing? Concrete?"

"Books, Bridget. All the books. You know, nerd stuff," he says, grinning and closing some of that metaphorical gap. His scent catches on the breeze and hits my face.

To hide my nose (which wants to sniff at the air like a hound), I duck under the table toward my own book bag. Might as well get a jump start on the ole homework. Theory is the stuff that's on top of my pile—ugh. But there's no way out of this mess but through it, so I pull out the worksheets Dr. Milhouse gave us to complete. I set the demon paper in front of me, scrawl my name on top with a brand-new mechanical pencil, and . . . that's it. That's as far as I get. It's literally like someone handed me an assignment written in another language.

I have never felt this way in my entire life. I am Bridget fucking Venus Bloom, Conquerer of All Things Academic. I have always been first in my class, first to raise my hand to answer tough questions, first to turn in tests. I learned to read when I was three years old and won the county spelling bee every year between fifth and eighth grades. Back in Lynch I was a Mathelete, on the Quiz Bowl team, and conference champion last year in extemporaneous speaking.

When it comes to school, I do. Not. Struggle.

And yet here I am, arms flailing wildly in the front row of the struggle bus. There's no way I'm passing theory, which is a Very Big Problem in the scheme of things.

The table lurches as Max stands to lean over my work. "Oooohhh, inversions, my favorite."

"You're a sick and twisted person." I look up into the sunflower irises, so yellow with sunrise gleaming across them.

He laughs. "I take it you're *not* into theory."

"You take it right. Theory is my kryptonite."

"Ah, but you're an amazing accidental poet."

I scoff. "You know, any other time I'd giggle at that. Right now I'm too messed up over this theory suckitude. I'm . . . not used to not getting things."

And just like that, I'm totally exposed. Here I am with my hair in a shitty bun, no makeup, in my effing *pajamas*, and now I'm sharing my shameful theory secret. I have no idea what I'm doing and I think maybe I'm a little too sleep-deprived and stressed out to goalie my words any better.

"Oh, come on. You got in; you can't be that bad."

I didn't get in. But that's one self-disclosure I am very, very not ready for. I shrug.

"Okay, show me your suckitude. Which inversion is this chord in?" He leans in closer as he points to a triad on my page, sending more waves of fresh soap my way. Lord, forgive my wayward nose.

"No idea," I say without looking down at it. I'm sure I don't.

"Well, do you know what key it's in?"

"Nope."

His eyes are more alarmed than I expect them to be, but you know, I guess it's probably shocking that an MFP student would be *this* awful at theory. Which is why I'm *not* in the program. I get it now. I do. But I *need* to get in. "Okay, yikes. Have you . . . ever studied theory?" He speaks tentatively, like his words might detonate a bomb.

They nearly do. "Of course I have! I'm a musician! I'm just really rusty." The thought of Max—or anyone—finding out that I'm faking the whole MFP thing sends spikes of anxious adrenaline right into my bloodstream. And there's a second feeling, a tiny pinprick. I think it's guilt. I'd rather not skirt the truth with Max, but here we are.

"I see," he says, though he's clearly not buying it.

This is *not* the conversation I'd hoped to be having with one of the two friendly people I've met so far at Richard James. I now feel less like puking and more like crying, because this is *embarrassing*. Humiliating, even. If only I could be as good at this asinine subject as Mr. AP Theory.

A fiery blaze ignites in my chest as inspiration hits, and ah, is it welcome here. "Hey, do you think you could help me? With theory?"

He crosses his arms over Freddie's mustachioed face and leans back in his seat. "You mean, like a tutoring situation?"

As the word *tutor* comes into play, I feel my hope shrinking. Effing reality, dousing inspiration once again. "Um, yeah. I guess I don't really have any way to pay you, though." My monthly spending is for damn sure not enough to cover academic coaching of any kind.

"Hmm." Max strokes his chin in an exaggerated kind of way. "You *are* offering me the chance to flex my theory muscles for a captive audience, which might be payment enough. Because, you know, explaining the circle of fifths in great detail is *not* something I get to do enough in my everyday life."

I laugh. I'm still embarrassed about asking for help, but Max is softening it. "By all means, flex away. I promise to be impressed."

"Although you should absolutely feel free to fawn over my vast theory knowledge, Richard James will pay me to tutor you, if we fill out some paperwork together."

I almost jump out of my seat. This is one of my first good-luck events since arriving at this school. "Yes! I'd do that paperwork yesterday!"

He grins, his teeth almost fluorescent in the rising sun.

And then I'm hit with *more inspiration*. I'm on a roll now. "And I can bring treats! I just won a semester's worth of free Razzles from the Pop Shop. Whatever a Razzle is." The Pop Shop is a tiny, on-campus convenience store—perfect for junk food emergencies. I won the Razzles by being chosen as having the best decorated room *in the entire hall*. (Suck it, Ruby.)

"A Razzle is soft-serve ice cream with candy mixed in—like a Dairy Queen Blizzard, but better, honestly." Max's eyes close, rapturous over this ice cream.

"Oooh. Sounds great."

"They are. So here's my offer: since you find yourself in an abundance of free Pop Shop merchandise, let's do tutoring and Razzles."

I guffaw, because Tutoring and Razzles sounds a lot like Netflix and Chill. "Is that a pickup line?"

I think I've made the poor guy blush. *Again.* And I didn't even mean to this time. He shrugs but manages, "Take it how you want to take it." Softly, while staring at the picnic tabletop.

This all seems like a hell of a deal. "I'd love to eat ice cream and learn about the stupid circle of perfect fifths with you, Freddie. You're on."

You know those people whose entire faces are transformed when they smile? Max is one of those. He's super-skinny, but when he grins his cheeks puff out in the cutest of ways, and his eyes almost disappear. It's all absolutely adorable.

I just hope I don't wipe that smile right off his face when he sees how truly abysmal I am at theory.

I sail into my second day of classes with bright aquamarine optimism. If Max is going to help me with theory, the rest of my course load should be cake. My first piano lesson is fine. Then it's on to AP world history *and* AP bio. The duo won't be easy by any means, but still conquerable. History of Musical Theater should be no big thing, as my whole life has been one long Broadway history lesson.

My shine starts fading around the time of my end-of-the-day group piano seminar, despite the fact that Liza's in there with me. She's a great player, I can tell, but there's no passion in her technique. I get the distinct feeling Liza chose the course because it was easy, to pass the time or something. And *that* feels like a hell of a waste at a place like Richard James.

As the school day winds down, most of the students drift back toward the Rot for supper. The newness of everything and the startling reality of not singing *at all* weigh on my shoulders like a tuba, and I've got zero appetite and a great restlessness eating away at me. So, I do exactly what my dads told me not to: leave campus and walk out into downtown Chicago, alone. Even though it's eighty-five degrees and humidity clings to my skin like a wet blanket. I don't know where I'm going or what I'm seeking, all I know is that I'm an actual hot mess inside.

I'm in my head so furiously, and for so long, that when I finally take stock of my surroundings, I don't know where I am. Richard James is nowhere in sight. I look to the sky, trying to use the sun as a directional guide, but it's no use. I suck at navigation. Dodge has always joked I couldn't find my way out of a Target without GPS.

While I've walked the streets of Lynch alone many times, this is different. Obviously. For one thing, Lynch has 750 people, and I know basically all of them. Chicago has, what—millions of people? And the few that I "know" are back at Richard James. (Would any of them even miss me if I was gone too long?) Lynch is a one-mile-by-half-mile rectangle that consists of three churches, two bars, one school, and a handful of businesses. Chicago is *metropolitan*. Sprawling.

I am alone. In an unfamiliar city. On an unfamiliar street. And I'm sweating not only because it's ungodly hot, but also because I'm getting a little freaked out.

Now lost in every sense of the word, I pay more attention to storefronts, ready to walk into any coffee shop or chain restaurant that looks somewhat welcoming. My plan is to sit for a few minutes, cool off, get my bearings, and use my cell phone to navigate my directionally challenged ass back to campus. If all else fails I'll call my dads, but this would be enormously humbling and I'm going to be eating more than enough humble pie just living that Richard James life.

On the corner, I spy something superior to a Starbucks or McDonald's. A godsend, really. Exactly what I was seeking but didn't even think to hope for.

The store's signage is plain but effective: When in Rome in simple black script on the picture window, a few beautiful pieces displayed on a platform beneath. I throw open the door, and the bell tied to it announces my arrival. As the glass whooshes shut, the chill of air-conditioning wraps around me like a hug. Dust motes swirl in the sun, coming to rest on the jewelry counter in front of me. I inhale wood varnish, mothballs, and must, so familiar. So safe. My blood pressure ticks down several notches.

It's an antique store. And when Blooms are having a bad day, we antique. I know I promised the dads I'd be careful with my money, but goddamn it, what's the price of peace?

This place is loaded. To my left is a large display of Depression glass (one of Dad's favorite things), and near the back, shelves and shelves of knickknacks and other awesomely old items stand waiting for my embrace. I've never been in here, and still, it smacks of *home*. My dads and I used to spend nearly every rainy Saturday in antique shops. But the sun blazes hot today, and I realize that my social calendar no longer lives and dies by rain like it does when your dad's a farmer. Yet another mysterious pang of homesickness rattles through me.

But I don't have time for longing, not now. I've had enough pain for one forty-eight-hour period without borrowing more. I firmly refocus myself on the present, starting with a pewter-handled hand mirror that's *so me*. A wooden door behind the glass jewelry case creaks open and shut, and an old white man appears, small, slightly hunched. He wears a sweater vest, trousers, and loafers with no socks. His white hair is downy and disheveled, like the wind's recently blown through it. He blinks at me from behind glasses with thick, round black rims. "Hello there. Have you found something of interest?"

"Yes. I love this piece," I say, brandishing the mirror.

He smiles gently. "No, you don't."

"Excuse me?"

"You don't love it."

"But I do!" I get the urge to stamp my foot but rein it in. Barely.

He shakes his head slowly, unruffled, and levels me with an unwavering brown gaze.

I stare back, nonplussed. Who does this guy think he is? "But isn't the customer always right?"

His shoulders start to shake and at first I worry he's having a seizure or something, because his face hasn't changed. But then it does. It breaks wide open, teeth exposed, head thrown back. He laughs, deep and loud, and I'm startled to hear this *rich* sound come out of this tiny man, no taller than I am. "That's one of the stupidest aphorisms in the book," he forces out, though he's wheezing.

"Aphorism?"

He composes himself, stands up straight. "Oh, just a fancy word for an old saying, dear. Though I am rather a fan of old, pretty words, I must admit." He gestures widely, to all corners of the store. "Just like I'm a fan of all kinds of old, pretty things."

"Is this your shop?"

"Yes. She's not much, but she's mine."

"She's gorgeous," I say, setting the mirror back down where I'd found it. "One of the best antique shops I've seen."

His eyes warm. "Thank you, Athena."

"Athena? You must have me confused with someone else. I'm Bridget. Bridget Bloom." I offer my hand, and instead of shaking it, he picks it up.

"May I?"

I nod, and he grazes the back of my hand with his lips. It's not creepy at all. In fact, it strikes me as exceptionally kind, very old-world, but this doesn't stop the blushing heat from washing over me. My face probably matches my hair now.

"I'm Hans, and I'm pleased to make your acquaintance. And I don't have you confused. I know we've never met. You merely strike me as an Athena."

"That's funny. My middle name is Venus, like Aphrodite. Goddess of love."

He closes his eyes and shakes his head again. "No, no. You're no love goddess. You're a warrior, I can see it in you. And clearly, a protector of household goods." He gestures with his head toward the mirror I've set aside.

This is easily the strangest encounter I've ever had at an antique store, but also by far the most interesting. This Hans guy is a trip.

"Anyway, feel free to look around, my dear. I trust you will be respectful of all my treasures."

"I will. Thank you."

I veer off toward the back of the store. I finger gold-rimmed mugs, ivory chess pieces, sterling silver salt and pepper shakers. I pluck books down from dusty shelves and inhale the yellowed-paper smell of them as I let my hands trail down their fabric-covered spines. I hold a satin wedding dress with lace sleeves—probably once white, now a creamy ivory—to my body. It's about ten sizes too small in reality, but in my imagination, it's a perfect fit. And there's this grapefruit-size wooden owl I keep coming back to, skimming my hands over its carved feathers every time I pass.

As I browse, my pulse settles, my breath comes easier. My shoulders shrink away from my ears. I don't need my voice to be me in an antique store. When I feel almost myself again, I wander back to the front. Hans leans over the jewelry counter, methodically checking and rearranging the costume rings, the beveled pendants. His face is placid, and he hums quietly to himself as he works. I almost hate to disturb him.

"Hans?"

"Yes, Athena."

"I think I'm good for today."

"That's fine, fine. You didn't find anything to take home with you?"

"You have a fantastic selection. I found a million things I love."

"No, you didn't, but thank you."

I push my lips together and to the side and squish my forehead down toward my nose, which is the face I make when I'm confused. "Why is it so hard to believe I would love something in your store?"

"Because you can't, Athena. Not today."

"Can you explain what you mean?"

"No."

Hans is a hoot, but damn if he isn't frustrating. "Why?"

"It's not the kind of thing that can be explained in a day. I assume you'll come back, though. People with a true affinity for old things always do."

And I know with a certainty that goes beyond bone level that he's right.

I let myself into the room without knocking. Ruby lies in her bed with her head propped against the wall and her knees pulled up, a history book leaning against them. "Hey," she says.

"Hey."

"Missed you at dinner. Again."

"Yeah." I head to the closet to choose my wardrobe for the next day. Black shirt, black jeans, black shoes. It'll be a day of mourning, for sure. Here lie the fabulous vocal cords of Bridget Bloom, RIP.

"How was your day?" Ruby sets her book aside and sits up.

"It was . . . okay." I get out my lint brush and start defuzzing my black shirt. "Yours?"

She shrugs. "Fine. About what I expected."

I nod at her and continue my task of lint obliteration. When that's done, I give the jeans the same treatment. Next, it's time for my nightly skin care routine, which will take me a hot minute (read: much longer than a minute). I grab my face kit and head out to the bathroom.

When I return a half hour later, Ruby's under the covers with her headphones on, laptop open, typing away. Of course she's blowing me off now—she's Ruby Deterding, cello genius, super-snob. It stings a little, but part of me is glad I don't have to pretend to be interested in her day. I hop into my bed and become her mirror image, headphones in, schoolwork pulled up on laptop.

Just before midnight, I lay my red head across the pillow (gently, to preserve my curls). In the space between awake and asleep, I consider whispering a wish or two to God, the Universe, whoever's in charge of futures out there.

But I don't. They'd all come out the same, like singing.

SIX

WEDNESDAY GOES BY IN A blurry repeat of Monday, minus the soul-crushing run-in with Octavia. But Thursday is different, because I have a new course on my schedule: the Advanced Solo Performance Seminar that Octavia agreed to let me into. I know if I was being truly *humble* that I'd be *grateful* for this opportunity, but truth is, the whole accompanist thing is a kick in the throat. Not only do I not get to sing, I have to sit and *watch* people sing for hours at a time, while playing their music for them. Blerg.

After an especially weird installation of bio—Dr. Vance dramatically whipped a sheet off the top of a fetal pig, which I think was meant to be funny in a shocking way, but this girl Taylor threw up on her desk—I trudge off in the direction of Triton 150 and see Liza's dark head a few steps in front of me, headed the same way. "Hey, are you in Advanced Solo Performance?" I shout.

She slows down to let me catch up. "Yeah, you?"

"Yep."

"Oh, you sing?"

I open my mouth to shout my enthusiastic, "Yes!" but snap it shut before I betray myself. Then I try again. "Not this year."

Liza's face is all confusion, furrowed brows and pursed lips. Like Max, she's assumed I'm in the MFP, since we have theory and piano seminar together. Basically, everything with my faux program is going to plan. The thing I didn't account for was the slippery, gross feeling that comes from lies of omission.

"It's a long story. I'll tell you another time, 'kay?"

"All right."

I like how Liza takes everything in stride.

Triton 150 is kind of a mini auditorium. There's a stage area but it's only slightly raised, like one big step. The rest of the room features regular classroom chairs with two grand pianos flanking them, and a drum set. Open shelves of musical instruments—everything from maracas to trombones—line the back of the room. It smells like valve oil and mixed shampoos in here, and it feels *right*. Immediately. This is where I belong.

But for today, I'll sit on the margins of this safe space. I'll plant myself behind one of the baby grands, rather than in the center chairs with the rest of the students, and I'll keep my vocal cords quiet. *If Ariel could do it, so can I.*

And then it happens.

He's here.

Duke Ericson saunters into the room, the usual gaggle of

groupies clinging to his sides. A few students in the room shout out to him, and he addresses them all, bro-hugging, fist-bumping. I almost wave at him, because for the love of Barbra Streisand, I feel like I *know* him. He's as familiar to me as my own reflection, from watching him for so many hours on YouTube. But I catch myself and manage to keep my arms held firmly to my sides, fists clenched.

He passes up the many peer invitations to sit with them. Instead, he makes himself at home behind the other piano and starts playing the iconic opening to "Don't Stop Believin'." Students whoop and clap as he rips into the opening lines, pretty notes rushing out of his pretty mouth. He raises one hand to the room to gesture for folx to join in, and soon everyone's jamming to the chorus. And I sit on my piano bench feeling deflated, because *of course* I know every word of every Journey song (thanks, Dads), and *of course* I can belt those huge, high notes and runs with the best of them. Not being able to sing is like having an itch I'm not allowed to scratch. And there's another problem: How will I ever get Duke to notice me if I'm not singing? Accompanists blend in like faded wallpaper.

Think, B, think.

Inspiration never fails me. As the song and its singers race toward the final rounds of "whoa" and "believin'," I mesh some quiet chords from my piano in with Duke's. Slowly, I play louder. And louder. Until the voices have died out and Duke's piano goes still. I have the pleasure of knowing, without looking, that all eyes in the room are on me.

My hands slow into the familiar, soulful opening riff to John

Lennon's "Imagine." My lungs are full and ready to breathe the words to life, but this time, it can't be me. I take a leap of faith and shout, "Liza, take it!"

Her head snaps up from the notebook she's doodling in, and for a second, I think she's going to blow me off. But then she shrugs and pulls her shoulders back, managing to look bored while also pushing out the first line of the song in this honeyed, jazzy-raspy timbre. My mouth literally falls open as her voice meanders its way into the heart of me. She keeps singing, students around her joining in, swaying and waving cell phone flashlights in the air.

Across the room, Duke shimmers with electric energy, and he's looking my way as he belts along with everyone else. I feel like the happiness radiating off him is meant just for me, and I catch it, like a lightning bolt to the chest. As the last words are sung, I nod to him, and he plays the song out with me. Our chords web and mesh, each naturally filling in gaps left by the other. Like they belong together.

As we hit our eighth bar of transition, he mouths, "Piano Man," and I nod as we launch together into the classic Billy Joel. He knows all the words, even the long-ass verses, though most of the rest of the class doesn't. Everyone knows the chorus, though, and they sing it so loud my ears ring a little bit.

We've just tackled the big finish when a side door opens and a slick-looking white guy in dark jeans, a Questlove T-shirt, and a fitted blazer with rolled-up sleeves strides through. His sneakers squeak across the tile floor. "Morning, y'all! I see you're warmed up already. Let's go."

Dr. Sebastian, who everyone calls Seabass, launches right in with no pretense or pomp and with no apology for being ten minutes late for class. He's animated, gregarious, all big dimples and sparkly charm. He reminds me of . . . well, me, and I'm not sure if I love him or hate him, just yet.

Students get up on the stage and sing. Afterward, Seabass gives a list of what went well and what could go better, and he also asks the class to provide peer critique. I, of course, make no peeps except what comes from my fingers on the keys. A few times while I'm playing for a student, Seabass does this hands-down motion at me, the universal music director gesture for "quieter." That itch inside of me swells as my bright purple bass and my hot-pink treble fade away, no more than a forgettable, gray background for my vibrant classmates.

Duke is easily the best soloist, but Liza's a strong second. I can't help but resent her, just for the tiniest second, when I notice Duke staring up at her, rapt, as she sings.

"Okay, class, good start, good start. I know it's early in the year, but it's never too early to begin prep on your final project for this course, which is the end-of-semester musical."

A low, excited buzz kicks up around the room; the energy is palpable. The academy's student-run musicals are crowning achievements for the MFP kids—and one of the main reasons I wanted to come here. I do the best I can to ignore the searing pain of loss in my chest.

Seabass ignores the hum of voices and continues. "As a class you will write, cast, choreograph, and perform a short show on the last weekend before classes dismiss for winter break. Any MFP student is invited to be a part of the cast, but Advanced Solo students are generally looked to for the big roles and creative leadership, which is why I let the musical count as a graded project for this course. Our theme for the semester is *historical*—so, get your thinking caps on."

The buzz in the room grows louder as Seabass dismisses class. As for me, I'd like to open up the piano bench and crawl in. Watching my academy peers all jazzed about the musical reminds me so much of being in Lynch, everyone else buddy-buddy and making plans, me on the margins, watching. Being sidelined like this makes me want to scream myself hoarse.

And I could, because it's not like I need to preserve my vocal cords for anything right now.

I'm wearily putting my music away when, out of the corner of my eye, I catch a tall, broad form that *could be* Duke moving in my direction. My hope-o-meter slingshots from zero to a hundred, yet I will myself to not look. I'm not *needy*. But still, all I can think is, *Please please please please please*—

"Hey, piano star."

I'd know that voice anywhere. I force cool onto my face but can't stop my insides from liquefying into a delicious, melty goo. "You're not too bad, either." I smile up at him from under my curled, mascara-enhanced eyelashes. He's even better looking up close than he is on the screen, and I didn't think that was possible. His skin is smooth, cheekbones mighty. His hair's longer than it was in his last video, now grown out into a curly 'fro. If

Bruno Mars and John Legend had a love child, it would be Duke Ericson. And I'm sitting here, chatting it up with him. Lucky. Freaking. Me.

"Are you new? I don't remember you from last year."

"Yeah, this is my first year, but I'm a junior. Bridget Bloom," I say, standing and holding out my hand.

He takes it and I'm zapped, tingles of warmth running from my hand straight to my ovaries. "Duke Ericson. Senior," he says, but he has to know I *know* who he is.

"You headed to lunch, Bloom?" *Bloom*. We're already on last-name terms, which we all know from young adult literature is *the* key to a burgeoning love story. I might pass out.

"Yeah."

"Join me?"

I'm ready to emphatically accept when I spy Liza leaning on the doorframe, thumbing her phone screen. Waiting for me. I groan internally as I remember we already planned to eat together, and an even louder internal groan sounds off when I remember Duke's face riveted on Liza as she sang in class today.

But I'm not going to ghost one of the only friends I have here. So I say, "Sure. Liza's going, too, so let's all sit together."

"Hey there, Liza," Duke croons in a podcast-host voice, oozing charisma.

She barely looks up at him. "Hey," she says, all casual.

I clear my throat, loudly. "Do you two know each other?" My nails are making little half-moons in the palms of my hands. This might be the moment I lose Duke's attention.

"I'd say more like we know *of* each other," says Liza, droll as ever.

"Just different social circles. So far," adds Duke, smiling in that impossibly charming Duke way. "You're a junior, Liza?"

Liza nods, returning to her Very Important Phone Business.

The knots in my back relax marginally as we chat, making our way to the Rot. Duke and Liza seem like an obvious pairing. Both insanely beautiful, extremely talented. Maybe they're made of the remnant dust of the same shooting star. I cringe as I imagine how otherworldly a duet between them would be. Or a *baby*. Good Lord.

And then I stand up straighter, imagining a string connecting my head to my spine pulling taut. *I* look like a star. *I'm* talented. And Liza's showing no interest in Duke whatsoever.

Why *not* me with him?

SEVEN

EVERY STEP I TAKE AFTER lunch feels like walking on clouds. I'm floating. I'm a nebulous ball of happy, still high on the amazing, possibly life-altering meal with Duke. He asked a million questions about my life in Lynch, and he laughed at all my jokes, and when I drank my entire glass of water (your throat gets dry when you're talking that much), he *refilled it for me*. Liza chimed in only the few times Duke tried to include her. It was obvious that he only *really* had eyes for me.

My happiness high carries me through the rest of the day, but my feet hit the ground hard by evening, because my theory tutoring session with Max has arrived. I saunter into Triton 212 five minutes early, armed with two Oreo and Butterfinger Razzles. As melty streaks of vanilla drip over the sides of the cups and onto the room's small table, I wonder if I will somehow start associating ice cream with theory, which I think would be about enough to develop an aversion to one of my favorite desserts. We're learning about classical conditioning in psychology, and wouldn't this be one sad example?

Theory. Tarnishes. *Everything.*

While I wait for Max, I sit at the piano and play the haunting opening bars of Adele's "Someone Like You," the tune just melancholy enough to capture how I'm feeling about the whole having-to-be-tutored thing. I open my mouth to start singing it, like I always do, but the note catches in my windpipe, falters. I can't take the risk of singing even in private, because the next thing you know, some kid will hear me and question why I don't sing at school. And admitting I'm not an MFP student (translation: inferior to them) and then maybe even having to explain the whole Octavia challenge thing is worse than not singing at all.

Plus: motherfucking *humility.*

I take the chance of humming along and get as far as the chorus, but this song's not as fun when you can't sing it. I chord and arpeggio my way out, launching instead into Mozart's famous "Alla Turca"—which for me is home and nostalgia. It was the first big classical piece I worked on with Grandma Evelyn, and if I close my eyes, I can still feel her sitting beside me on the bench, her head bobbing in time to the music, my bouncy left-hand repetition setting the pace. Though Grams has been gone for over a year, when I play the piano, she's still here—a stirring in the air, a presence not seen but felt. *You're destined for stardom, little B,* she'd said, more times than I can count. Did she say the same kind of thing to my mom, when Mom was growing up? I'll never know. What I do know is that I took Grams at her word—I still do. I'm meant for more than Lynch. I'll do what Mom never got to.

I finish with my head bowed, eyes still squeezed shut, willing Grams to stay just a little longer. Her hands upon mine, demonstrating a technique. A wave of goose bumps and then one of heat come on me in turns, and I sit and let it happen.

Gentle pressure comes to rest on my shoulder, right where Grams used to lay her hand when she would watch me play. The touch is pianissimo soft, but it might as well be a sledgehammer with the force of my startle. I jump off the bench and whip around.

"Holy Moses, Max! You scared the shit out of me!" I put my palm to my chest, as if I can slow my heart by pressing my skin down into it.

"I'm sorry. Truly. You were like . . . really zoned out. I said your name a few times and you didn't even hear me."

"Oh. Well, I've got some mad focus when I'm really into something."

"What were you into, just then?"

Conjuring my dead grandma and making plans to avenge my mother's foreshortened legacy, as one does. "Just thinking about music. And theory, I guess. By the way, your Razzle's over there. Better hop to it before it melts."

He sprints to the table—I'm not kidding, it's the fastest I've seen him move. "Oh, God," he says through a mouthful of ice cream. "How did you know this is my favorite blend?"

"Lucky guess," I said, digging into my own melty cup. We sit in a few moments of companionable slurping and chewing before he starts riffling through his bag. "What's this?" I wiggle the stapled packet of papers he's pulled out.

"That's your pre-tutoring assessment."

"My what-what? That sounds an awful lot like a test."

"It is."

I grimace. "Is it the one we all take for theory placement?"

"Oh, most definitely not. Those puppies are locked down like the U.S. nuclear codes. I made this one up."

"You . . . made it up?" I flip through the pages. It looks almost exactly like the test I took online for the MFP program. "How long did this take you, man?"

The tips of his ears go pink, but that doesn't stop him from shoveling in more Razzle. "Don't worry about that. It was fun."

"Your idea of fun and mine are two very, very different things."

"Hmm. Do you like outdoor concerts?"

"Sure," I agree, recalling an excellent indie band amphitheater show the dads took me to last summer.

"How about spending rainy days camped out on the couch with a book?"

"If there's coffee, yes. Bonus points if I can borrow someone's cat." I love cats, but Dodge is allergic.

"See, then. We're not so different." And his smile is so unguarded that now the proximity of his body and mine feels A-OK. "Should we get to work?"

Ugh, reality crashes in. "I guess," I say, pulling his homemade test closer.

My face must say it all as I fail my way through the thing. When I start to falter and slow down near the bottom of page one, he says, "Don't worry. The point of this thing is just so I can see where you're at. We'll get you into top theory shape in no time."

"Lordy, aren't you a confident one."

"Only because you give me a reason to feel that way. I watched you play for a few minutes before I came in. Also, I heard through the grapevine about your sick piano skills, courtesy of the Advanced Solo kids. With all that in mind, I have a hunch." He reaches into his bag and pulls out a guitar songbook, then pushes it across the table. "Could you play these songs on piano with just this music?"

I flip open the book. "Well, yeah. It's got the chords. I know where to put my hands on the keys for each chord."

"If you know chords, you know theory."

"Tell that to my test score."

"I'm serious, Bridget. Somewhere inside of you is an understanding of theory—that much is clear from what you can do on piano. We just have to help you unlock it."

"I'd say it's locked down pretty tight. My brain's apparently like the Bastille. Or Alcatraz."

"Not bad at history either, eh?"

I smirk. "Theory is my Achilles' heel, really."

"Oh, and a little mythology in you, too."

"Tons of mythology."

He crosses his arms and squints at me, which I assume is him going for "piercing scrutiny." His freckles and peach fuzz undermine him, but it's not a bad look. One might say it's cute, really, in a sweet shelter animal kind of way. "So clearly, you're great at learning stuff. Theory is just another brand of stuff."

"Whatever you say." I lean back in my chair and match him, pretzeling my arms against my trunk.

He smiles in a frustrated-but-humoring-me way. Like I'm a kindergartner. "Just keep working."

"Fine." I heave a huge sigh, the kind that's intended to be heard *and* get a point across. Good old Midwestern passive aggression is a fun party trick.

I grudgingly dive back into the packet, but once I start a thing, I don't do it halfway. I answer as much as I can. The very basic stuff—which notes are which, anything to do with note duration and rests—I know through and through. I'm okay with meters, basically know my scale and key signatures. After *that*, things get dicey. Tonic, diatonic, harmonic, the terms roll through my mind like a cruel nursery rhyme. I have no idea what's going on. A little over halfway through the test, I shove it away. "I've done what I can. The rest is Greek to me."

He uses a pen to guide his eyes as he peruses my work, circling things, making arrows, and jotting notes. He's a studious little professor, in jeans and a washed-out Led Zeppelin T-shirt that just *might* be actual vintage. "Okay, you've got the basics."

"Sort of have to, to play piano."

"Right. It's the more theoretical stuff you don't get."

"Obviously."

"Explain this, though: How can you go play a diminished

72

seventh on the piano, when you see the chord notation, but not be able to draw one on the staff?"

"What can I say? I must be one of life's great mysteries."

He smiles, crinkling up his sunflowers. "Indeed."

Indeed? What a dork. I don't mind that I made him smile, though.

"So, where do we start?"

"Looks like . . ." He flips to the first of the pages that's covered in pen. "Intervals and inversions."

"Sounds terrible."

Just when I thought he couldn't smile any bigger, he does. "I'll make it as painless as I can."

For what it's worth, he does. He walks me patiently through more kinds of intervals and inversions than should even be allowed in music, because holy shit why. He even helps me get a head start on my Milhouse theory assignment for the week. It's not the worst hour of my life, and that's a high compliment to Max, considering the subject at hand. He must agree that our time together wasn't heinous, because he volunteers to meet with me weekly, if we can move the standing session to Wednesday evenings. I readily agree. I can already tell it's going to take both help and a Christmas-level miracle to get me through theory.

"Big plans this evening?" he asks when we leave Triton 212.

"Not really. I'm heading to supper now."

"Mind if I join you? I promise we don't have to talk about theory."

"If you swear on Freddie Mercury's grave."

The side of his face I can see is grinning. "Oh, if we're invoking

73

Freddie, then totally. Consider the word *inversion* temporarily struck from my vocab."

"Also, can we keep this tutoring thing between us? I'm kind of embarrassed that I'm *this* bad at theory."

"Your secret is safe with me."

We get our trays and head out into the seating area. Duke's sitting at a table with some kids from Advanced Solo, including Liza. He sees us and waves.

"Bloom! Max! You two know each other?"

The grin has dropped off Max's face. He doesn't look unhappy, exactly, but his playfulness has made a hasty disappearance. "Yeah, we met at breakfast the other day," he says. Which is technically true.

I try to thank Max with my eyes while sliding into the seat nearest Liza.

"Hola, chica," she says. "You're late." The food remnants left on her plate are dry and wilted. She's been here a while.

"Yeah. I got some homework in before heading down here."

"So studious." She leans into me, bumping her shoulder into mine.

I lean back. "You know me. Class act, all the way." I chew and swallow a few bites of Caesar salad, then decide to satisfy the question burning up my insides. "Duke, how do you and Max know each other?"

"Are you kidding? Max is my main man! My A number one! Hell, he's even my roomie!" Duke bro-claps Max; Max shoots him a withering smile. "No, seriously, Max and I have known each other since we were little kids."

"Really?"

"Yeah! We grew up on the same street. Max basically lived at my house."

All eyes are on Max, and he seems to pick up on it, though his eyes are riveted to his roast beef sandwich. "It's true. Duke's mom was my second mom. Then I got older and she got hotter and now I can't think of her in a motherly way anymore."

Duke punches Max's arm as we all bust up with laughter, even Max.

We leave the Rot as a foursome, with a few other kids from Advanced Solo class also tagging along. I'm right in the middle of the throng, laughing, joking. I'm a *part* of this group.

Finally, finally, I've found the place where I fit. Where I belong.

As soon as I get my official acceptance to the MFP—and Duke—I'll be so much closer to everything I ever wanted.

EIGHT

THREE WEEKS INTO THE ACADEMIC year, and I'm starting to hit my stride. I nail my first English paper ("EXCEPTIONAL" written across the top, go me), get a 95 percent on my first trigonometry test, and am basically an AP bio legend due to the fact that I am so fearless with slicing and dicing. Everyone wants to be my lab partner, and who can blame them? I'd much rather dig around in a cow's eyeball than sit through theory lessons, which, for the record, I am *also* butchering—not in the useful, "cutting up an eyeball" way, but more in the "I super-suck at theory" kind of way. Don't get me wrong—I'm trying. Theory is just effing hard.

Getting into the MFP is still my ultimate goal (obviously), but I have to admit to myself that I don't mind living this Chicago academy gen ed student life on a temporary basis. My social life is booming, I'm (mostly) dominating my academics, and I've even got my off-campus haven at When in Rome. Which is why on Sunday night's video chat with my dads, I'm finally comfortable enough to confess I haven't been admitted as an MFP student. Besides, I have to tell *someone*. No one at the academy knows but Piper and Octavia, and the secret is burning an anxiety ulcer into my stomach lining.

Dodge's caterpillar brow sinks low across his eyes. "So what does that mean, being a gen ed student?"

"It's not that different from being in the MFP. I'm still allowed to take a boatload of music classes. The only thing I can't do is perform."

At that, Dad's and Dodge's faces go stricken. Absolute devastation. "Oh, honey," breathes Dad.

I'm touched by their sympathy, so much that my eyes start to burn. "I know. It'll be hard not doing what I do best, and obviously now I can't try out for the big end-of-semester musical. But I'm making the most of it."

They blink at me, and then they exchange a Look. Dodge clears his throat. "Sweetheart. If you can't perform, that means no sponsorships this year, right?"

I nod.

Dad looks like he might actually cry. "We didn't want to have to tell you this, but we had to sell a parcel of land to pay for this semester. One that Grandpa Bloom left us when he died."

Holy *shit*, they did *what*? I suck in a huge breath, my mind handing me an echo of my late grandpa Bloom, *Never, ever sell the land.* Farmland is precious in a place like Nebraska—not just because of supply and demand. It's a pride thing, a family thing, to pass land from generation to generation.

But me getting my Richard James education is *also* a pride thing, a family thing. I guess the dads swapped one legacy for another.

Dad continues. "We'd counted on you getting a sponsorship to help pay for the rest of the semesters."

My face must fall, because Dodge's voice ticks up about an octave. "It's not your fault, B. We know you tried your hardest for the music program."

My bottom lip trembles. I really had tried.

"Oh, lovey. Let's come back to this another night, okay? We'll figure something out."

And I grasp on to that with all of my being. *We'll figure something out.* My dads always had. I know they'll come through for me again.

I've pushed all of *that* firmly out of my mind by Thursday night. Ruby is ignoring me as always when there's a four-knock rap at our dorm room door. Liza. That's our signal—four slow knocks, because no other weirdos would knock that many times at that pace.

I call for her to let herself in and then immediately find myself purring, "Heyyyyy," as she comes into view. She looks—I kid you not—like a rock star. An *actual* rock star. All in black, her jeans and T-shirt hug every curve of her willowy body, makeup strategic and stunning, hair recently straightened and as shiny as ever. She's an Artemis, for damn sure. Goddess of the hunt.

"Don't stare. You're making me uncomfortable," she says, shoving her way into the room. She waves at Ruby, who's in bed with her fancy-ass laptop. Ruby returns the wave but not the smile, and though her head doesn't move, I can see her eyes are eating Liza up. Who wouldn't?

With no further announcement, Liza hot-steps her way into my closet and begins a survey of my hanging clothes, moving some articles aside, pulling out other things, and draping them across her arm. I step into the closet with her.

"What the hell are you doing?" I watch as she holds up yet another shirt, scrutinizes, hangs it back up.

"We're going out."

"Out?"

She strides back out into the room, throwing the clothes onto the bed. I trail behind her, silent for once in my life. Awestruck. Liza's never taken up this much emotional space in the whole time I've known her. "Come here," she says.

Liza holds shirt after shirt against my chest. Finally, she settles on a flowy emerald-green tank top. "Put this on, and wear those black jeans you have. And a black leather jacket if you've got one."

"Duh. Wardrobe staple," I say, pulling the day's T-shirt off and replacing it with what she's chosen. I know a lot of girls are more modest about changing in front of others, but I've always been like, a body's a body and I've got what I've got. Now I just need about a half hour to fix my hair—

"I know you probably want to take ten years to work on your hair, but I'm telling you, it's fine as it is. We'll spruce up your makeup in my room, then go."

Damn, she's good. And bossy, too, when she wants to be. I'm

too caught off guard, and frankly hella intrigued, to lodge any complaints. "All right," I say, grabbing my wallet and my smallest purse.

"See ya, Ruby."

"Later," she says, not even bothering to look up.

One half hour and one fresh face of pinup-girl makeup later, Liza's sneaking us out. Usually, if we leave campus after eight, we have to check out using our key card and then check in again by eleven—and if we're not in by curfew, our parents are called. Somehow, she has a special key with no ID, just marked "Guest Faculty," that she uses to let us out the back door of the dorm, and then we're out into the streets of Chicago. Free birds.

"Where'd you get the key card?" I ask.

"I've got a 'don't ask, don't tell' policy on this bad boy. The less other people know, the better."

For the love of Tina Turner, she sounds more like a CIA operative than a teen at music school, but whatever. My pulse picks up, and it has little to do with the walking. I've never been a delinquent. Until now. "I can't believe we're doing this."

"Oh, believe it, girlie."

She hails us a cab—so cosmopolitan! I've never even seen anyone do this in real life!—and tells the driver an address. Ten minutes later, we're parked in front of a place called Helter Skelter. A bar, by the looks of it.

"Um, spoiler alert, but we're minors. Hot minors, but minors."

"It's technically a bar and grill. We're good." She slips her arm through mine and pulls me inside. Bodies push up into each other, vying for personal space. Liza leads us to the packed bar, where by some miracle that probably has to do with her cleavage, she is served our two Sprites immediately. After handing me one of the glasses, she slinks like a Bengal tiger toward the seating area. In her second miracle, a two-seater comes open and we pounce on it.

I'm only just settling in when something hard bounces against my knee.

"Here. For your Sprite," Liza says as I grasp what she's offering me. I sneak a look under the table, and it's a small metal flask in my hand. Holy shit.

"What *is* this?" I whisper, though then I have to say it again so Liza can hear me. We're in a loud effing bar, after all.

"Vodka," she says. Like it's just the most natural thing in the world.

"How'd you get it?"

She shrugs. "I have my ways."

I try to casually hold my Sprite in my lap and pour in the tiniest slug of liquor before hustling the flask back over to Liza. She does the same, then holds her concoction up to me. "Cheers," she says as we clink our contraband drinks together.

I venture a sip. It's citrusy with an edge, the familiar childhood lemon-lime sliced through with the promise of grown-up memories.

"This is really good," I say, shouting at Liza over loud music.

She takes a long pull of hers. "Never had one?"

I think of Lynch and the popular kids who drank together at road parties every weekend. Parties I was never invited to. "Wasn't really part of the drinking crowd back home."

"Welcome to the drinking crowd," she says, tossing back another slug. Hers is half gone already.

Applause and whistles charge the air in the room, and I turn in my seat to see that in the corner, someone holding a microphone is bowing, flushed with pleasure. She hands the mic off to a guy standing behind a podium, and this guy says, in a movie-announcer voice, "Thank you, Nicki, that was great. And now we need Tim! Tim, please join us at the front of the room!"

Tim's name and a song title, "Take On Me," flash up on a big screen above the podium guy.

Delight rushes through my bloodstream, straight into my sweaty toes and tingling fingertips. "Wait. Is this karaoke?"

"Yep." She rolls her eyes. "That's kind of why I like to come here. I play *American Idol* judge in my head all night. It entertains me."

I reach across the table and grip her arm. "I've never seen live karaoke!"

"Ouch, jeez."

I relax my grip, but my eyes stay fixed on Tim, who's now dancing to the frantic eighties groove.

"Is it everything you hoped it would be?" I can tell from the curve of her mouth and the dryness of her voice that she's teasing me, and I don't care.

I'm mentally running down the list of Bridget's Perfectly Singable Songs when it hits me, a thud of truth that echoes in my hollow gut: I can't sing in front of Liza. Her knowing about my non-acceptance into the MFP would be almost worse than a stranger knowing. I don't want to be "less than" her. I want us to be equals.

"It is," I reply, guzzling the rest of my vodka deliciousness in one long, gulpy drink.

"Ready for another?" Her tone is sardonic. I'm pretty sure she's expecting me to say no.

"Sure."

She gets up and returns with two more Sprites just as Tim manages to tackle the extreme falsetto finale of "Take On Me." I cheer and whoop with the rest of the appreciative patrons as Liza and I furtively doctor our drinks. The atmosphere of the room is rubbing off on me, and I pour a little more vodka in this time.

Liza and I chat as best we can, but it's hard to get into a deep convo. The place is loud. Plus, I'm fighting a pretty heavy internal battle regarding whether or not to get onstage at this bar. On one side of the line stands my pride and the promise I made to myself to not sing *at all* this year; on the other, recklessness, liquor, and also pride. Pride is a fickle master, let me tell you.

Also, I'm completely distracted with critiquing the singers, who range from awful to impressive.

"She was pretty good on the big notes but really pitchy in between," I say to Liza after a woman finishes "I Will Always Love You," which, as far as I'm concerned, is a song that should be sung only by Whitney but which people forever seem hell-bent on massacring.

"Agreed," says Liza, twirling her straw. Now that she's halfway through her third drink, her eyes have taken on a filmy glaze and her shoulders are even more slumped than they usually are. "You know, you sure know a lot about singing for someone who doesn't sing."

83

I'm halfway through my third drink, too, and feeling bold. Recklessness and liquor are winning. "So about that—" I start, but then the applause goes up for the latest singer, and the karaoke guy says, "And now we need Bridget Bloom! Bridget, you're up!"

I flash wide-eyed Liza an apologetic smile as I make my way to the front of the room. And to my destiny. You see, when I got up to go to the bathroom after our second drink, I also visited the karaoke guy and handed him a little slip of paper with my name, my song choice. It was the most thrilling moment of my life.

And it's about to be usurped.

Ever since I landed my first lead (Annie, age seven), I've been chasing the high of the stage. Those front-row faces, all lit up with joy and appreciation—they cleanse me, clear me of all self-doubt. Up onstage, I am Bridget mothertrucking Venus Bloom, a force. One of a kind. I know I am loved, but on that stage, I *know* I am loved.

I've never been addicted to any substances, but I might just be hooked on that feeling.

I step up to the man and grab the microphone out of his hands as the opening bars to "Respect" kick in. The previous karaoke wannabe couldn't handle Whitney, but I sure as hell can do Aretha some justice.

And I do. By the end of the fourth line, the crowd's eating out of my hand, wolf whistling and catcalling. I make eye contact with my audience like every music teacher I've ever had has taught me, telling them the story of this song. It must work, because well before I get to the big spelled-out finish, they're clapping along, big rosy grins on faces throughout the room. I spy Liza sitting with her mouth hanging open but turned up, a shocked sort of smile. Finally, I've done something to faze the impenetrable Liza, and I'm not gonna lie: it feels good.

I finish to raucous cheering and yelling, these patrons every bit as loud as I hoped they would be for me. This is a dream come true. This is the best. Night. Ever.

Humility is fucking overrated.

I pick my way back to my table to scattered compliments and slaps on the back, and when I get there, my half-full drink remains, along with a full glass of something neon yellow. "Thanks, but I'm not sure I need another one," I say, gesturing at the new drink.

"I didn't get it. Someone bought it for you," she says, pointing to a brunette in boyfriend jeans and a tight T-shirt, one arm fully sleeved in tattoos, leaning up against the bar. She's maybe about our age—probably a little older, given all that ink—and cute as hell. Her smile sends a dizzy surge of adrenaline through me, along with something that feels like a full-body glow. For five seconds, chatting her up seems like *the only* thing that makes sense—but I check myself. I've got enough on my plate right now without trying to launch an off-campus romance. I mouth, "Thank you," to the gorgeous one I let get away and turn back to my bestie.

Liza leans closer. "When were you going to tell me that you sing?"

"Um, never?"

"*Why?* You're good. Really, really good. And I would know.

85

I've been dragged to every kind of singing camp, class, and workshop you can imagine."

The time to come clean with Liza is now or never, and the vodka seems to be saying "now."

"Okay, here's the deal. I'm not a music focus program student. I didn't get in."

"*What?* Why? How?"

"I totally bombed the theory test. Like, probably worse than you or anyone else in Theory for Dummies. Because of that, the admissions people didn't think I could handle being an MFP student. I'm trying to prove them wrong, by the way. And not just because I want to perform, but because I *need* to. I just found out we might not be able to afford for me to be here if I don't get a sponsorship."

Liza's face goes blank. "Well, that's a lot."

"Yeah."

"Why not sing for funsies, like in classes and stuff, though? I've never even heard a peep out of you."

I sigh with the force of a martyr. "*That* is self-imposed. Octavia told me I needed to work on my humility. Not singing at all is my way of doing that."

Liza sits back in her chair, blowing air out of her mouth with puffed cheeks. "For someone who seems to love it like you do, that's heavy. Almost cruel."

"Tell me about it."

"Do you miss it?"

My throat feels unexpectedly huge and swollen, and everything above my chest hurts a little. Grief chose this moment to sneak attack my body. "Yeah. Every single day. Singing's what I love the most about music, and the whole reason I wanted to go to Richard James."

Liza sips at her drink. "I'd give up my spot for you, if I could."

"Don't be silly. You obviously deserve to be in the program."

"Deserving and wanting are two different things, though."

Move over, grief—the shock hits me right in the breastbone. "Wait. You don't want to be in the program?"

She shrugs. "I mean, it's fine. But mostly I'm in there because my mom insisted. Said if I didn't do it, she wouldn't pay for college."

"That's . . . heavy. Almost cruel," I say, her past words mapping perfectly to this scenario.

"Tell me about it," she repeats with a rueful smile. "I intentionally failed my theory final last year, to see if it'd get me thrown out of the program. Didn't work, obviously. They just put me back in Theory for Dummies."

"So this is your *second* time in that class?"

Liza nods, not even bothering to look ashamed.

I cringe as a wave of something like jealousy sweeps over me. She tried to throw away the very thing I want. "Do you hate music that much?" I ask, working hard to mask how incredulous I feel.

She shrugs. "You know when something is shoved down your throat so hard-core, and for so long, you can't even really tell how you feel about it anymore? Like, you used to love tater tots, but then the school cafeteria served them every single day, and then you can't stand the sight of them?"

"Yeah, I get that. We watched *The Princess Bride* as a family every Christmas. Now I've seen it so many times that I don't know if I actually like it or hate it."

"That's me and music. I love all things artsy, but I'm more into creating things that people can look at without looking at *me*. I think maybe I could be a decent architect. But Mom was always *determined* to make me a music star. She said music was in my genes, so it was my destiny."

"Wow." Her genes. Her destiny. She took the words of my life and spat them back at me, but in reverse. "I *know* I'm destined to be a star. My dads have always said so, and my Grams, too. *And* my genes."

"Oh yeah?"

"Yeah." I typically don't share a lot about this stuff with others—and actually, back in Lynch, I never had to. Everyone knew everyone in that town, so all the kids there knew my story, without me ever having to tell it. But Liza isn't from Lynch, and she doesn't *have* to know anything about me. She wants to. She asked. So I tell her—about my dead mom, my dads adopting me, all of it.

Liza sits with her eyes uncharacteristically wide for the second time tonight. I'm two for two on Liza shockers, not bad. "Do you know anything about her? Your mom?"

"She was really loud and also really smart, but almost failed high school. Grams said her standardized test scores were always off the charts but she didn't always care about showing up for class. She was an amazing singer; Dodge showed me some videos of her from high school. She wanted to get the hell out of Lynch and make it on Broadway. So . . . maybe that tells you a little about why I'm the way I am?"

She nods. "Totally. What about your bio dad? Anything from him?"

"No idea. He was kind of a one-night thing, from what Dodge has told me, and happily signed his rights away before Mom died. I don't know who he is. And I'm not super-inclined to go looking for him."

At a surface level, none of this stuff is really so bad to think about. These are the facts of my life, and I'm used to them. Also, I ended up with the two best dads in the world. And yet. Occasionally I let my mind wander and I think about baby me, whose biological father never wanted her at all and whose mom-made-of-star-power died before she could ever launch, let alone see *me* ascend.

Every time I think about *this* part of my history, I want to sing loud enough to pop a blood vessel in my eyeball. I want to shove my way to the front of a stage, the spotlight hot and bright and filling my vision so entirely, there isn't room for anything but the moment and the glory. Anything to remind myself of how special I actually am.

In other words, the center of attention is my safest place.

Liza finishes her drink and slumps low in her seat. "So let's get this straight. You're dying to be in the MFP so you can do what you love. I'm forced to be in the MFP, which forces me to do things I hate. And we both have at least one sucky bio parent."

"God, we are a tragic pair. We belong together." I look down at my phone clock. "Twelve fifteen. Should we head?"

"You're not gonna finish that one?" She nods at my still-full fourth drink.

"Nah." When she reaches for it, I bat her hand away. "And you shouldn't either. Let's go."

We duck safely back into the dorm using her enchanted key card and stand at the point at which we need to head into different stairwells.

"Thanks for tonight. It was fun," I say.

Liza pulls me into a hug so tight, the air is shoved from my rib cage and an involuntary gasp pushes out with it. I'm flummoxed. She's not the hugging type, but then again, I'm not the drinking-and-sneaking-out type.

We're casting our identities to the wind at Richard James, she and I.

NINE

I WAKE WITH MY MOUTH glued shut. Prying it open results in
no better fate—tastes like something died in there. Effing. Gross.
I reach for the bottle of water on my bedside table and take four
greedy swallows before letting my too-heavy head fall back on
the pillow. I've smashed the snooze button, so I'll have to suffer
through one more loud round of "Firework" despite feeling like a
complete dud.

A lamp across the room flicks on, and I flinch under its glare.
Ouch. When did light become so deadly?

"Rough morning?" Ruby sits up in bed and turns toward me.

What? Ruby is talking to me? Is hallucinating also part of a
hangover?

"Yeah, you could say that." My voice comes out in a croak and
I put a hand to my throat in horror—*how will I sing today?*—before

remembering that I'm not allowed to sing. For the first time in my life, *that's* a relief.

She snickers. "Figures."

I squint over at her. "What do you mean?"

"Don't you remember last night?"

I dig back into the foggy memory of my return home. I remember letting myself in, throwing my clothes around haphazardly as I sought pajamas . . . Ohh.

I rarely get embarrassed, yet this memory's enough to make me want to crawl back under the sheen of my bedspread indefinitely. Even if it *was* just Ruby who saw. I groan, not bothering to stifle it, and press a pillow over my face.

"To be fair, you're a good singer."

Last night, as I entered the room, I launched into a roaring rendition of Sinatra's "New York, New York." For reasons unfathomable to sober me. Then, I undressed in time to the music, tossing a shoe off to one downbeat, a sock to another, then my pants and shirt, and you get how this must have looked to Ruby.

But another memory comes poking in—Ruby and I singing the song's big finale together. I'm pretty sure I high-kicked in just my bra and underwear. (I look under the covers and check: affirmative. That happened.) And then I giggled and collapsed in my bed, and it's the last thing I remember.

Wait. Ruby joined in? Ruby had *fun*? With *me*? No, no. Impossible. Surely, if vodka can screw this badly with judgment, it can also screw with memory. I've already put Ruby solidly into the "doesn't like me/not friend" category, and it's too confusing to get her out of there.

Plus, she's an instrumentalist. Instrumentalists are, as a rule, not fun.

Shit, did I *say* anything? Ruby would be the worst person to know about my undercover MFP operation. And I can't have her finding out about my less-than-ideal financial situation, not that she can't already tell I don't come from the privilege that she does. The thought of her lording any of this over me makes my feet sweat. "Did I . . . say anything? Anything weird."

Her half smile is hard to read. "I guess it depends on your definition of weird."

"Like, any unexpected confessions?"

She looks taken aback. "Other than professing your undying love for Frank Sinatra, no."

Whew. She could be lying, but I don't know what her motivation would be. "I know I acted like an ass last night. Weird request, but can you please not tell anyone I was singing?"

Her eyes narrow. "Lemme get this straight. You come home roaring drunk and the thing you're worried about me spilling is that you were *singing*?"

She's got a point. "Okay, I'd appreciate your discretion about the drinking, too." The discovery that I'd been drinking could earn me a one-way ticket out of Chicago, I realize with a start. How could I have been so stupid? Next time—if there is a next time—I'm gonna be more careful.

She's looking at me like she wants to say more, but instead, she slumps back down on her bed. "Whatever. I won't say anything about the singing or the drinking."

"Thanks."

An hour later I drag myself into the Rot, barely making it in time to grab something before I have to head to class. Liza's nowhere to be found, which isn't unheard of, as sometimes she sleeps through breakfast. Our habit on these days is to meet on the bench outside of the Rot to chat for a few minutes before we head to our respective first classes, so I take my Pop-Tarts to go.

Yet when I get to the bench, she's not there either. I mean, I feel a little like death from those vodka Sprites (and how can something that was so delicious last night sound like absolute shit today? I wouldn't touch one with a ten-foot bassoon), but surely she's not so hungover that she'd skip?

I'm ruminating on this and munching sweet strawberry goodness when I hear voices from around the corridor. Liza's one of them—good, she's up and at 'em. I get up to greet her but get no farther than heading around the corner when I halt in my tracks and turn back.

I'd seen a flash of high heels, straight posture, red nails. The other voice is Octavia's.

"I know what you said, but I'm asking you to please, *please* reconsider." Liza's voice, with this much raw emotion in it, is almost unrecognizable.

"How many times must we discuss this? I haven't changed my mind. My decision is final." *Our decision stands.* She's a fan of hard stances and ultimate authority, Octavia Lawless, dean of students, MFP chair. I take in her words just as I did when she said them to me, with equal parts dread and fear.

"But *please*, if you'd just hear me out—"

"No, Liza. End of discussion." Followed by the staccato of sharp pumps clicking on tile floor, growing fainter by the second.

A few moments later Liza comes around the corner, wiping her eyes. Her hair is lank and pulled back into a ponytail, and her face is oddly bare. Just as I suspected, she's a stunner even without her signature thick black eyeliner—maybe even more so—but it also feels weird to think of anyone this sad as stunning. Lines of pain stretch across her usually smooth forehead.

Ugh, if anyone knows the awfulness of being smashed like an insect under Octavia's four-inch heel, it's me. I rush to Liza. "Are you okay?" She doesn't shy away when I put my arm around her shoulders.

"I'm fine. Just more of the same," she says through a sniffle.

"What, you're in the habit of arguing with Octavia Lawless?"

She looks me over, her face so close to mine, I can smell the mint on her breath. She brushed her teeth, thank God for small favors. "I argue a fair amount with her."

"Seriously?"

"Don't you ever argue with your dads?"

I gawp at her, confused. "Sure, I get into it with my dads once in a while. But what in the French toast does that have to do with you and Octavia?"

Liza eyes me warily. "Octavia's my mom, B."

"What?"

"Ouch! Dammit, I know when you have feels, they're big feels, but you've *got* to stop it with the whole squeezing my arm thing."

I realize I'm clenching her bicep with some serious force and relax.

"My last name's Lawless. Didn't you put two and two together?"

Nope, because I never even thought to learn Liza's last name. In my mind, she was just Liza and that was good enough. I shake my head.

Astonishment peeks through Liza's overall look of despair. "I thought for a while maybe you only sat by me in class *because* I was Liza Lawless, daughter of the famous Octavia, who isn't *only* a Broadway star, but is *also* the dean of the whole school. You looked like the type."

"The type?"

"You know how when girls throw themselves at football players, they're called jersey chasers? There are also folx who throw themselves at famous people or anyone who can help get them closer to the famous person. Star catchers, I call them. No offense, but I thought you were one of them. I've grown up around them my whole life, and you fit the bill."

This one hits me right in the gut. She's right. That's exactly why I initially introduced myself to Max—to get closer to Duke. And if I'd known Liza was Octavia's daughter *before* shit hit the fan with Octavia, I probably would've tried to be Liza's friend. Because she was a Lawless.

"What changed your mind?"

"I kept waiting for you to ask about my mom, or what it's like to be her daughter—star catchers always do this. You never did. And *then* you sang in front of me, even though Octavia told you to be humble if you wanted to get into the program for real. You wouldn't share information I could use to hurt you if you didn't trust me. Really trust me. That's when I knew our friendship was real."

Huh. I'd had no idea with whom I'd shared that information—and if I'd known, no way in hell I would've shared.

But on the other hand, I'd had no idea I was being tested. I wouldn't have passed if I'd known Liza was *Liza Lawless*. For what it's worth, because of the way everything went down, I like Liza because she's Liza. Period.

I hug her to me. "It's real, friend."

Liza has the grace to not ask me if I would have done anything differently if I'd known Octavia was her mother. And I'm much, much too ashamed to admit to her that I didn't know her last name. In contrast, Liza knows *tons* about me. All about my dads and some stuff about Lynch. She knows my favorite color is purple and it takes me an hour to do my hair and I have a weird penchant for bacon in my chocolate-chip cookies. What do I know about her?

Nowhere near enough, clearly.

"Good, because I really need a real friend right now. My mom sucks."

Truth. I know firsthand. "I'm sorry."

"After our talk last night, about how your dream is to be in the MFP, and mine's *so not*, I thought I should give talking to her one last shot. I tried to convince her to let me apply for the visual arts program next year, or even just go to a normal school. But you heard how well that went."

97

"Yeah."

She pulls a Kleenex out of her jeans pocket and blows her nose into it, making an absurdly loud honk for such a delicate person. "Anyway, thank you for being here."

"You're welcome."

We stand in semi-awkward silence as Liza uses her tissue to sop up her face. Good thing she came makeup-free today. I wonder if she predicted the talk with her mom would go down like this and preventively skipped the cosmetics. Poor Liza.

"Umm . . . probably bad timing, but you're not going to tell your mom about the whole singing thing, right?"

I get a dry look, some semblance of Normal Liza swimming to the surface. "Bridget Venus Bloom. Think this through. What would I say? 'So Bridget and I were out drinking at a bar when she gets up and sings this unreal cover of Aretha.'"

We both laugh and walk toward the classrooms, her hips in line with mine, like we're marching into battle together.

Because we are, of course.

TEN

"AH, ATHENA. YOU RETURN AGAIN," Hans says, removing his reading glasses. He sits on a stool behind the jewelry counter, writing in a ledger. Hans's records are all still handwritten, which I find both horrifying and enchanting. I visit When in Rome at least once a week now, usually on weekends. The silver and knickknacks, the smell of dust, Hans himself, somehow—they're all familiar, and thus safe, in a world where almost nothing feels familiar anymore.

"Guilty as charged. New stuff?"

He waves me to a cardboard box sitting an arm's length away. "See for yourself."

I peer inside the open cardboard. Inside, various things: a few pieces of silver, a small tabletop clock, several trays of costume jewelry. I open one longish white box and gasp: it's a stunning necklace, its round pendant a swirl of the brightest aquas and blues. I've never seen anything like it.

"That's abalone," Hans says, peering at the necklace over my shoulder.

I hold it up to the light, the stone sending jets of blue and green reflection off the walls. "It's to die for."

"Well, something did. That bauble used to be the shell of a marine snail."

"That's one good-looking snail," I say, picturing droves of Technicolor gastropods crawling around on tropical terrain.

"Not especially. The pretty part of an abalone shell is on the inside."

I wrinkle my nose. "Seems like kind of a waste, doesn't it?"

"You tell me, Athena."

We stand quietly admiring the piece for a few seconds longer, and then I slowly lower it back down into its box. "I'd tell you I love this necklace, but we've been down this road."

"Ah, yes. You've decided to dodge the inevitable response today?"

"Yep."

Hans removes all the pieces of jewelry from the box, setting them on the counter. "Would you like to help me clean and display these?"

"Absolutely."

The last few times I was here, Hans put me to work. Just little things: dusting shelves, sweeping, polishing silver. But at the end of my two-hour visits, he's slipped me some cash. I think I have a job at When in Rome. Even though first-year academy students are discouraged from seeking employment, in order to "focus fully on their studies and adjust to student life," *some* of us don't come from money and could use all the help we can get.

I help with the jewelry, and then he sets me loose with a dust cloth on some shelves of knickknacks. I take note of what has recently sold. One chess set, though now there's another in its place. A set of gold-rimmed mugs is gone. The hand mirror I'd admired during my first visit was sold by my second, but I wasn't nearly as devastated about it as I thought I'd be. Guess Hans would've been right on that one: I apparently didn't *love* it.

Working at Hans's shop has an added benefit: time to think, without Ruby judging my every move, and without the constant chaotic drone of singing and instruments blasting—the status of our dorm at all times except the few enforced "quiet hours." Today I've got a real life conundrum to toss over. As I dust the compact wooden owl (hello, little fella) and the chessboards and books and baubles, I mull over my friendship with Liza. Our night out was amazing and special and even life-affirming, but something about it just isn't sitting right. I feel closer to Liza than I've ever felt to anyone outside of my dads. I *thought* I knew her so well. Yet I didn't know some of the most basic details of her life, such as her last freaking name. Or who her (famous) mother is. A jolt of surprise runs up my middle as I realize I don't know anything about her father or whether she has any siblings. Let alone if she has any other good friends.

I've come to no amazing conclusions on how this happened by

the time I finish dusting. Hans asks me to take inventory of some merchandise in his back room and hands me a clipboard with a list of items. A half hour in, I'm already almost through the list when something catches my eye. It's a wooden box, tucked away on the top corner of a shelf apart from the rest of the goods. Only the ornate floral carvings on its front are visible until I pull it down. Enough dust flies off it that I sneeze *four times*. I wonder if Hans has forgotten this little treasure, or if maybe it's up high enough that he's not able to see it anymore. (He told me he has shrunk a few inches over the years. Can you imagine? I'm not looking forward to ever walking around in the world at anything less than my five feet seven inches.)

The scent of cedar wafts as I pull the box's lid from its bottom. Inside is a stack of yellowed papers bound together with string. The writing on the top page is faded but still quite legible.

My Dearest June, As I drifted off to sleep last night, your face was the last thing I saw. Every detail, like you were lying right here with me. Your brown eyes. Red lips. Those dimples and all that hair. And wouldn't you know it, when I was rudely awakened by the foghorn this morning, your face was still there, right where I left it, and that's how I knew everything was going to be okay.

I work my way through a series of letters to June, signed Socks, and the return letters from June. There are probably over a hundred of them. Socks was away at war, stationed near Da Nang, Vietnam, where he worked on aircraft as a mechanic. June lived on a farm in Nebraska. (Nebraska!) They were engaged to be married when Socks came home—even though they'd met only one time. The letters are like reading a real-life Nicholas Sparks novel, I shit you not.

An hour later I'm still reading. Simple curiosity is one motivator, but it's also more than that. I'm not just intrigued—I'm *invested*. I hear the voices of June and Socks speaking to me like movie characters and somehow feel like this is my story as much as it is theirs.

I'm about halfway through the tale of June and Socks when I realize the light's shining in the big shop window in an afternoon kind of way, and I still need to get some homework done before supper. I carefully replace the letters in their box, finish taking inventory, and return to the front of the store, where Hans is still hard at work at his (archaic) ledger.

"Ah, she returns. How did it go?"

I hand him the clipboard. "Everything accounted for."

Hans shifts in his chair, pulling the clipboard back from his face to read it. "You've added a line here. A box?"

"Yeah, there was a small wooden box with carvings up on a top shelf. It wasn't on the list."

His brow furrows but then smooths, and he holds one index finger into the air. "Ah. With letters?"

"Yes. What an incredible story."

The corners of his mouth turn up. "Indeed."

"You've read them?"

Hans nods.

"There's something about them I'm not sure I understand." *And something about me, too.*

"I can try to help."

"It's kind of a big question."

"Try me, Athena."

I tug at a curl as I work to somehow smash my complicated, nebulous thoughts into words. "It's about—how do you know you *know* a person? Socks and June are engaged, but at first they seem to hardly know each other. Like, Socks asks June, 'What's it like for you, being one of fourteen siblings?' And June asks Socks, 'What's your favorite color? I want to sew you a shirt for church.' Stuff I'd assume people who knew each other enough to be engaged would already know."

"An astute observation." Hans scrubs at the lenses of his reading glasses with a rag. "I noticed you said, 'at first' they hardly know each other."

"Well, yeah. I'm about halfway through the letters. Now they're getting a little more casual, using more shorthand to refer to different events, that kind of thing."

"They seem closer, at the halfway mark."

"Yes."

"I agree. How do you think they achieved this, even at such a distance?"

I scrunch up my mouth and dig deep. "I guess it has to be the sharing of information. Since they couldn't *do* anything together, they had to build shared experiences through the written word. She tells him about her life, and vice versa. And they ask questions about each other."

"Yes, questions. Very important, Athena."

Well, holy crap, there it is. The answer to June and Socks *and* to Bridget and Liza. The reason I didn't know Liza's last name or anything about her family is that I never *asked*. If our relationship were documented like Socks and June's, all the letters would be in my handwriting.

So Liza knows me really well. But I don't know her.

"Thank you, Hans. I have to go for now, but would it be okay if I looked at the letters again sometime?"

His smile crinkles his eyes *and* his nose—this must be his Best Smile. It warms me like hot chocolate after playing in the snow. "Of course."

I walk back to Richard James dead set on my task: I'm gonna get Liza to write me some metaphorical letters.

ELEVEN

MY HEAD IS BROILING MY forearms. Am I getting a fever, maybe? I hope so. Sickness *might* get me out of this tutoring session. Might. Max is hardcore.

"Hey. Bridget. Earth to Bridget."

"What?"

"How's the worksheet coming?"

Does he mean the worksheet currently smashed under my arms and head? "How does it look like it's coming?"

Max's sigh is audible even though one of my ears is crunched into the crook of an elbow. I wonder how much longer he'll put up with me. I always show up, but I'm never an exemplary student. He keeps telling me I'm making great progress, and in any other arena of my life, I'd be eager to eat up that kind of praise. But his for some reason slides off, like I'm Teflon and his words are grease.

I hate theory so much. So, so much. Even though I'm well aware it stands between me and my dreams, I can't seem to get into it.

Fingers tousle my hair, digging gently into my scalp.

I rear up. Anyone who knows *anything* about naturally curly hair *knows* you do. Not. Disturb. The. Curl. With. Your. Hands.

But Max's hair is as straight as a Westboro Baptist churchgoer, so I suppose he wouldn't know.

I smooth a hand over the crown of my head and glare at him.

"Ready to work?" he asks, face full of hope. That, and ice cream. He's making great headway through this week's peanut butter cup Razzle. I finished mine before we got going, and now it congeals in my theory-hating stomach.

Though it pains me greatly to do it, I pick up the pencil and try again.

Five minutes later, I'm as far as the second item on the worksheet and pondering gouging my eyeballs out.

Maybe if I start a conversation, he'll let me quit trying on this thing. I know very little about this boy, which is weird given we spend at least an hour together every single week.

Someone I do know a lot about now? Liza. I've spent the last week focused on balancing out my relationship with her. By asking lots of questions, I've learned what her childhood was like (not great), who her dad is (musical genius sperm donor of Filipino heritage), and even her most embarrassing moment (peeing her pants in front of her entire second-grade class when her awful teacher refused to acknowledge her raised hand for many minutes). Now if our relationship were a series of letters, there'd be a stack in her blocky, all-caps handwriting.

I also know a fair amount about Duke, as he's around at every mealtime. I know that his favorite cereal is Cap'n Crunch, and that he's lactose intolerant, and that occasionally the sound of chewing sets him off. His very first crush was Arwen from *The Lord of the Rings*, but he'd also make out with Legolas. We could add more than a few Duke letters to the pile that Liza has now written me.

I don't have many letters from the ever-quiet Max Griffin. And I'm not above diversion tactics.

I lean back in my chair, stretching. "I need a break."

"You just *had* a break." He looks up from the worn composition book he's been scrawling in, the same one he brings every week. It's maybe about a billion years old, every corner dog-eared, the cover barely hanging on.

"Well, I need another. Let's talk about you for once."

If his head were see-through, I'd see gears churning and grinding up there right now. He wears a look of intense concentration, like my request to have a conversation is *a big deal that must be carefully considered*.

Finally he matches my posture and leans back in his chair, pushing back from the table slightly. "Fine. Shoot."

"What were you like as a kid?"

Instead of answering, he shovels in another massive bite of Razzle, drawing the spoon out slowly. He swallows, his Adam's apple bobbing hugely in his lean throat, and something like pleasure hums through my midsection.

Why do I so enjoy watching Max eat? A weird fetish, if I've ever heard of one.

"Well?" I prompt.

"Shy, scrawny, and idealistic. Obsessed with learning. Teachers loved me."

"Same as now?"

He grins. "Pretty much."

"Favorite movie."

"*Amélie*."

"Never heard of it."

He leans forward, gripping the table. "Seriously? Never?"

I shake my head.

"Well, let's watch it sometime."

"You promise it's not stuffy?"

"Promise."

"Okay, then." I pause and scrunch up my face, because you know what? Sometimes thinking up questions is hard. "What artist or band, living or dead, would you see in concert if you could choose any in the whole world?"

"Queen."

"Oh yeah. Duh. Favorite Queen song?"

He groans. "Ugh, the impossible. Maybe 'Under Pressure.' The Bowie collaboration pushes it over the edge."

"Good choice. I like 'Fat Bottomed Girls,' because homage."

He laughs, and I like it so much that I join in.

"You should solo it sometime. Just for me," I add.

His laughter cuts off and the happiness drains away from his face. "Yeah, I don't think *that's* going to happen."

"A different song, then."

"Nah. I'm not much for singing in front of people."

Now *this* is odd language for a music focus kid. He might as well have said he was considering a whole-face tattoo. "What? Why?"

"I'm just not. Not really my thing anymore."

Something clicks into place in my noggin, and I sit forward in my chair so quickly that I bonk my knees on the bottom of the table. "Wait. Do you have stage fright?"

His brows push down as he leans even farther back in his chair, like now he's the one who wants to get away from me. "You know, you're one to talk. It's been weeks here at school and I've *never* heard you sing. Duke told me you're a student accompanist for solo class, not a singer. What's up with that? Do *you* have stage fright?"

My blood goes carbonated and I nearly burst. Duke was *talking about me* outside of class! Huzzah! And yet, the content of Duke's sharing was less than ideal. My insides start exploding in a different way, panicky feelings replacing the excitement. If Max finds out I lied about being in the MFP, will he keep tutoring me? He's kind, but he's also a rules guy, and I just can't see him looking past this.

My jaw clenches. "Singing's not really my thing, either."

"That's not what you said the day we first met."

Damn him and his weirdly good memory.

He squints. "I don't get it. You look like a musical theater kid, act like a musical theater kid, and can play circles around most of us on the piano. But no singing."

His savvy face tells me he's about three seconds from seeing right through my lie, but for some reason my panic over this gives way to another feeling. Goddamn having to *pretend* to be a music focus kid and goddamn *humility* and goddamn Max for being smart enough to defraud me. This erupting fury is hot to the touch, but it's dynamic. I latch on to it, using it to propel me forward. I pick up my pencil, because even doing stupid theory worksheets is better than being scrutinized by Max. "Guess we're a matched set, me and you." I train my eyes back on the worksheet.

"Guess so." Patches of red are sneaking up his neck, but I find no pleasure in them this time.

For whatever reason, I'm able to figure out the six remaining items—the ones that were impossible just a few minutes ago—with no problem.

I push the sheet across the table and Max flips through, his red pen poised above the pages but never dipping onto them. "Every single one of these is right. Nice work."

I can tell by the tone of his voice that he's gobsmacked at my sudden theory abilities, but I somehow already knew my answers were correct. And his cheerleading is nice, but as usual the kindness doesn't stick. Maybe it's because every success I have in theory feels more like luck than learning.

I slide back from the table. "Are we done here?"

"If you are."

"I am," I say, and it comes out shaky because now that my anger is dissipating, other feels are sneaking in. Things like sadness. Like a desperation to be *seen*, really seen—and a flash of cold white fear that no one wants to even look at me if I'm not singing.

"Bridget?"

"Yeah?"

"Why don't you sing?" His voice is gentle, and the question is . . . real, for lack of a better word. I think he wants to see *me*. Just plain old me, without my voice.

I close my eyes and for a split second, I'm going to say it. It'd be so easy, and wouldn't it feel good to be real with someone other than Liza? Something about Max is breaking me down. Maybe it's his freckles or his unapologetic obsession with all things nerdy, but more likely it's the fact that he shows up for me week after week even though I'm a hot mess when it comes to theory. He could tutor anyone and make the same amount of money. But he chose to help *me*.

Yet when I again picture the possible outcomes of this—no more theory help, Max telling everyone, *Duke* knowing I'm less than he is—I inwardly cringe. If my MFP secret gets out, it'd be like Lynch all over again—not belonging, no matter how hard I try.

It's too risky.

"It's a long story," I say, and quickly exit the room. Tears would be another thing I wouldn't be able to explain.

Wednesday night theory gives way to Thursday morning chaos. An emergency before-school meeting for the MFP kids has been called by Seabass, because the student-run musical is inching closer and we still haven't come up with a plotline, let alone written any music. Apparently, "historical" as a theme has everyone scratching their heads.

Yes, I've noted how deeply I'm entrenched in my own lie, now thinking of myself as an MFP student to the point of attending the meetings. But I *have* to show up to this thing, because if I don't, my cover's blown.

The whole program congregates in the Rot, where chairs have been turned around, auditorium style, to face the front. I plunk down by Liza, her apathetic face nose-deep in her phone. "Morning, sunshine," I say, and all I get in response is a grunt.

Max appears at my other side. "Hey," he says, in such a loaded way that I turn to face him, though our chairs are altogether too close for this to be a comfortable eye-contact situation. I'm nervous he's about to try to continue last night's questioning, but I don't see any curiosity, or even playfulness, on his face. I see only concern. My anxiety instantly fades because I know—I just *know*—he's not going to force me into more conversation. As I soak in his sad brown eyes, something else sneaks into the place anxiety carved out. Something . . . warm. Hell if I can name the feeling, though.

Duke, though he's shouted down by half the school (*Hey, man! Come sit with us!*), sits on Liza's empty side. Ten bucks says he would've sat by me if there'd been an open seat.

Seabass claps his hands and the room's chaos settles to a simmer. "Okay! You all know why I called this meeting—we need to make some progress on the musical, people! Let's hear it. Who's got an idea?"

Max nudges me. Leaning in close, he whispers, "FYI, this 'emergency' meeting happens every year. The faculty knows that if they light an urgency fire like this, we'll all take the whole thing more seriously." When he leans back out, my curls move with him, as a few clumps have stuck to his cheek. We grin at each other as I pull them away.

A second-year raises his hand and pitches a Sacco and Vanzetti musical, which is quickly squelched as being too dude-centric. Someone else offers the idea of "something Prohibition era," but no one has much to say about it or add to it. Too vague, no meat.

This could be my moment, if I could just *think* of something. *Think, Bloom, think think think* . . . I feel my forehead swelling with unthought thoughts.

And when it *does* hit me, it's such a revelation that it punches me in the throat. I cough, choking on my own excited spit, and my hand flies up so fast and with such force that Liza is a casualty. "Ow, B," she mutters, rubbing her arm.

"Ms. Bloom! Whatcha got?" says Seabass.

I stand, which I know is extra, but I can't help it; this idea is making me buoyant. "So, I recently came across these letters between lovers who met during the Vietnam War era. The guy, Socks, was a soldier and had gone on leave to Nebraska with a buddy. The girl, June, was one of eight sisters in one rural Nebraska family. Socks saw June across a clothesline and it was basically love at first sight. They only knew each other a few days before Socks left for war, but still, Socks asked her to wait for him—and she did! But the thing that is *really* cool about this is that their love story is all in letters. We could use them to drive the plot—the story, the songs, we could even do some voice-over stuff, like read right from the letters."

There's a glow on Seabass's face that has nothing to do with his fake tan, and I see it in my schoolmates, too. An excited hum kicks in, a hive of words swapped among my peers.

Max touches my wrist, so lightly I almost don't notice. "This is an amazing idea. Why didn't you bring it up before?"

I shrug. "I didn't *have* the idea before."

I spy Ruby sitting a few rows away, looking tremendously un-impressed. I ignore her.

"Vietnam-era romance. Based on a true story," says Seabass, crossing his arms over his chest in a satisfied way. "What do we think, folx? Is this our musical?"

Duke vaults to his feet, clambering to stand beside me. "I second this idea. I think it's perfect. Who's with me?" He's so close I can feel the heat radiating off his body, even through my sweater. He smells clean, but different from your typical boy—almost like baby powder.

I know this is it. Duke is the Pied Piper of Richard James, and if he wants this musical, it's happening. Sure enough, hands all over the room fly up, a few people let out little whoops of support. I've just become the OG author of the Richard James musical. Oh well if I don't know even one iota about music writing. We work with what we have.

"Okay, it's settled. Form a battle plan, troops!" Seabass claps once and moonwalks out of the room. I'm not kidding. He actually moonwalks.

A familiar safe but fizzy energy stirs in my chest as every eye in the room lands on me. The spotlight, my home away from home. Now, I'll know for sure I belong here, even if I'm not *technically* in the program. I'll be seen, and if I'm seen, I can't be worthless. Relief is the sweetest song.

Except then I realize the eyes aren't on me. They're on Duke. Of *course* they'd look to Duke. The triumphant tune in the heart of me quiets to a whisper as I too turn to face our unofficial-official leader. He shifts from leg to leg, also just realizing the room is waiting on him. "Um, okay! So, uh . . . hmm, I don't know how this works! Should we meet again like this in a week or so and talk progress? Everyone bring ideas?"

I'd roll my eyes at his terrible leadership if he weren't so darned endearing. Giving zero actionable items to specific people will lead to zero progress. We just learned all about diffusion of responsibility in psych.

No one else seems to notice, though, and everyone nods and shoots a thumbs-up at Duke as they cram stuff into their backpacks, preparing to leave for their first classes.

"Hey, may I?" Duke gestures at Liza's seat, and she shrugs and slides over into his old one. Duke wants to sit by *me*, just like I thought. He plunks down, close enough that his denim jacket slides against my sweater. "Bloom, you're a genius with this letters thing."

I smile so wide that my bottom lip splits open a little. Worth it.

Max stands, straightening his jeans. "Look, ten bucks says no one is going to have any great ideas by next week without actual tasks to work on, and we really don't have that long to get this thing together. We can take the lead on songwriting—like, maybe us four can work on it, have some ideas to share with the big group next week?" He nods around at me, Duke, and Liza.

Max also apparently understands diffusion of responsibility.

Duke shrugs, apparently unconcerned. "Sure, let's do it."

As for me, I'm *thrilled* to be included on this MFP-only task, and I nod so hard that I poke myself in the eye with my hair. "I'll take some photos of the letters so we've got something tangible to work with. Maybe I can write down big-picture ideas, too," I offer.

"Genius," says Duke, again, squeezing my knee before he takes off for class.

His praise and that squeeze and this moment—it all makes me feel bigger than the spotlight, brighter even than Venus. I am the sun.

TWELVE

THE KIDS IN ADVANCED SOLO are all losing their shit.

Their first graded performances of the year are coming up, and everyone wants to nail their songs. It's not just about the grade. It's about the pride. The bragging rights.

If it were me, it'd be about being the best. And in this group I might just be, with the exception of maybe Liza and definitely Duke.

Yet I'm forcibly reminded every day: I'm *not* a vocal soloist right now. I'm an accompanist. And I'm responsible for sitting through extra practices with these divas as they perfect their craft—it's part of my grade. "You won't have to invest the time into prepping your own solos, so you are expected to practice with your performers"—the edict of Octavia Lawless, chair of the MFP. She arranged this with Seabass after she let me into the course.

It's maybe the worst kind of torment. Like making a person addicted to gambling work in a casino, slapping his hand away every time he even *thinks* about pulling a slot machine lever. I bet Octavia meant for this to be the case. She had to know this particular course assignment would hurt me. Maybe she even means to break me. Which is part of why, of course, I grin and bear it. Humbly. I can't let her win.

"Bridget. Measure forty, please."

I snap to attention. This girl Madison stands in front of the piano, a hand on her popped hip. She thinks she's the next Céline Dion, but she's flat on the front end of every big note and her phrasing is bad. Not that I'm going to tell her that.

I'm just the lowly accompanist, after all.

We launch back into her song and run the midsection over and over, until there's probably blood running out of my ears.

Once Madison is finally satisfied and hauls herself away from the piano, I work with another student. And another. The last student of the night is Duke. My insides tingle with anticipation. I hadn't expected him to sign up for practice time, as I'd assumed he'd accompany himself for the graded solo—but I'm not gonna lie, I fist-pumped when I saw his name in the online sign-up system.

He knocks lightly on the practice room door as he lets himself in, and I smile my most winning smile.

"Fancy meeting a girl like you in a place like this," he says, sidling up to the piano. He leans down onto the top of it, resting his head in his hands.

Is he this comfortable with everyone, or is it just me?

It's probably me. God, please let it be me.

"Fancy that."

"How's your night going?"

"Oh, you know. Another night, another six soloists. I do what they tell me to, they sing, they leave. Same old."

"Isn't it weird, how the kids who don't play piano are the most entitled ones? They have, like, no consideration for the work accompanists do."

"Exactly. That's so true." This boy speaks the language of my heart.

Funny how I don't mind this tiny box of a room so much when Duke's in it. It felt oppressive with the other soloists, but with Duke, it's cute. Cozy. Ripe with possibilities.

"Well, just in case I forget to say it later: I appreciate your hard work, B. I know accompanying isn't glamorous, but it shouldn't be thankless. Without you, there'd be no solo."

Holy wow. YouTube Duke is popped-collar charm, a voice like a caramel sundae. But in-person Duke? He is even more than that. He understands what it is to be a musician, an *accompanist*, even.

What I want to say: *OMG, just kiss me now. You are so deliciously smooth and sweet, I want to slather you on a piece of toast and eat you.*

What I say: "You're welcome, but it's my pleasure, really."

"Last year, I didn't trust the student accompanist, so I played for myself. This year it's different. I've seen what you can do. So I figured it was as good a time as any to practice singing without the piano under my hands."

Wait 'til you've got ME under your hands.

"Aw, don't blush. I'm just giving you some props," he says, mistaking the reason for my rosy cheeks.

Out of nowhere, I shiver—you know the kind that happens when you're either really cold or really *something* (BIG feels) and it just happens? That kind.

"Hey, I saw that." Duke slips his arms out of the sleeves of his denim button-up and lays it across my shoulders. "Is this better?"

I was roasting hot even without the denim, but I'll be damned if I admit that, not with Duke's baby-powder-and-peppermint-scented clothing on my body. It's the next best thing to Duke himself being wrapped around me (which is hopefully also about to happen).

"Thank you," I say as I cuddle deeper into the shirt.

"Of course. Shall we?" He hands me sheet music for what looks like an eighties-era power ballad, "I Want to Know What Love Is." Unlike a lot of the sheet music I get handed—on plain eight-and-a-half-by-eleven paper, printed from a digital download—this is an old-school copy, probably purchased at a music store, and well loved. The cover is creased, pages slightly yellowed.

"Where did you get this?"

"From home. Mom plays piano and she has a ton of sheet music."

"My grandma had a similar stash. It's like a treasure trove when you're a music geek."

"Totally." He grins.

"Why this song?"

"Seabass told us to do contemporary, not from a musical, and to choose something that challenges us. My upper register is where I struggle most, and this song is *all* about the upper register."

I wonder what I would've chosen if I'd gotten to pick a song for myself for that assignment. Singing's so easy for me—figuring out my challenge would have been the challenge.

I arrange the music in front of me and experiment with the first bars, familiarizing myself. "I'm ready when you are."

Struggle with the upper register, my ass. Duke hits every note right in the middle, molasses voice wrapping all the way around every single word. He apparently knows the lyrics already and I catch him looking at me as he sings, rather than his music. He's singing about love and wanting to feel it and wanting someone (*please* let it be me) to show him, and by the end of the song I'm all quivery. Sweat drips down the small of my back.

"That was . . . good," I croak as the song winds down.

"Eh." He shrugs. "I can do better. Did you notice, in that part right before the chorus, that I missed some notes? I was off. I could hear it. Sharp."

I hadn't, but maybe my perspiration-inducing focus on Duke's face had something to do with that.

He comes around to the back of the piano and sits with me on the bench, flipping the music back to the first pages. He points. "See, this, right here." His left arm brushes my breasts as he reaches across me, and he draws his hand back quickly. "Oops, sorry," he says, laughing.

"It's okay. They're everywhere," I say without thinking, accidentally slipping into an inside joke that I have with Liza re my ample chest.

He laughs harder, and I can't help but start in, too. His left arm pushes into my right; his thigh rests against mine, all of it rubbing together as we giggle. Much more friction, and we're gonna start a fire.

"Anyway. Like I was saying. Right here." He plays the melody and sings along, then does it again.

"I can do that for you, you know." I cock an eyebrow at him.

He draws his hands back from the keyboard. "Old habits die hard."

"Here, try it again. I'll play."

We run through the section he thinks he's struggling with several times, lines about a life of heartache and pain and wanting to change his lonely life. He sings it like he means it and I wonder if he does.

Can a heart explode out of one's chest if it feels enough things all at once? If so, we're about to have a bloody mess in Triton 212.

He finishes his "tough section" once more and then sits quietly, staring at the music. Uncharacteristically quiet. This is a guy who's always laughing, joking; he's basically one big charismatic smile of a person.

Or so I thought.

"Where'd you get the idea for the musical?" he asks, now noncommittally chording "Hey Jude" on the piano.

"Funny story: I found the letters purely by accident in an antique store."

"Wow. Amazing. Any ideas for songs yet?"

I pull out my phone, show him the pictures I took of some of the letters. "A few. I've been toying with the idea of an ocean since they've got one between them."

"Like, across an ocean, something like that?"

"Sort of, but that's been overdone."

He whistles. "Shrewd one, aren't you?"

"I'm just a girl who knows what she does and doesn't want." In a fit of boldness, I look right at him. There is zero space between us on the bench and not very much between our faces. He has to see the meaning in my eyes. Has to. Our eyes lock and everything south of my navel stirs.

And then he's up and ambling around the room like nothing happened at all. But I know it did because my arm and my thigh are still warm from contact with his body.

"Well, keep brainstorming on that song! I will too. Can we go through my solo again, say, early next week? Day before it's due?"

"Yeah, sure, absolutely." I don't know if I have openings in my accompanist practice schedule, but I will *make* an opening for Duke. Obviously. There's nothing I wouldn't do for him, especially after tonight.

One parting movie star grin over his shoulder and he hustles out of the room.

I feel my shoulders slump as the tension drains out of me and into the floor. Absentmindedly, I put my hands on the keys and start an Adele standard, "Make You Feel My Love," allowing myself to hum, though I'm burning to sing.

I get back to my room pretty late because I stayed and played piano after Duke left. It was a good night to feel all the feels. Without singing in my life, it's sometimes hard to remember what music means to me. Even piano has become a thing not completely mine anymore. Most of the time I'm playing for someone else.

Tonight I reclaimed music for my own. It was only an hour's worth of piano just for me, but I feel at home in my body and more sure of my purpose than I have for a long time. Richard James is working its magic on me, even without the official MFP status. My dads have to find a way to fund me for next semester. I don't let myself think much about the alternative, but when I do . . . ouch.

"Hi," says Ruby, perched in her usual way on the bed, laptop on lap.

I hang up my bag and things. "Hey."

"Long night?"

"Yeah, but also a good night."

"What'd you do?"

Why does she care all of a sudden? "Just homework and accompanying stuff."

"I think it's cool you're an accompanist."

I am so confused and, honestly, too tired to really process Ruby's sudden attempt to Be a Good Roommate. "Thanks." Now in my pajamas, I grab my caddy of nighttime routine stuff and head off to the bathroom.

When I return a half hour later, Ruby's got her earbuds in. Thank goodness. One less weird interaction to have to muddle my way through. I slip into bed and put on my noise-canceling headphones—carefully, so as not to disturb the curls, of course. My phone reveals a missed text from Max.

> Freddie: FWIW, I love your idea for the musical and I already have a few ideas. Can't wait to work on this with you.

Which is such a Max thing to say, because Max *loves* working on anything nerdy. I send him a thumbs-up emoji.

Mozart piano concertos become the background for my thoughts, which are something between a daydream and a night dream, in which Duke and I finally kiss and in short order become a legendary musical couple, like Johnny Cash and June Carter or Sonny and Cher. Our children will have light brown skin and maybe also freckles, so many curly heads, and they'll basically be musical savants because duh.

I indulge myself and switch the music to my Duke YouTube playlist, and his voice is the last thing I hear as I drift off to sleep.

THIRTEEN

IT'S SUNDAY NIGHT AT EIGHT and it's almost time for my weekly video chat session with my dads. Problem is, I can't find my laptop cord, which is asinine, because how many places can a person really put a laptop cord?

Desperate times call for desperate measures. "Ruby, have you by any chance seen my laptop cord?"

Ruby's avoidance of me has been at an all-time high, ever since the night she was weirdly nice. Her lunch group is gaining speed. Every day her table now includes a pimply blond viola player, a percussion guy, and an unidentified instrumentalist named Lily with long black braids who has been to our room a few times. They're all, apparently, in a suspended state of anger, and if they could get paid for dirty looks at me, they'd be rich by now.

"Nope." Doesn't even bother to look up from her copy of *Rolling Stone*.

Great.

I'm about to FaceTime the dads from my phone instead when Liza comes bounding in—or, since we're talking about Liza, walking slightly faster than slow, but for her that's an enthusiastic bound. Lo and behold, she's carrying my laptop cord. "You left this in my room," she says, tossing it onto my bed.

"Thank God! This is just like when the three kings brought gold, frankincense, and myrrh."

"You do realize you just compared yourself to Jesus Christ, messiah to Christians everywhere."

"If the shoe fits."

Liza laughs, and as I bend to plug in the cord, I catch Ruby rolling her eyes. I'm *this* close to having a verbal throwdown with that girl.

As soon as I'm plugged in and booted up, my dads are ringing us. "Hi, guys!" I say as their heads pop onto the screen.

"Hi there, rising stars," says Dad.

Liza waves at them. "Hi, dads. You look good. Dodge, is that a new cap?"

Dodge tugs at the bill and grins. "Good eye. Chad ordered it for me last week."

"Online shopping is a blessing and a curse, I tell you," says Dad, shaking his head.

"Anyway, what've you girls been up to?"

I give them the basic update on academics and music stuff, and Liza talks mostly about her upcoming solo performance test, which she is the opposite of enthused about. "I picked a bad song."

Liza's gotten into the habit of joining in on Sunday video chat night, which is why we use the laptop instead of my phone. She thinks my dads are hilarious, and when we talk with them, she shares personal details that she only rarely shares with anyone else. Even *feelings*.

I jump in. "No, you didn't. Your song is great! And you've got the best accompanist around."

"That much is true," she says, punching me lightly on the arm.

"Awww. You two are the cutest friends," croons Dad as he and Dodge beam at us through the screen.

Ruby's *Rolling Stone* hits the floor as she gets up, slides her moccasins on, and leaves the room. The door slams behind her, jarring my mirrors.

"What was that?" Dad's words, but he and Dodge wear the same startled expression.

"Just my roommate. Who knows what's up with her," I say, ready to move on.

Dad's brow lowers with worry. "Are we being too loud, I wonder?"

"Nah, she's gotta be used to this by now. We do this every Sunday."

"Why don't we ever talk to Ruby?" asks Dodge.

"Eh. We're not exactly close, remember?" I've mentioned my Ruby woes to the dads a couple of times, but either they keep forgetting or they keep thinking I will at some point befriend her. They just don't understand how impossible that is.

A few pleasantries later, we're wrapping up the chat. Liza sighs as we say goodnight to the dads and close the laptop. "It's been years since I wished for a dad, but yours make me want one again. Actually, they make me want two."

"Don't worry, I'll share mine as long as you keep helping me with stupid theory." I've enlisted her help occasionally because I'm afraid of wearing poor Max out with my many, many distress texts every time I do homework.

We work through some problems involving diatonics and harmonics and probably some other -ics until my brain melts. "We need to stop," I say, rubbing my eyes.

"Gladly." She puts the notebook away.

"I still can't believe I made friends with the one person in Theory for Dummies who doesn't actually suck at theory."

"Lucky you."

"Isn't there some irony in you, the daughter of the woman who kept me from getting into the MFP, now helping me get into the MFP?"

Liza scoffs. "You're right. I've accidentally managed to find a tame but still subversive form of Mom-rebellion. Anyway, I think you're getting a little better at theory. How's the tutoring going?"

"Eh. Fine."

"Max seems like a good guy." She side-eyes me.

"He's okay."

"He's way cooler than Duke."

"Wait, what? Why would you say that?"

Liza shrugs. "Max seems real. Duke's all right, he's just kind of . . . smarmy? Glib? I'm kind of over the whole hanging out with stars thing, if you know what I mean."

"But you hang out with me all the time, and I'm *going* to be a star. I'm just . . . a late bloomer," I say, batting my eyelashes.

She shoves my shoulder. "For now I like hanging with Bridget, just Bridget, before she was a star."

And that's a statement that I let settle into the heart of me.

FOURTEEN

THE FOLLOWING WEDNESDAY, I START my day with two text exchanges, the first from Max:

> Freddie: Good morning, Red. How's everything? Did you get through your theory homework?

> > Me: Red? That's like . . . the most unoriginal nickname ever for a redhead. Try harder.

> Freddie: What's your middle name? Also, you dodged the homework question.

> > Me: LOL, it's Venus. Yes, like the flytrap, but I focus more on the love goddess aspect. As for theory: yes, teacher, I'm all prepped for class AND will see you later.

> Freddie: Venus it is! Bring your homework

and your creative cap—we're going to be

branching out during theory tonight.

The groan bursts out of me automatically. Branching out during *theory* sounds about as fun as spending a day with Ruby.

The second text:

Duke: Can you fit me in for a last-minute

practice? Sorry, I forgot to sign up!

Me: Sure! Come at 5:40.

Which was *not* an open time. In fact, it's my only free moment between classes and theory tutoring tonight, and after that I'll go straight from dinner to a required floor activity, but who needs rest when there's a chance to hang out with Duke?

He waltzes through the door of Triton 212 about seven minutes late. "Hey, you." I've learned over weeks of observation that he has a stage smile and a real one, and only the real one moves his ears. Today his ears bounce ever so slightly, and any annoyance I had about his tardiness flies out the door.

"Hey, Duke."

"Ready to work?"

"Born ready."

As we launch back into his song, I again wonder what we're doing here. He's got this. He *owns* this. There's only one reason he'd be doing all this extra practice: an excuse for alone time with me. I smile up at him as I play the ending. "That was *fantastic*."

"You think so? I thought I sounded pretty blown out by the end. Maybe I need to hold back more in the middle."

"I personally think that bit of rasp you've got going on at the end adds authenticity. You're singing your guts out to someone in this one, you know? Sounding tired at the end of an intense emotional disclosure works."

A look of surprise and dare I say *wonder* has crept onto Duke's face. "You sure know a lot about performing for a nonsinger."

My cheeks flame with Jekyll and Hyde emotions—flattery, fear. "You learn a lot about singing when you accompany."

"Uh-huh." Now he's brought just one eyebrow down comically low and he looks . . . curious.

Diversion tactic, *stat*! Duke's the *last* person I need finding out I'm not really in the MFP.

I put my fingers back on the keys and start to play a tune I know by heart, one I've been working on over the last year.

"Hey, you're playing my song!"

I grin up at him and start back at the beginning, nodding for him to join. And he does. "You finished all my sandwiches / As if they were yours / All you left of me was crumbs / You swept me away."

Verse two, then he hits the haunting chorus. "And now you're long gone / Were you ever there / The frames are empty; the pictures are torn / I'll finish my sandwich now."

Soon we're in the homestretch of the song and it takes everything I have to not chime in on some harmony. "I'll finish my sandwich now / I'll finish my sandwich now." He holds the last, amber note for the perfect amount of time before letting it die out.

Because Duke is perfect.

"How'd you learn that? I haven't released any sheet music to the public," says Duke, coming around the piano to sit by me on the bench.

"I can play just about anything by ear. I'm sure it's the same for you."

He looks at me like I'm a precious jewel. "Well, no, I've had to work a bit at what I know, and I use a lot of chord markings when I play. But you . . . wow, B. That's incredible."

I'm a puddle. I'm going to have to be sopped up with a rag after this meetup. "Thank you. It's a great song." I pick up one of my curls, twirling it around my index finger. "I've always been curious: Who'd you write it for?"

Duke's face changes, going from tuned in to blank in a hot second. "Um, just someone I used to know."

Shit, I said the wrong thing. He must not be ready to talk about this lover who left him behind as summer ended. This one who used to finish his sandwiches.

I lay a hand on his arm. He's warm. I'm warm. I'd say our bodies are exactly the same overheated temperature, and I wonder if it's the room or the music making or the *us* that's making us this way. "It's okay. You don't have to talk about it."

He claps his hand over mine. "I appreciate that." God, he's so *real*. I'm tempted to pinch myself to make sure.

We sit for an indeterminate amount of time with my hand under his. Then he starts to lean toward me. This is the moment I've been waiting for, dreamed of, prayed for, hoped for, yearned for. This is *my* moment. Our moment. The first day of the rest of my life.

I part my lips slightly and let myself lean right, melting into him. There's a tiny scar on his left cheek, invisible at arm's length, obvious at this distance. And maybe there's even more he's got hiding under his pop star persona, because he says the next words like they cost him something. "There's something I need to tell you. Something I've never told anyone."

Ohhhh man, we're going to start right off with the L word? I'm surprised but not surprised, and I brace myself for the amazingness of *Duke Ericson's voice* delivering me words of affection.

I'll be able to say it back, no questions asked. I've loved Duke since the first time I saw him on YouTube, singing the song he just sang in this room.

The door to the practice room swings open, with enough force that it smacks the doorstop and bounces. Duke and I jolt away from each other like lovers caught in the act. Which we *were about to be.*

Max meanders into the room, headphones on. He sees us and jumps—literally jumps. "Jesus! I didn't know there was anyone in here!"

Obviously.

Max yanks his headphones off and levels a wary gaze at us. "What're you two doing?"

Duke's up, taking his sizzle—and whatever he was about to say to me—with him. The disappointment is smothering. I feel like I can't even get a full breath, it's that crushing. "B and I were preparing for my graded solo." He looks down at me and grins. "She's whipping me into shape."

I get my full breath as I absorb his smile. Maybe all hope isn't lost. Maybe . . . maybe it's just on hold.

Not that I'll ever forgive Max for interrupting what was sure to be the most beautiful, meaningful moment of my life.

"Oh. Cool," says Max, whose eyes slip away from mine every time I look at his face. Just like the lover does to Duke in "Sandwiches."

"Wait. What're *you* doing here?" says Duke. "You don't even have your guitar."

"I uhhh . . ." Max puts his hand on the back of his neck, rubbing it, and his head points to the floor. "Sometimes I hang out in this room when I write. Quiet. The piano. Inspiration. You know?"

Bless him for keeping my theory tutoring secret, but still, his timing sucks.

"Makes sense, dude." Duke grabs his backpack from the table and heads to the door. "I'll see you both later. Thanks for another great practice, B."

"Sure thing," I say, desperate for just five more minutes alone with him. Five more minutes could have changed the course of my whole life.

But Duke's gone, and instead now I get to do a theory lesson with Max. One that starts ten minutes early, apparently.

"I'm, um . . . sorry?" Max addresses me, sounding confused.

"For what?" I ask, but it comes out monotone, more of a statement than a question.

"I'm not sure, but judging by the look on your face, I've done something very wrong."

I roll my eyes. "Chill, Max. Let's do theory."

"Well, I'm a few minutes early."

"You don't say. I didn't even have time to grab our ice cream."

"I was going to play for a bit, but we can just get started now." The tips of his ears are red as he pulls papers and his trusty composition book out of his bag. Are his hands shaking?

My stony insides soften. "Hey. I'm sorry if I looked pissed off or whatever. You know how I feel about theory."

"Yeah. I always know how you feel about everything. One of your charms." A half smile on an otherwise droopy face, no eye contact.

I sit across from him and hand over my homework, as he's gotten in the habit of looking it over for me. "What's on the agenda today?"

He pushes another of his gross homemade packets across the table. "Here."

"What, no lesson? I thought you said to bring my creative juices or whatever."

He shrugs. "Later. First, you need to review." He grabs his composition book and opens it to a page with scribbles and crossed-out words and a few unmarked lines of writing. I'm not gonna lie, it looks like the workings of a madman.

"What's that?" I say, pointing my pencil tip at his page.

He yanks the notebook away. "It's nothing. Just some writing."

"What, are you an aspiring novelist, too?"

Return of the vague half smile. "No, silly. Songwriting."

"You write songs? Like Duke?"

"Yeah. Like Duke." I see his teeth flaring out through his cheeks and realize he must be clenching his jaw.

"Can I see?"

He slams the notebook shut. "I'd rather you didn't."

"Oh, c'mon. It's just little ole me."

"No." His face is stony.

"Jeez, okay." What's his deal today? He's acting as if Freddie Mercury died all over again.

"Just focus on the worksheets, all right?"

"Fine." These sessions are bad enough *with* the somewhat engaging lesson-plus-conversation Max and I usually have. Subtracting interaction from the equation equals absolute torture.

And why does he get to be all salty with me, whereas I swallowed my anger and disappointment to be decent toward him? Typical gender bullshit.

Righteousness swells within me as I barrel through the review packet, one stupid question after the next. It's all ridiculous, pointless, but somehow I'm flying through it. Before I know it, I'm done and shoving the completed stack of sheets to Max. "Happy?"

He wears a look of contempt. "Okay, you couldn't have actually *tried* and finished in"—he looks at his phone—"fifteen minutes."

"Guess again."

He hitches an eyebrow but picks up the packet. His second eyebrow slowly creeps up to join the first as he flips pages. By the time he reaches the end, he still hasn't made a single correction mark. He throws it down on the table. "How did you do that?"

"I don't know."

His face is all lit up, obviously excited, meaning his mood has gone from foul to fantastic in a matter of minutes. All because I did okay on some theory packet? I may never understand this kid. "I don't know either, but you did it! You are unbelievably quick, you know that?"

Despite my anger and confusion, I bloom with his compliment. "Thanks. Didn't know I had it in me."

"Which is a great segue to the *next* part of theory!"

"There's *more*?"

He shoves yet another packet of pages at me, but this one's a bunch of blank staffs, and that's it.

"What in the name of Lucifer is this?"

"That's a staff, Venus."

"I *know* that, but what am I supposed to do with it? Where's my worksheet on tonics and Dorian scales and diminished whatevers?"

"It's time to take theory into the practical realm."

"Which is?"

"Songwriting."

He looks at me like Phil looks at Judy during the first big dance sequence of *White Christmas*—a little punchy, a little lovestruck. His eyes turn down to the empty staff paper, and I swear he looks like he wants to marry it. Leave it to Max to project a massive crush onto *songwriting*. God bless his nerdy heart.

Entertaining as this whole scene is, I'm confused. "I don't get it."

"What's there to get? Songwriting is a natural extension of theory. It's what theory is for!"

"You are way, *way* too jazzed about this, sir."

"I am exactly the right amount of jazzed, and when you get into this, you will be too."

I roll my eyes. "So what do we do?"

He motions for me to follow him to the piano. "I think it's easiest to work on music writing from here."

I sit, and by necessity I'm closer to him than I've ever been. Whereas Duke smells like baby powder, Max's skin releases something cleaner, and something earthier. Laundry detergent and bar soap and . . .

"Sage?" I say, then snap my jaw tight like a bear trap. I hadn't meant to say it out loud.

Max's face, already reddish from blissing out over songwriting, blushes deeper, to approximately the color of pickled beets. "If you're talking about the way I smell, yeah. It's an essential oil."

"My grandma burned sage in her house every week after my grandpa died. Said as much as she wanted him around, she needed his spirit to not live in her house."

I expect him to make some kind of judgment face, but instead he just nods. "Sage is good for that. Clearing homes."

"Why do you wear it?"

"Helps me with nerves. I don't really know why, just does."

"What are you nervous about?"

He laughs, short. Kind of like a bark. "I'm *always* nervous. About everything."

I sort of want to touch his hand or something, a nonverbal "it'll be okay," but that would probably be weird. Instead, I shift us back to business. "So, about this songwriting . . ."

"Right. Okay. Close your eyes."

I squint one eye. "Do I have to?"

"No, but I think it helps."

"Fine." I press my eyes closed, knowing his are probably still open, looking at me. I feel oddly exposed.

"See if you can think of a tune in this key. Something original." He plays a chord.

"It's C major," I say without opening my eyes.

"Show-off."

My responding grin is wide and rogue. It's sad that *this* is my only means of showboating these days, but I'll take what I can get.

"Anyway, back to the task. Write me a melody, Ms. Perfect Pitch."

This is exceptionally difficult, starting from a blank slate like this. I open my eyes and shoot a couple of dull daggers at him. "Wouldn't it be easier to write words first?"

"Well, maybe. Do you have some words?"

"No."

"Well, then. Let's start like this. Just try. If it doesn't work, we'll switch gears."

I close my eyes and breathe deeply. Maybe if I just pour enough hope out into the open air, the Universe will gift me with a stunning original song.

And then, the Universe delivers. A tune worms its way in, something *like* songs I've heard before but not *exactly* like any song I know. Without hesitation I hum it, at the same time opening my eyes to find the notes on the keyboard.

Max's head is nodding so fast it's frightening. He looks like a bobblehead doll on speed. "Good. Great!" He shoves a pencil into my hand. "Write it down. Doesn't have to be pretty or follow rules of music, just get the notes of that melody on the staff."

We go on like this for an unidentified amount of time, Max throwing in suggestions, even quietly singing little bursts of ideas. I'm quickly realizing I sort of adore his singing voice—what I can hear of it, anyway.

"What about this?" I say as I play out an idea for a bridge.

"Yeah! Or what about . . ." He lays his hands on top of mine and plays his variation on my idea, pressing my fingers down, which pushes the keys in. This all sends a zing of raw *yes* through me, something warm and alive and magical.

. . . The melody, I mean. The melody is pure magic.

"So, I maybe do have some words. For the musical. Could this be a musical song?"

Just when I thought Max couldn't smile any bigger—voilà. "Of course it could! What are you thinking?"

"I've been playing with the imagery of an ocean, since there's obviously a big one between Nebraska and Vietnam."

"But not like 'across the ocean.' That's overdone."

Is he a mind reader? "*Exactly.* I've been messing more with the weight of an ocean, and how that might be kind of like the weight of keeping a relationship together long distance."

"Holy shit, that's money. Let's free-associate. Weight of the ocean, weight of the sea, waiting . . ."

"Heavy. Holding." When I say "holding," our heads snap up, like we somehow both know this is *it*. "'Holding Up the Ocean,'" I say, words tumbling out in an excited jumble.

"Bingo. This is gonna kill." Max bends over his notebook, ferociously scribbling every idea we come up with.

By the end we've got a bare-bones melody for verses, chorus, and bridge, with chords jotted above each section of notes. The page brims with beautiful, semi-structured chaos. My handwriting's in pencil, Max's in pen, and our gray and blue scribblings tango across the paper.

I snap up the finished product and hold it to my face, still stunned at what has just happened. I wrote a song. *We* wrote a song. I had no idea it would feel like this. I don't know that I've ever been prouder of anything I've done.

Which is saying something.

Over the page I grin at Max, unbridled, huge, probably toothy. "I can't believe we did this."

"I can. I knew from our first theory lesson that you were capable."

I scoff. "Right. Theory all-star, right here."

"Hey. I mean it. When I saw what you can do with music using only your gut and instinct, I *knew*. Don't cheapen this for yourself." His voice is sterner than any seventeen-year-old should ever sound, because he's a dork like that, but his eyes are soft. The middles are sunflowers at the peak of August bloom, the very outsides are the color of the best cup of coffee you've ever sipped. I drink it up for a few seconds before turning away.

Why is my chest so tight? I straighten myself up on the bench, roll my shoulders back. Then I start playing our song again, from the beginning, trying to guard myself against forgetting how it sounds. "So, what's next for us?"

"What do you mean?" The piece of skin that's visible in his V-necked T-shirt has gone patchy red.

"I mean . . . how do we tackle the rest of the musical?"

"Oh." His bright eyes dim for a wink, then flicker back to full power. "I say we share this one with the big group to see what they think. And then when we get together again, we can start working on another song."

"When we get together again?" I glance at my phone clock— we've already been at this for over an hour. "Wow. Time flies when you're writing songs."

"Welcome to my world."

I had a supper date with Liza that started ten minutes ago, and my growling stomach won't let me forget it. As I gather my things, I drop a weird truth bomb. "I can't believe I'm saying this . . . but tonight was pretty great. Thanks for this, Max."

But he's already opened his composition book. "Sorry, had an idea. Gotta practice what I preach, you know." He gnaws at his bottom lip as he scrawls across the page, quickly neck-deep into this new thought.

I take that as my cue and let myself out.

Liza's already eating when I plunk down across from her in the Rot. "How was tutoring?" she says.

"Great!" I take a massive bite of Caesar salad and chew heartily.

Liza's head snaps up. "Theory was great?"

I swallow. "Yeah."

"Are you being serious right now?"

"Yep."

She holds her hand to my forehead. "You're freaking me out, Bridge."

I maintain that theory is stupid. But maybe, just maybe, I'm not hopeless after all.

My growling stomach is almost appeased with the salad and nachos I'm slamming down (this is how I do balance), but there's another hunger still burning in me. Duke's face is the only thing that can take care of it.

As if summoned by my desire, he saunters through the doors of the Rot, Max at his side. After loading down their trays with burgers and tater tots and an array of fruits, they join us.

"Long time no see, B." Duke's smile is . . . knowing? Teasing? The smile of inside jokes that only lovers share? Ugh, I can't tell.

"You know I can't go much more than an hour between meet-ups with you," I say, my tone splitting the difference between sarcasm and flirtation.

"And I you," he says, matching me.

What. Is. Happening?

"Hey, Max," I offer, and he barely nods at me. Which is whiplash, as literally ten minutes ago we were on songwriting fire together.

Liza's watching all of this go down, head on swivel like we're engaged in a Ping-Pong match. "Um, yeah. Bridget, what're you doing tonight?"

"Floor activity. Mandatory fun. Which means a whole night of Ruby, ugh." I crane my neck around and spot her sitting with her morose peeps a few tables away. She sees me looking and glances away, now whispering something in Lily's ear.

Pu-lease. That is some weak-ass gossiping. I've survived worse.

"What activity are you doing?" asks Liza.

"Painting pottery at some indie craft place a few blocks off campus."

She drops the French bread she'd been picking at. "Really? Can I come?" Her voice pitches high with excitement. This is definitely the most excited I've seen her, ever.

"Please. I need all the help staying unmiserable I can get."

"Well, I've got one better." Liza leans closer and lowers her voice. "After pottery, we're sneaking out again."

"C'mon, Liza. We can't do that again. It's too risky."

"That's what makes it fun. Please, B. I need this."

Duke's head pokes between us. "What is it you need, Lawless?"

Liza rolls her eyes and shoves Duke's head away. "None of your beeswax."

I'm seized with the best idea since people have been having ideas. Why didn't I think of this before? I grab Duke's collar and pull him back toward us. "Liza and I are sneaking out tonight. Wanna come?"

"Bridget!" Liza looks horrified.

"What?"

I flash puppy-dog eyes at Liza, who heaves a sigh so huge, any martyr would be proud. "Fine. Duke, you want to hang out with us tonight? Off campus?"

Duke's grin is totally decipherable: devilish. My knees go watery. "You bet I do," he says.

"Max, you too," Liza throws in.

Wait, what? Max, too? The ultimate rule follower? He wouldn't possibly.

But Max salutes her with two fingers and smiles a tiny smile. He's in. I can't help but be the tiniest bit impressed, though I'm also disappointed—the plan I'd been hatching was much easier with three people than with four. But, you know me: I'm unstoppable. Nothing and no one's gonna get in the way of my kissing Duke, tonight.

Not nerves.

Not circumstance.

Nothing.

FIFTEEN

AT EIGHT ON THE BUTTON, Piper's overly enthusiastic voice comes ripping down the hall: "Social time, girls! This is a required activity!" Even from behind our closed door I hear her knocking, tracking down the other residents of our floor.

I glance at Ruby, who is, as always, sitting on her bed with a magazine propped up against her knees.

"So, you ready for this social thing?" I ask innocently enough.

"I'm not going."

"What?"

She slams the magazine onto the bed. "Did I stutter?"

I rear my head back. She might as well have slapped me. "Jeez, sorry. But seriously, you have to go. It's mandatory." And I leave the room posthaste. Whatever Ruby's got going on, I do *not* want any part of it.

About twenty other girls mill around in the hallway. I approach Emma, who I've met in passing but don't have any classes with. She's short with a head of raucous brown curls—tighter and frizzier than mine. "Hey, Emma."

She'd been looking cagey and now she smiles at me with gratitude. "Hey, Bridget. How's it going?"

As we wait for the activity to start, I magpie information about Emma. She tells me she's a French horn player, with aspirations to play for one of the major symphony orchestras someday. This is her first year at the academy. She's from St. Louis and she has a brother and a dog. Her parents are divorced.

See, I'm getting good at this whole "asking questions" thing.

I've just finished telling Emma about Nebraska and my dads when my room door flies open and Ruby comes stalking out, Piper's arm slung around her shoulders. Ruby's cheeks are blotchy and her eyes are red rimmed. Has she been . . . crying?

I'm surprised. I didn't even know Ruby had a soul, let alone the capacity for tears.

Piper moves into the approximate center of the clump of girls, her lips mouthing numbers as she does a head count under her breath. "Gang's all here! Let's go!"

Emma drifts to the back of the group and I fall back with her. Yet when I realize Emma's objective, I balk. She goes right up to Ruby and squeezes her shoulders. "Hey. Whatever it is, it'll be okay."

"Thanks, lady."

I goggle at their apparent closeness. Ruby is *approachable*? Down is up and up is down. As we hit the streets of Chicago on our way to the art place, Panache Paint, Ruby and Emma talk shop: which cities have the best orchestras, which conductors are epic, etc. It's all Greek to me, and not only that—I hadn't expected to feel like the odd one out on this floor social. *I* belong at Richard James . . . don't I?

"What about you, Bridget? What do you want to do when you grow up?" Emma's move to include me feels good, but of course she hits me with a hard one.

"Oh. Um." The whole time I've been at the academy, I've only ever been asked this by Liza—and by the time she asked, I didn't have to lie to her, because she'd heard me sing. "I want to be a songwriter."

A songwriter? I pulled *that* one out of my ass, given that I've written one total song ever.

"Oh, like Duke Ericson?" Emma asks, her face brightening. "That boy is *goals*."

And I'm about to score. When I lay one on him tonight, he'll go up in flames. And I'll burn with him.

"I don't get what the big deal is about Duke Ericson, anyway. I bet he doesn't even write his own stuff," comments Ruby, rolling her eyes.

"What? Of course he does." Ruby's words have stoked the coals of my Duke-loving heart.

"How do you know?"

"Well, I don't know if you noticed, but Duke and I are friends."

"Oh, you think? Every other thing you say when you're hanging out with Liza is 'Duke this' or 'Duke that.'"

Heat rises to my face, and I have to work hard to tamp down the lethal combination of anger and embarrassment that's churning in my midsection. I take a solid five seconds before I respond. "Whatever, Ruby."

Out of my periphery I see Emma looking somewhat horrified. I change the subject, for her sake. "So, Emma, weigh in: favorite Razzle flavor."

We manage to make it the rest of the way to Panache Paint without incident. Liza's loitering around the entrance, trying to look nonchalant—and succeeding, because that's just how Liza looks.

"Well, what a *coincidence*," I say.

"Indeed, my dear," Liza replies.

Ruby shakes her head and *rolls her eyes again*. If she keeps this up, her eyes are gonna get stuck up there. Which may be for the best, for humankind.

Ruby, Liza, Emma, and I seat ourselves at a four-top. After a brief departure to choose a piece of pottery and our paint colors, we return to the table. I have chosen—wait for it—a mirror. It will be perfect for my collection, even if it's not an antique.

"Seriously? Another mirror?" Ruby speaks under her breath, but I know she meant for me to hear.

"Yep. Because some of us pay attention to our appearance," I say.

I can feel the weight of her glare but won't give her the pleasure of looking up.

Emma, who might be an emotional barometer of sorts, takes this as her cue to speak. "So, who's trying out for the musical?"

I swallow a sigh. Sure, I've enjoyed my little foray into the other side of musical theater, thinking up ideas and writing music. But I still can't try out; still can't perform. And it still effing sucks. Suddenly, my head feels like it weighs a hundred pounds.

Ruby speaks up. "I'll probably try out for the orchestra pit."

"Me too," says Emma.

"Bridget, you'd be a perfect pianist. You're the best accompanist I've ever worked with." Liza smiles at me as she hands me the paintbrush I've been waiting for.

Bless her. My head feels marginally less weighty. "Thanks. Maybe I'll try out." I have no idea if that's a sanctioned role for me, but it's worth looking into.

"This might be weird to say," Emma chimes in, "but Bridget, I would've mistaken you for the musical theater type. You're so animated. I could totally see you onstage."

Liza shoots me a coy glance and I kick her under the table. The last thing I need is Liza's cheeky attitude blowing my fake-MFP cover. "Yeah, I get that sometimes," I say, tethering all my attention to the mirror frame I'm painting. Much as I usually *love* talking about myself, this particular topic needs to drop.

And it does. Ninety glorious minutes fly by. As much as I'm looking forward to the next part of my night, it feels good to be with Liza, hanging out like besties in TV shows do. I haven't had a close friend since seventh grade, and I'm only starting to realize how sorely I've missed this.

Ruby and Emma take off with Piper, who gives me and Liza her blessing to wander back to campus when we finish, as long as we check in at her door later—which is fine, because we have to meet the boys back at the dorms before our Big Night Out. I've been framing it up for myself as a double date: me and Duke, Liza and Max—especially since Liza thinks Max is "pretty cool," which for her is an enthusiastic endorsement.

I finished my work of art ages ago, but Liza's still at hers, carefully adding an art deco–like design to her already flawlessly painted vase.

"Are you about done, Picasso?"

"Just five more minutes," Liza says, tongue against her upper lip as she completes another tiny detail. "Are you sure you still want to go out? I could honestly go for staying here and doing another piece."

"Are you serious right now? You're the one who *insisted* we go out again. 'I need this,' remember?"

"Well, yeah, but that was before I discovered Panache Paint," she says, wiggling her eyebrows at me.

I pout my lip. "Come on, the boys are counting on us."

"It's just Duke and Max. They'll get over it."

"They'll get over it?" I am one pushback away from a temper tantrum.

"Ugh, fine. Let's go," she says, putting one final touch on her vase, then taking it to the counter to pay.

We schlep back to campus, our matching tan suede boots perfect for this damp October night. Thank God all the precipitation finished up while we were painting, because curly hair hates the rain. Its smell lingers, though. Rain on pavement, just like every

154

antiquing afternoon with Dad and Dodge. A quick but very real flare of homesickness zings through me, but I dismiss it. Tonight is for joy, not sadness.

Liza nudges me. "You've done a full one-eighty over the past couple of hours. Remember when going out tonight was 'too risky'?"

"Yeah, well, I'm mercurial."

"Truth."

"Why'd you invite Max, anyway?" I try to keep the irritation out of my voice, but I'm pretty sure I fail.

"Why not invite Max? He's nice, he's funny, he's our friend. He was sitting right there, so it would've been sort of shitty *not* to invite him. Plus, he's clearly into you."

I stop short, my heel sliding a tad on the slick pavement. "Um, no. He's my *theory tutor.*"

"C'mon, friend, I wasn't born yesterday. I know what attraction looks like when I see it, and I see it when he looks at you."

For the love of Rihanna.

Max and I have all vanilla interactions, right down to his Razzle eating—*nothing* like the chemistry between me and Duke. Liza's delusional. I shrug it off. She can think whatever she wants, but this changes nothing about tonight's objective. Operation Sitting in a Tree with Duke is a go. Liza will make a killer wingwoman.

We check in with Piper, then go to my room to change. Ruby ignores us, like we hadn't just spent two hours together. Whatever. A half hour later Liza and I are out the door again and headed to our meeting point, the dorm's back exit.

They're waiting for us when we walk up, Max with a cool leather jacket on over his usual T-shirt and jeans, Duke looking like . . . well, like a pop star. The most delicious variety of pop star.

"You good, B?" Duke's eyebrows come together in concern.

I blink heavily, twice, realizing I'd been staring at his mouth with a ferocious intensity.

Cool your jets, Bloom.

Wait for it.

SIXTEEN

HELTER SKELTER IS A LITTLE less busy tonight. Still, most tables are full and there's a line at the bar.

Not that Liza has any difficulties getting served. She's well aware that one flip of her long sheet of hair and one coy, closed-mouth simper has the power to summon any bartender of any age or gender.

She's on her way back to our table after a successful refill trip to the bar, somehow balancing four glasses of Sprite. We're on our second round, the boys agreeing that Sprite and smuggled vodka is *the* drink of the night.

Duke clinks his glass against Max's. "Remember the last time we tried to hit up a bar?"

Max flinches. "Do we have to talk about that now?"

"We totally do. It's a funny story, man—even you gotta admit."

Max keeps his head turned down as Duke launches into the tale of their last bar visit. It was the night before they left for school this year, their last hurrah of the summer. They'd taken an Uber to Kansas City's Power & Light District, which Duke explains "is like an outdoor mall but instead of peddling clothes, it's all liquor." He says it's where the college crowd tends to flock. They had fake IDs, so they thought they'd be in, no problem.

"And then the bouncer guy at the entrance—who was as big as the two of us combined, by the way—crosses his arms over his barrel chest and says, 'Yeah, I don't think so, friend,' and turns Max away. Literally, grabs him by both shoulders, turns him back toward the street."

"Oh my gosh. How mortifying," I say, slurping my drink.

"Yeah," says Max, neck red as ever.

"So we walked down the street and grabbed a pizza and went home," finishes Duke.

I laugh along with Duke but quickly shut it down when my eyes fall on Max, whose clear discomfort makes me squirmy.

"Here's to being older and wiser!" Liza holds her glass in the air, and we all clink with her.

Karaoke has just begun, at least according to George, our overly enthusiastic host: "Weellllcome to Helter Skelter, where *evvvery* night is another opportunity to *slayyyyy*." I get the distinct feeling that George didn't have many friends in high school.

The first song starts and our table is a hotbed of harsh criticism.

"Ugh, pitchy," says Liza as a Madonna imitator launches into the second verse of "Like a Prayer."

"Not as bad as that 'Unchained Melody' guy, though, am I

right?" We all nod in unison, Max actually cringing at the memory of the middle-aged man who completely butchered the most love ballady ballad of all time, just minutes ago.

I'm dying to sing. Literally dying—I feel my life force oozing out of me and mingling with the rest of the fluids that stain the carpet of this bar. I sometimes wonder if it'll ever get better, this urge, this craving. Once in a while, when I'm steeped in some challenging English paper or engrossed in a dissection in biology, I think maybe it will. Maybe.

And then I get around other singers and all hope is smashed.

Tonight it's taking every bit of self-restraint to not march on over to the karaoke table and put my name in for a song. Any song. It could be "The Hokey Pokey" for all I care. I need that rush, that inimitable thrill of being in front of a crowd, all eyes on me. I need to be reminded that I'm special, worth seeing. Worth knowing.

I'm gonna have to have a talk with Liza about why we even came to Helter Skelter tonight. The girl had to realize this was going to be agonizing for me. Couldn't she have picked a different place? I give some consideration to saying to hell with caution and singing, blowing my cover with Max and Duke and letting the chips fall where they may.

And then I imagine the feeling of having to admit my conditional acceptance to Duke. He'd never look at me the same, and he'd never want to be with someone less than him.

No, singing tonight is not a chance I'm willing to take. Much as it hurts my heart to not share the thing I love the most with the man I love the most.

"Duke Ericson, we need you at the front!"

"That's my cue," Duke says, hustling up to the stage. He does a hilarious yet somehow sexy version of Miley Cyrus's "Party in the U.S.A.," complete with sweet dance moves, which I *so* did not expect but which makes me love him more. Apparently, his performance has the same effect on the crowd, as the whistles and catcalls are earsplittingly loud.

As the cheesy synth ending fades out, Duke leans over and whispers in the karaoke guy's ear. The karaoke guy gestures him back, and together they lean over a computer, typing something and watching the screen change. Whatever they're doing, they must succeed, because soon they're fist-bumping. The karaoke guy picks his mic back up. "Liza Lawless, please come up," he booms.

Liza's mouth drops open, and she shakes her head.

"C'mon, Liza. I need a partner for this," says Duke, speaking into the microphone in a TV announcer–deep voice.

She throws a helpless glance at me, then shrugs and gets up. Duke whispers something into her ear and she nods back at him. To anyone else in the crowd, I'm sure she looks like her usual too-cool-for-school self, but I know her well enough to know she's ruffled. She's blinking too fast. Her color's off, too pink, and she's fidgeting with the hem of her shirt.

The piano opener starts, and my feet hit the floor, jarring. *No. No. No.*

This can't be happening.

I love Liza, I really do, but in this moment I *hate* her. She's getting exactly the moment I've always dreamed of—and worse yet, I have to sit and *watch* it.

How many times have I watched Duke do this duet with Blythe Rosen, pop sensation, on YouTube? It was *the* quintessential Duke Ericson video, the one that put him on the map. How many times have I imagined myself as Blythe, standing at Duke's shoulder, his delicious music pouring out of my mouth and my eyes locked on to his?

"You finished all my sandwiches / As if they were yours," sings Duke. He sings, as always, like the words are his truth. I guess that's what it's like to sing stuff you've written yourself.

Liza's playing it cool, eyes on the floor. But when her cue to sing comes, she picks up her head and stares straight to the front, singing the words by heart. "You took away my loneliness / You said I was home." Her face doesn't own the music the way Duke's does, but something in her simplicity makes her believable, too. She has no pretense. She sings like a girl with nothing to hide and nothing to lose.

Unlike me, who has everything to hide, and I've just lost what I wanted.

I gulp my drink and burn with envy as Duke and Liza hit the chorus, and of course their harmonies are spot-on. It's sickening.

"Their voices work together. Similar in timbre, you know?" Max moves to sit in Liza's vacated chair, closer to me.

He's right, but I'm not going to say it.

"I sort of hate this song, though."

Now *this* gets my attention. It's the first time I've ever heard Max say anything even remotely negative about Duke. "Really? Why?"

Max downs the rest of his drink, his lean throat bobbing. As usual, I can't peel my eyes away. My fascination with Max's throat is a weird quirk. "It's kind of a long story. But yeah. This song is dead to me."

I snort. "Dead to you. That's funny."

"You're not laughing, though." His eyes are a little glassy, face a little sad. "What's going on, B?"

How does he see right through me, every time? What I want to say is that *my insides are shriveling*, and I very nearly do, because Duke and Liza are still killing it onstage and I'm not.

What I say instead, because God knows I need the distraction, is, "Tell me a secret."

"A secret?"

"Something no one knows about you."

"You already know the sage thing. And now the Power & Light bar humiliation! What more do you want from me, Venus?"

"I always shoot for the moon," I say, tossing my curls over my shoulder.

"Noted. Now, a secret . . ." He tips his chin into his hand and stares into space. "Okay. When I was little, I was painfully shy."

"You don't say."

"Okay, I know I'm not exactly chatty, but I'm *miles* better than I was."

"You being a shy kid isn't the most embarrassing thing I've ever heard."

He smirks. "I'm building up to it. So, it was a lot of just me and Mom, growing up. My dad was gone a lot—he's a lawyer, and some of his clients are international."

"No siblings?"

"Eventually my little sister came along, but I was already nine by the time that happened. Mom stayed at home with me when I was little. I *adored* her. I still do. When she would drop me off for kindergarten, I was the kid crying and clinging to his mom's leg."

There's something sweet sliding around in my chest, like maple syrup coating my ribs. "Max, that's adorable. Not embarrassing, but adorable."

"Wait for it—here's the big reveal. Promise not to tell anyone."

"I swear on Freddie Mercury's grave."

"That's serious shit."

"I know."

We're quiet for a second, mutually taking a moment to absorb the spectacle of Liza and Duke. They're now well into the homestretch of "Sandwiches" and killing it, like pros would. I suppose that's because they basically *are* pros, though a part of me wonders if the perfection of this performance has more to do with a compatibility that was there all along but that I didn't let myself see. So many tank-topped bodies sway with the song's andante beat, evidence that the audience is loving this duet way more than Max and I are.

Max taps my hand, bringing me back to him. "Okay. So. I need you to know, I am *not* inviting you to call me this. You can't say it at school. Ever."

I lean in, happy for this distraction and also thoroughly intrigued. "Oh, do go on."

"When I was little, my mom called me . . ." I marvel as two red dots appear in the apples of his cheeks and his usual neck flush goes from red to redder. "Cuddlepuppy," he mutters.

I choke on a sip of vodka Sprite. "I'm sorry, *what?*"

"Cuddlepuppy," he repeats, marginally louder. "Because I always, always wanted to be cuddling with her."

My cuteness capacity has blasted into the danger level, and I feel like my chest might explode, thinking of little Max and his big brown eyes and his mom, snuggled up together on a couch watching cartoons. But he watches me tentatively, and I know he's serious about not leaking this info. I mime locking my lips and throwing away the key. "I won't say it out loud. I promise. But you can't stop me from this." I change his contact name to CPuppy in my phone and flip it around to show him. He's still red, but his smile looks a little pleased.

The bar goes up in loud applause and yelling, and I remember to be miserable. Duke and Liza are on their way back to the table, looking mutually shiny.

"Bravo, friends," I say, drawing deeply from my super-inner reserves of nice. Duke might be slipping away from me, but surely he's not all the way gone. Yet.

"Yeah, great song," says Max. Apparently his mood has also soured upon Duke and Liza's grand return. His voice is casual, but his eyes, which danced even through the blush of his Cuddlepuppy story, are full of venom. Duke yanks at his collar, as if it's suddenly too tight.

"Welp, it's been fun, but I'm gonna head back," says Max, already slinging his jacket over his shoulder.

"What? Why?" I say. I mean, I need him here. He's my best chance of distracting Liza so I can cozy up to Duke.

"Tired. It's been a day. You want to come with, Venus?"

Is he kidding? "Nah, I'm gonna stay."

He shrugs. "Suit yourself. See you tomorrow, folx." And he stalks off, never looking back.

"Hmph. That was weird," says Liza. She slurps at her mostly empty glass through a straw.

A round of drinks for Duke and Liza appears at the table, purchased by random bar patrons. And then another. And then somehow, Duke acquires a shot of tequila.

Thirty minutes later, Liza's three sheets to the Windy City, and Duke's about seven. As the sober-ish one of the group, I take it upon myself to get my pickled entourage out of the bar.

The three of us pile into the back of a cab, Duke sandwiched between me and Liza. Liza and Duke start singing again, giggling their way through it. Duke boops Liza on the nose with his index finger. "Can't believe you know all the words to my song." His words run together, like watercolor paints sliding across a wet canvas.

She swats at his hand. "Don't go getting a big head, now, Ericson. I only know that song because I like Blythe Rosen."

"Nah. You know it cuz you like *me*."

"I know all the words to all of your songs, Duke," I say, wanting to somehow remind them both I'm here.

"Do you?" Duke turns his head and considers me. I try to send him telepathic messages, using just the force of my eyes. *I love you, Duke. Just keep looking this way.*

He turns back to Liza. "You need to be more like Bloom."

Liza laughs. "That's impossible. B and I are like spinach and artichokes—we go together, but we do not come from the same plant."

Huh. I kind of like Liza's drunken wisdom.

The cabdriver drops us off near the back entrance of the dorm. I loop one arm through Liza's and the other through Duke's and pull them to the door. Liza pulls her magic key card out of her back pocket for me, and I use it to gain entry.

I whisper, "Okay, here's what we're going to do—" But I stop short, ducking all but one sliver of me back behind the door.

Because there's something in the stairwell.

Someone.

A scary, crimson-nails-clicking-the-stairs someone.

SEVENTEEN

AS OCTAVIA PUSHES UP FROM her seat on the stairs, her face comes out of the shadows, now fully visible. The scene strikes me as very film noir, and *this* strikes me as a highly inappropriate time to be having such a thought.

Liza's forearm catches me in the chest, hard. It hurts like hell, but I'm able to see the gesture for what it is—a message of "You stay, I go." I stand back as Liza takes a massive yet woozy step forward, shutting the door all but a crack behind her. While standing as still as possible, I grab the cold metal handle with my available hand. I need this door to stay open, but not open enough for Octavia to notice. Once Liza leaves her position, taking her key card with her, Duke and I have no other way in.

"You," Octavia spits, voice sharp as nails.

"Me." Liza says it deadpan. Fearless.

Duke's head lolls on my shoulder, like an out-of-commission marionette. I pray to whoever's listening that he stays quiet for just a few more minutes.

"I'm very disappointed in you."

To my absolute horror, Liza starts laughing, in big, slurred-drunk guffaws. "Oh, this is just too good. *Too good.* One to tell the grandkids one day, amiright, Mom?"

"Do you have any idea how much trouble you could be in for this, Liza Jean Lawless?"

I note the use of Octavia's word "could" and file it away.

Also filed away: Liza's middle name. Jean. Classic. Timeless.

Liza snorts, which is very un-Liza-like, but then again, drunk Liza is a beast of an unknowable color. "What're you gonna do? Kick me out?"

"No. I won't give you the pleasure of an early departure."

Liza snorts again. "Figures."

"We'll discuss consequences tomorrow. For now, let's get you to my apartment."

"Ugh, you're gonna make me walk all the way to faculty quarters? Come on, Mom."

"Yes. A night in with your mother is just what you need."

I feel Liza's foot, which she had been using to lodge the door open, pull away, then two sets of footsteps echoing up the stairwell, one at a dull thud, one at a sharp staccato. Liza's faint protests fade in time with the footfalls.

I nudge Duke. "Hey."

"Mmhmph?"

"Can you do a flight of stairs?"

His eyes come blearily open, squinting, though this stairwell is not brightly lit. "Yeah."

With my arm around his waist, we take the stairs one labored step at a time. Funny, when I'd pictured my arms around Duke's body, it didn't look at all like this. Still, being this close to him, this *responsible* for him, is exciting in its own way.

Thankfully, his room is just on the second floor, and we make it up the ten stairs without incident. I pull him down the hall toward the number he says is his—217. "Where's your key?"

He pushes his right hand into his pocket and fishes but quickly gives up. "I can't find it, but I know it's in there. Can you just get it?"

For the love. Of. Madonna.

I daintily put my hand into Duke's right pocket and feel around, careful not to inch too close to the center of his pants. I am unsuccessful in locating a key, and because I'm starting to feel inappropriate, I take my hand out. "Mmm. Don't stop," says Duke, actually giggling.

I slap his arm. "Don't be a perv."

I try the left pocket and come up empty. Finally, in the back left pocket, I strike gold and pull out a key attached to a small Kansas City key chain. "Got it." I twist the key in the lock. "Will we wake Max?"

"Nah. He'll be practicing now. Always is."

Sure enough, the room is pitch-black and silent upon our entry. Once my eyes adjust to the dark, I note the bunk beds.

"Please tell me you sleep on the bottom," I say, still having to haul him forward.

"You're in luck," he slurs. He collapses into his bed fully clothed. I take his shoes off and lay them on the tile floor, but that's about all the clothing I feel comfortable peeling off a person without consent. Softly, I sit at the foot of his bed, wondering if he's okay to be left alone like this. His eyes are closed and he's breathing heavily; he looks like he's already asleep. Or passed out. So much for Operation Sitting in a Tree. My chest aches with the loss of it, and I don't trust that tomorrow will feel the same as today did. Today was special. Magical. There was something there between us. I know it.

And now it's gone.

I turn away from Duke, prepared to return to my sad dorm room and think sad thoughts, but a hand catches my wrist. His eyes are closed, but a smile plays across his lips. "Stay," he says. "Stay, just a little while."

He pulls me closer and lays my hand on his chest, and I leave it there, watching it rise and fall with his steady breath. I can feel his heartbeat underneath my palm. I wonder what it would be like to lay my head there, my ear to his beautiful heart.

"You feeling okay, Duke?" I whisper.

"It's Delbert," he whispers back, his words sloshing together.

"Excuse me?"

"My real name is Delbert. Delbert Ericson the fourth."

I stifle a laugh. "Oh, my."

I have to hold my hand steady, to stop it from acting on the mind of its own. It wants to wander, up to his chin, up to his jaw. It wants to hold his face still while I whisper my truths and finally, finally kiss him.

But he's too drunk. I won't do it.

"Maybe you should lie on your side," I say, remembering something from health class about drunk people dying when they choke on their own vomit.

He obliges, turning onto his left side, curling toward me. My body now rests in the curve of his waist, hand on his shoulder.

"Better?"

"Yeah."

For a time we sit quietly. I admire his magnificent lashes, curving up against his cheekbones. Why do boys always get such long eyelashes? One of nature's mysteries, I suppose.

He mumbles something.

"What? I didn't hear you." My whisper is as quiet as I can get it to be, but still loud in the silence of this dorm room.

"Sing something."

Oh.

Well.

What could it hurt? If Duke has questions about me and singing after this, I'll fess up. I'll just have to deal with him knowing all the truths about me if he has questions later. It's only a matter of time, I suppose—when we get together, I'll have to come clean with him about not being a real MFP student. Relationships are built on honesty, right?

I choose the song my dads have sung me at bedtime for as long as I can remember, "I'll Stand by You," originally recorded by the Pretenders. The ultimate love song. You're telling someone you'll be there for them in their darkest times, when they're sad, mad, wrong, ashamed. It's the perfect thing to sing to Duke as he drifts away, breathing heavy and deep as I reach the final chorus.

I'd be there for him again, if he needed me. Like he's needing me, right now.

EIGHTEEN

THIS MORNING'S OUTFIT WAS SELECTED with precision. Plum-purple shirt, because this is the color that does the most for my eyes and complexion—my lucky color. The color of royalty. I tug on the jeans that hug my curves in all the right places. My hair cascades over my shoulders and down my back, each red-gold curl a work of art. My wine-colored lip stain is on point, my eye shadow is understated but flawless, and my fingernails are freshly polished.

I'm ready for my first day in the world as Duke Ericson's paramour. How could he not fall for the girl who took such tender care of him?

The only hiccup will be if, due to the vodka haze, he doesn't remember. And if that's the case, I'll just have to remind him.

I leave the room early, before Ruby's even dragged her ass out of bed. This is doubly gratifying, as every moment I don't have to talk to Ruby is a gift. Yet the real motive for today's hyper-punctuality is to give myself more time with Duke at breakfast, to figure out where he's at, emotionally—and possibly, if things go really, really well, we'll have time to sneak away into a practice room for a quick make-out sesh before first classes.

I keep my eyes peeled for my prince as I make my way to the Rot. But the boy I run into in the hallway isn't Duke.

"Hey, Venus," Max says, throwing me a half smile. "Perfect timing. I was just about to text you."

"Welp, here I am. Thanks a lot for leaving me alone with Drunk 1 and Drunk 2 last night."

"Yeah, about that . . ."

He trails off as I glance over my shoulder.

"Looking for someone?" says Max.

"Um, well . . . I'm hoping to have a chance to talk to Duke. I helped him get up to the room last night and I wanted to check up on him."

Max's stony face tells me nothing. We've gathered our respective breakfasts (oatmeal and fruit for him, dry toast for me, uncharacteristically black coffees for both of us) and sat down across from each other before he says anything.

"I doubt Duke makes it to breakfast. I saw him in the bathroom before I came down here, and he looked like shit."

I flinch. "Yeah, I thought he might have a rough morning."

Max gulps at his coffee, then wipes his upper lip on a napkin. "Listen, there's some stuff I need to tell you about—"

Liza plunks her tray down on the table beside me. On it: a glass of water, a slice of American cheese still in plastic wrap, and a bottle of ibuprofen.

"Yikes," I say out loud, without really meaning to. Liza's all in black, which is typical, and with a naked face, which I guess is normal for the mornings after she drinks. But the deep blue, puffy circles under her eyes are not normal, nor are her dark-rimmed glasses, which I've only ever seen her in when we've stayed the night in each other's rooms. I know damn well she didn't take a shower this morning, because I can still smell liquor on her (is it emanating from her skin?). Yet somehow her hair, pulled into a simple side ponytail, is still exceptionally gorgeous. There's no justice in the world.

"Shut up." She plops heavily onto the bench.

"Breakfast of champions you've got going on there," quips Max, who looks like he's trying not to laugh.

"Shut up," she repeats, putting two ibuprofen in her mouth and drowning them with water. She drinks the entire glass in one go.

I slide my half-full glass over to her. "Is that all you've got today? Words a little difficult?"

She closes her eyes for longer than a blink. "Zip it."

Max and I exchange an amused look as Liza fumbles with the wrapper of her cheese. Her hands are shaking.

"Here," I say, unwrapping it for her.

She shoves the rubbery slice unceremoniously into her mouth. "Thanks."

"How was your sleepover with Mommy?"

Liza levels an icy glare at me.

"I'll take that as a 'great.' I've heard faculty living quarters are posh. Anyway, Max was just about to tell me something, and it sounded important." I look up at him with raised eyebrows.

"Oh. Um, it can wait. It was just some tutoring stuff."

"Shh! Keep it down!" I duck my head like I'm trying to dodge shrapnel.

"What?" He lowers his voice to just above a whisper. "I thought you said Liza knew about the tutoring."

"She *does*, but no one else does. *No one*," I say pointedly, hoping he understands this includes the missing wheel of our usual foursome, Duke.

He has the grace to adopt a sheepish look. "Oh, yeah, sorry, okay." He grabs his tray and stands. "I gotta go anyway. See ya later."

"Later," I say as he leaves. Liza grunts her farewell. Her head's on the table, one arm serving as a pillow.

"Come on." I yank her arm. "It's time for class."

"Don't think I can do it, B," she says, looking up at me blearily.

"Wait here."

Two minutes later, I'm shoving a bottle of Mountain Dew, her favorite granola bar, and a stick of beef jerky into her bag. "Drink the pop during class, and eat when you're ready." I help her sling her bag over her shoulder and we walk to class.

"How do you know so much about hangovers? You said you didn't drink, back at your old school."

"Nah, but I watched what the other kids did. Lots of coffee, energy drinks, and greasy, salty food was what everyone always wanted. I figured this was the cure."

Liza's eyes widen. "And just when I was starting to think you were too self-absorbed to be observant of others."

Me, self-absorbed? Ha.

A couple of hours later and finally, it's time for the moment I've been waiting for: Advanced Solo, the only class I have with Duke. And he'd better show up, because it's graded solo day. I arrive a few minutes early, and much to my relief, he's already there, playing something from the Romantic period, Schumann or Chopin or something. Minor key, soulful, sad. Not very Duke-like.

I close in on his piano.

He smiles, a small one compared to the normal ear-to-ear. He looks tired and a little wan, but other than that, not too bad.

"Rough morning?"

His smile widens, but his ears stay put. "I've had better." He pauses his song long enough to pat the bench beside him, and I sit. Hopeful. Blood rushing out to my extremities, heartbeat pounding in my fingers and toes.

"Did you have a good time last night?"

"I did. You?"

"Yeah. I mean, any time spent with you is good." I turn my body on the bench to make it open to his. There's no way he could not see *love* written all over me.

He keeps playing, the song swelling into a melancholy bridge. "You're sweet, B."

Taste me, if you think that was sweet. "Just being honest." I close the already tiny amount of space between us. My jeans push up against his.

Finally, he looks down at me . . . and his eyes, which should be full of knowing, are full of something else. Surprise? Confusion?

"B, I—"

"Good morning, my pianoforte wonders!" Seabass, ebullient as ever, has chosen this day to be early. This. Day. For the love of Kelly Clarkson, this is frustrating.

"Morning, teach," says Duke, grabbing his music and vacating the bench. I'm left in his warm wake, alone. Again.

Students start trickling in. I resign myself to another lost opportunity. When, *when* will I get my happy ending? Or new beginning, depending on how you look at it.

Liza comes straggling in, still looking as wretched as someone like Liza can look, which isn't even in the vicinity of wretched. I watch Duke's body go stiff as she takes her usual seat, and he sits by her instead of where he typically sits. She shoots him a questioning look, and he stares back at her with . . . urgency?

Liza looks utterly confused, but also like she's too tired to really focus on whatever's going on with Duke. She chugs the last bit of her Mountain Dew and gets up to pitch the bottle.

"Musicians, I trust you are all ready for your graded solos today?"

Students clap and fist-pump and make verbal affirmations of confidence. Which I find to be hilarious, given most of them were total stress cases when they were meeting with me for practice.

"Would anyone like to volunteer to go first?"

Liza jets straight from the trash can to the stage. "I'd like to get this out of the way," she says with her patented lack of pretense.

"Ooookkay then, let's give a warm welcome to Ms. Liza Lawless." I wonder if Seabass maybe missed his calling as a game show host.

We cheer politely as Liza arranges her ponytail and finds her place onstage. She makes eye contact with me when she's ready and nods.

Despite her extreme hangover, Liza's solo is impeccable. She's one of the lucky few who are simply natural talents. I mean, did she do extra practice? Yes, but I'm pretty sure she only came because she likes hanging out with me. This girl could be a star today, on Broadway or in the pop world, if she wanted . . . but that's the thing. If she wanted.

"Excellent, Ms. Lawless, excellent!" Seabass is rosy and overflowing with approval.

Liza says, "I'm going to the bathroom now," and beelines from the stage to the door.

A few singers later, she returns, a shade paler than before.

With minutes winding down in the class period, Duke stands. "I'd like to go now." He wipes his hands on his pants. Surely he isn't nervous.

"Yes, Mr. Ericson, you're the natural choice, given you're the only one left."

The class titters as Duke takes his place at center stage. A bead of sweat makes its way down his forehead, something I've never witnessed during his practice sessions. *Jeez, Duke, simmer down*, I want to say. *You've done this a million times and in front of millions of viewers. You were a total ham just last night, for crying out loud.*

He nods at me and we start the song we've been through so many times. But instead of looking at me, he's looking out into the class. Which I initially chalk up to just advanced technique, because you're supposed to engage with your audience when you sing.

Then I realize he's not engaging with the audience. He's engaging with *one person* in the audience. His eyes are locked on to her with laser focus, never looking anywhere else.

Liza.

And it's noticeable. The class is looking back and forth from Duke to Liza. Liza's looking like she wants to sink into the floor.

Well, okay, so he settled for focusing on one thing, which is something you can do when you're too nervous to look at other people. You're really supposed to choose a wall or empty seat or something, but he chose Liza. Whatever. Friends are safe.

Duke finishes the song and the class claps their approval, myself included. But then he starts singing something else. The song *I* was singing last night, in his bed, when I tucked him in. My bedtime lullaby.

My chest constricts.

Oh, Duke. I'll stand by you.

He does the first verse a cappella with his eyes closed. When he opens them, he looks at me with such fire that my marrow turns to magma and melts all my bones. It's happening. It's finally happening. He remembers.

And then he says, "B, would you?"

Oh would I, would I, does he even have to ask? My legs are tensed to stand and go tackle him, when he turns his gaze back to Liza and continues to sing. Second verse.

Wait, what's happening?

He finishes the second verse and then says, "Okay, now," and waves his hands at me in a musician's gesture of "start the music."

Oh. He wants me to accompany. I join him at the chorus and at the same time try desperately to catch his eye. Now is really *not* a great time for him to use Liza as a comfort person in the audience. Why can't he look at me, if he's singing to me?

He steps off the stage, still singing. When he reaches the middle of the room, he turns a chair around and straddles it, right in front of Liza, who looks like she's about to die. During the third verse, he picks up her hand, which sends an instant flame across her formerly pale cheeks. She bites her lip and tucks her chin closer to her chest but doesn't look away from him, doesn't take her hand away.

My cheeks are also burning, but not just from the heat underneath. The tears dripping down my face are also pretty hot. So much for my perfect makeup. So much for my perfect moment.

My destiny is slipping away and, sickly, I'm a *part* of it. I'm aiding and abetting my own destruction with my hands on these ivory keys. And I'm background, just background for Duke and for Liza, the stars of the show.

NINETEEN

THE SMELL OF TARNISHED SILVER and yellowed pages has never been so welcome.

I collapse into a chair behind the counter, not even waiting for Hans to invite me back.

His head comes poking out of the back room door, white hair as floofy as ever. "Athena! You're early."

Which is a funny thing to say, because it's not like I have a set schedule here. Yet, I think I know what he means. Usually I roll in on weekend afternoons, after a nice sleep-in those mornings. It's nine a.m., currently.

I am early, indeed.

"Yeah," I say, and I want to say more, but I can't get any more words to come.

Hans furrows his brow at me. "I'll be out in one minute."

I stay put and stare off into space. I might not be quite awake. I couldn't sleep at all over the past two nights, thoughts racing, memories playing out over and over in front of my eyes, like movie shorts. Duke and Liza at the dinner table on Thursday night, making disgusting bashful faces at each other. Which escalated to Duke asking Liza if she wanted to "hang out" after dinner on Friday night. Max and I looked on as they left the Rot hand in hand, probably headed to a practice room, because many types of "practice" are known to happen in those rooms. My stomach turned as my mind played out the imagined scene of Liza and Duke, alone, his hands all tangled in her silky hair, their movie star faces all mashed together.

I tried everything to stop the repulsive, intrusive thoughts. On Thursday night I pumped too-loud music through headphones, an attempt to drown out the noise in my head. When that didn't work, I got up and paced the room. And when it *all* failed, I yanked out my journal and wrote shitty hate poems: one for Liza and Duke, one for Ruby (for good measure, and because I *know* she could hear me up and struggling but didn't even bother to check on me). But it's hard to write hate poetry for people you don't actually hate.

By last night my patience was worn even thinner. Four sweat-drenched, mostly sleepless hours in bed were all I could handle before I yanked myself up and out, exhausted but also wound tight with nervous energy. Autopilot dragged me to Triton 212. I needed that hum of my vocal cords, the pleasure of my voice's bend and pitch along the top of my comfort songs. I needed to *sing* my way out.

I sang for the loss of everything. Duke. My hopes and dreams that involved him. My missing, uncertain identity. Could I sustain a friendship with Liza, now that she had everything I always wanted? Without Duke and without performance, what was I even doing here? The notes, the words, poured forth from a trembling mouth and shaking shoulders.

I stopped singing and resorted to just plain piano by seven fifteen, as the overly ambitious weekend practice crowd started trickling into the other practice rooms.

By eight thirty I was tired of playing. My wrists hurt, my head hurt, my heart hurt. The thought of being back in the room with Ruby was deplorable, and the thought of seeking out Liza was almost as bad. I walked, almost without conscious thought, to a place that now represents comfort and safety: Hans's shop. It's away from school and all the pain, and maybe I'll get some good ideas for the musical while I'm here. If my brain can even generate creative thought in a state like this.

Hans walks carefully in from the back room with a tray that holds a teapot, two mugs, and a plate of croissants. "I assume you haven't had breakfast yet?"

I shake my head. I don't know how he would know that, but I stopped trying to figure Hans out long ago. He just knows stuff.

After pouring green liquid from the teapot into both of our mugs, he holds his cup up to his face, right under his nose. "Ah. Jasmine silver needle. Nothing better."

"I've never had it."

"You're in for a treat. These leaves are divine, special ordered from China." Only the very corners of his mouth are visible over his mug, but it's enough to see their upward curve. "I am somewhat of a tea snob."

My exposure to tea is plain iced with my dads and occasionally a cup of hot brewed from a Lipton tea bag with Grams. I sniff the mug cautiously. Flowers? Flowers go with tea? I blow into the mug to cool it, then take a tiny sip.

Florals and perfume and pungent tea, way different from Lipton's, wend their way into my nose as I swallow. "This is good," I say, going for another taste.

"It was my wife's favorite, and I'm afraid she got me rather hooked."

Was. Hans has never mentioned his wife before. "*Was* her favorite?"

Uncharacteristic sadness sets in behind his usual placid gaze. "She passed away last year, unfortunately."

I've never been very good at knowing what to say on the subject of dead people. It's so awkward. Even with Hans. "I'm sorry," I say weakly.

He offers me a croissant and takes one for himself. "So am I."

We sit and chew our respective pastries, taking sips of tea between bites.

"You don't seem yourself today, Athena."

"I'm not."

"Care to talk about it?"

I take my time in finishing my croissant before I answer. "I'm not sure."

Hans nods and swirls the tea in his mug. "I understand. Some things are hard to talk about."

The night's restlessness settles back upon me, like a pink cloud of rabid energy. I sweep buttery crumbs from my lap. "I'm going to do some dusting."

As usual, a few items of merchandise are gone, and many remain. The owl is still there, thankfully. Today I move a lace doily and place him on it, then flank him with two pink Depression glass plates. I know setting him up so lavishly makes him more likely to be noticed and bought, and this brings me a pang of sadness, yet I want the best for him. I want him to go somewhere he will be loved.

Two hours of dusting, arranging, sweeping, and polishing later, the past two sleepless nights are catching up with me. My shoulders ache, and my feet are weighted with anvils. I return to my usual seat behind the counter and drink cold tea out of my mug. Note to self: jasmine silver needle is also good chilled.

When Hans sees I've returned to the front of the store, he shuffles over. From under the counter, he pulls out the letter box. "Why don't you rest and do some reading. And research. Take more pictures, if you need." Hans is *all* on board with the musical and has been my biggest creative supporter.

"Yes, I'd love to. Thanks, Hans."

He bows his head and returns to the windows.

I read with a different kind of fervor than before. I've already read all the letters, so I know the outcome of Socks and June's love story. Today I don't need *whats*. I need *hows*. How did Socks get June to fall in love with him so quickly? And how did they *know* it was love? I'm hoping for backstory, clues to what happened in the short time they shared together before the letters. For the musical. But also . . . for me.

About thirty minutes in, I get a little something in one of the letters from June.

I have to confess to you that sometimes, my mother seems to doubt me and this commitment you and I made. How can I possibly explain to Ma the connection I felt with you, more immediate and more real than anything I'd ever felt with anyone? I suppose the simplest way of saying it is that as soon as I met you, I knew I wanted to be around you. I wanted you to be in my life in some way, always.

See, I swear this is how I felt about Duke. *Feel* around Duke. Being in his presence makes me happy.

I snap a picture of the letter, then sigh and push them all away.

"Not as satisfying today?" Hans asks, leaning up against the counter.

"Still some of the best things I've ever had the chance to read. I'm just reading them with a different lens today, is all."

"And how has your lens shifted?"

"From hopeful to confused."

"Ah."

Slowly, I begin the process of repacking the letters into their box. I spend extra time holding them, letting the delicate paper linger on my hungry skin, willing their knowledge and magic to somehow seep into me via osmosis. I must have missed something in them, some message, some meaning. Must have.

Because unlike every other time I've visited Hans's shop, today I'm going to leave with more questions than answers.

TWENTY

I'M STILL IN A CRAPTASTIC mood when I arrive back at my room, around noon. My whole weak 'n' shaky vibe has me fumbling with my keys—yes, that's right, I'm at the point in my academy existence where I can't even manage to unlock a door without failure. When I finally get it open, I slam it behind me. Mirrors rattle. Ruby rattles, too. She throws her notebook on her prissy white comforter and glares at me with the force of a thousand missiles. She might be scary if she weren't so pint-size—and if she weren't wearing a bright pink shirt with My Little Pony on it.

I'll admit that her black eyeliner, which grows thicker and sootier by the day, *is* a little scary. At this rate her entire eye area, from brow to cheekbone, will soon be nothing but two inky circles. I shall call her Ruby Raccoon, and life will be marvelous.

I grab a granola bar out from my stash under the bed and hastily tear the wrapper off. When the wrapper misses the trash can, I don't bother to pick it up. I'll get it later. Instead I palm a bottle of water from the mini-fridge and flop on my bed, for once not caring that I'm totally crushing my hair.

In a flash, Ruby is up. She snatches the wrapper off the floor and hurtles it into the trash can. Every motion is big and exaggerated, like she's an actress playing a bit part, Girl Who Picks Up Waste. Wrapper safely where it belongs, she stands in front of me and glowers down, one hand on a jutting hip.

"What?" I say, mouth full of honey oat mash (which currently tastes like sand, by the way).

She says nothing, just keeps trying to kill me with her admittedly frightening eyes.

I try again. "What?" I sit up in bed so I can wash down the last bite of bar with a swig of water.

"Don't you *ever* think about anyone but yourself?"

"Um, I've spent the entire day thinking about people other than myself, if you must know."

She scoffs. "Could've fooled me."

"Ruby, I *really* don't have the energy for this today. What the hell are you even talking about?"

"Could you have been *any* louder when you walked in the room?"

"Jeez, sorry. I didn't know you were in here."

"Like it matters. You *always* stomp around, throw your things everywhere, like you're the only one who lives here."

A flash of something red and dangerous slices through me.

189

"Maybe if you weren't such a terrible roommate, I'd make more of an effort to be courteous."

"Oh, *I'm* a terrible roommate? That's funny, Bridget. Really, really funny." She laughs in this way that raises goose bumps on my arms. A cackle, heavy with sarcasm. "Whose water you drinking there?"

I look at the sixteen-ounce store-brand bottle in my hand. "Ours."

"Hmm. I don't remember you ever pitching in to buy any water. Though I can think of many, many occasions in which you've helped yourself. Did you even notice that the one you're drinking is the last bottle?"

I rack my brain—surely I've picked up water for us on one of my and Liza's weekly CVS trips—but, sadly, Ruby's right. I can't remember ever buying water, because I'm sure I'd remember lugging that heft home on foot.

And no, I hadn't noticed the bottle I'd just grabbed was the last.

"I'll get the water next time," I say, picking at my fingernails.

"If only that would make us even."

I sigh—it's more like a huff, really. "You know, it's impossible to communicate with someone who's clearly hated me from the get-go."

"What're you talking about?"

I toy with a loose thread on my silky bedspread. "C'mon. You've been shitty to me from the very first day."

"Give me *one* example of how I've been shitty to you."

"The mirrors."

Return of the cackle laugh. "Oh, we're back to *that*? Seriously? Did you ever stop to think about that day from *my* perspective? I get to our room for the very first time, and there's this redheaded stranger flying around, talking a mile a minute, and the room's already all decorated with *her* stuff. I was overwhelmed. I hadn't even seen the place and already, I felt like there was no space for me."

"I put up the mirrors *to be nice*. To save you from having to decorate."

"You're missing the point. The mirrors are *your* thing! I have other things I like. Why would you assume I'd be into your style?"

I cock my head. "Because my style is awesome."

"Unbelievable." She throws her hands in the air and grasps, like she's trying to capture air in her fists.

Which is pretty much a metaphor for what this whole "discussion" feels like.

"Also, your parents were mean to me," I add.

"My parents are mean to everyone!"

I *knew* they were snobs.

Ruby presses on. "I *did* ask you to come to supper with us that first night."

"That would've been a thrilling time, I'm sure. Dinner with the two stuffiest people I'd ever met, and the roommate who thought I was obnoxious."

"But I *did* invite you."

"Fine. You did. Big deal."

"And you turned me down, and you've turned down *every* other attempt I've made at trying to engage you. I've asked you to go to the Rot. I've tried to have conversations with you, to get to know you. And at every turn, you blow me off."

No, no, no. This girl is deluded. *She's* the one who's blowing *me* off constantly. *She's* the one who thinks she's too good for me.

"You know, come to think of it, the best night we ever had together was that night you came home drunk. You were like a different person. I mean, you were still loud, but you asked me about my day, and about my friends, and how my classes were going. You were considerate. Nothing like your sober self, all self-centered and too busy to give me the time of day."

"Oh, *I'm* too busy, Miss Earbuds Always In?"

"I started doing that after it was clear you wanted nothing to do with me."

I snort.

But she's crying now, little rivers of black running down her mottled cheeks. "I've never even had a real conversation with your dads, and you talk to them every week. Only Liza is good enough for that."

This one sucker punches me. "I had no idea you'd want to be a part of that."

"Yes, because you never bother to ask me what I want, or how I feel."

I've run out of words to defend myself, the weight of her accusations caving in on me. This whole time, when she's thrown a rock, I've thrown it back. And then she threw a brick, and then a boulder, and those were too heavy to push away.

The longer I sit with Ruby's fury, the more I see truth reflected in her version of events. And the truth is heavy. The heaviest of heavies.

So instead of defending, instead of throwing another stone her way, I give up the fight and crumble under the avalanche. I lean back against the dorm room wall. The cold from the cinder blocks seeps through my shirt, chilling me from the outside in, just as a cold fear steals over me from the inside out. I'm stuck, and I'm frozen. I'm a block of ice trapped in a room with rock walls.

Ruby swipes at her nose and eyes with her hands. She speaks one last sentence before she leaves the room, in a voice that's no longer cold, but wobbly and miserable and sounds like it took her an awful lot of effort to squeeze out.

"Who do you think put the bottle of water by your bed the night you were drunk?"

I lie in my bed for a long, long time after Ruby leaves. My head's been spinning for so long, I think it plain runs out of juice, like what happened to Dad's car battery that time I left the dome light on all weekend. I sink into my bed, limbs so heavy I'm waiting for them to crash through the mattress and into the unyielding tile floor.

The whole time, my eyes are stuck to the one mirror I can see myself in from my bed. It's my favorite, the one with delicate seashells all along the borders.

That girl staring back at me, her hazel eyes so dull, hair a wreck: Is she an awful person?

Because probably only an awful person would lust after her best friend's boyfriend.

And probably only an awful person would blow off her roommate for months, while not even noticing that said roommate was trying. I'd let my first impression of Ruby become my *whole* impression, seeing only what I wanted to see after that, not what was actually there.

Yes, these are the habits of a not-so-good person.

I keep my eyes on the glass, trying to divine some goodness in the face of the wench in the mirror. Do I even know her?

My legs move of their own volition. Without a conscious thought as to what I'm doing, I'm up, now standing point-blank in the mirror, body almost pressed against it. I get close enough to it to kiss my own reflection, as if by getting closer physically, I'm also closer to the truth about myself.

But the mirror fails. I look and I look and I *look* and no knowledge comes. So I grasp it by its frame, one hand on each side. Gently, tenderly, I carry it to my closet. Next, the one above my dresser, the one Dad got me in Omaha for my thirteenth birthday. It comes down, and I lean it against the shell mirror. Slowly, but steadily, they all come down, all go into the dark safety of my closet.

When I'm done, I have no way of looking at myself.

Which I'm learning might have been the case all along.

TWENTY-ONE

I SPEND BASICALLY THE WHOLE rest of the weekend locked in Triton 212, "practicing." Yeah, that's what we'll call it. Avoiding, pouting, hurting, crying, obsessing . . . those are other names for what I do in that room. Just me, the piano, and a bottle of water I continuously fill in a nearby drinking fountain. A jar of peanut butter and the trusty box of granola bars are the weekend's sustenance. I'm not ready to go back to the Rot.

Liza texts a million times, and a million times I make excuses to not see her. Not feeling well. Tired. Homework. Gotta practice.

All this quality time with yours truly brings on an unexpected rush of homesickness. For stupid Lynch, of all places. On Sunday night I open my laptop right from Triton 212 and choke down a sob as my dads' heads pop up on-screen. I will *not* let them see me cry. Instead, I plaster a clowny smile on my face, which I know is fake but my screen tells me is passable. Acting skills: check. "Hi, Dads!"

They both look uncharacteristically tight. "Hey, lovey," says Dad, gnawing on his thumbnail. A dollop of foreboding hits my gut, because Dad only bites his nails when he's worried.

We make small talk, and I share lies about how great everything was this week. When they ask after Liza, I say, "Cramps," and there is no further probing.

After a weird silence, Dodge clears his throat. "There's something we need to talk to you about, and it's kind of a hard thing."

I mean, why not? I'm already devastated; what's one more blow? "Okay?"

"I know we don't generally talk to you about money matters, because it's not your job to worry about them. But now we have to explain a few things. Richard James tuition is a lot. As in . . . a *lot*, B."

"You get what you pay for, though, right?" Which is something Dodge has said literally a gagillion times.

He cringes a little as he continues. "You already know we had to sell some land to pay for your first semester."

My stomach churns as I await the next sentence, because whatever it is, it isn't good.

Dad takes over. "Sweetheart, Dodge and I have been crunching numbers to see what we can come up with . . . but as of now, unless we sell more land, we just don't think we can afford for you to go back to Richard James next semester."

"Unless you sell more land? Is it a possibility?"

Dodge looks like he's about to crumble. "B, we need the land. That's how I make money over time, with the crops I plant and harvest every year."

"But *I* need this school! Don't you see? This academy is my every-thing." My eyes leak rivers of tears and mascara, and my voice comes out so loud and pathetic that the *ing* of *my everything* echoes off the tile floor and reverberates. Lingers. In its aftermath an unfamiliar silence settles over me and my dads, and I'm sure even from miles away, they can sense its grossness.

"We are so, so sorry," says Dad.

And just when I thought things couldn't possibly get any worse, they absolutely do.

On Monday I skip classes. I know, I *know*—it's not good. But I *just can't do it*. I can't face Liza, can't inhale the musky apple scent of her burnished hair and take in the wonders that are her perfect voice and perfect skin and now perfect boyfriend. And honestly, what's the point? I'm not even going to be here next semester. More granola bars and peanut butter during the day, which I spend holed up in the practice room again, but Monday night finds me in my room with a growling stomach and fantasies of excommunicating anything in-volving nuts from my existence for the rest of time.

When I return from my self-imposed exile, Ruby's banging away at her laptop. I've been slinking in and out of our room at off hours, so this is our first awake encounter since Saturday's nuclear fallout.

I flip open my laptop to order pizza from the restaurant Liza and I usually hit up—it's cheap *and* good, some kind of pizza miracle. I'm *this* close to ordering a Hawaiian pie, my personal fave, when my finger stills on the track pad. Might as well go for broke—what do I have to lose?

"Do you have a favorite kind of pizza?" I speak over my shoulder at Ruby, still not ready to look at her.

Long pause. In fact, it's so long, I start to think she's ignoring me and square my shoulders back to my computer, ready to complete my order after all.

"I like pepperoni," she says finally.

I change the order to half pepperoni, half Hawaiian, and hit submit. Thirty minutes later, the pizza arrives. I pull two paper plates out of the supply I keep in my desk drawer, hand one to Ruby, and keep one for myself. I set the pizza itself on top of the mini-fridge, which is more or less the Mason-Dixon Line of our room. A demilitarized zone.

Eating cheesy pineapple-y goodness from the comfort of my bed feels like nirvana after so many granola days in the practice room. Ruby fetches a piece, and would you believe she actually *ate food on top of that white bedspread?*

We consume all but two pieces in complete silence. I put the leftovers away. Usually I'd leave the empty pizza box on top of the fridge with a plan to take it out to the dumpster in the light of day, but come to think of it, the box was usually gone by the time I got back from the next day's classes. Ruby.

Tonight, I take the pizza box straight out to the trash.

An hour later, I'm changed into my pajamas and my face is freshly washed. My wrists ache from the long hours of piano, and, weirdly, I'm so sick of music that I can't bear to even put in my earbuds. I pop two ibuprofen and instead of my nightly wind-down with tunes, I dig out a comfort book, *The Secret Garden*.

I've just started chapter two when Ruby's voice cuts through the sleepy silence of the room. "Thanks for the pizza."

"You're welcome," I say, and promptly fall asleep.

Tuesday morning I contemplate skipping class again. It's Advanced Solo day, which means I will almost inevitably witness the item formerly known as Duke and Liza. Also, as aforementioned: Does it really matter if I fail all my classes now?

I'll make my decision about class after I meet with Piper. I got an email from her yesterday afternoon, asking if I'd be willing to "check in" with her this morning. Which brings me back to the comfort library, aka the Place Where Dreams Go to Die. Can't wait to see what Piper's fixing to destroy me with this time.

"Morning, Bridget," she says, breezing into the room with her perfect beachy waves.

"Hi."

"So, I'll cut right to it. You ever seen a piece of celery that's been left out too long?"

What. In. The. Hell?

"Sure," I reply evenly, though my insides are throwing a confusion rave, darkness paired with a strobe light.

"That's what you look like these days. Usually you're tense but in a passionate way. Full. Like your heart comes out in everything you say and do. But the past few days you're just . . . limp celery." Her cobalt peepers blink at me.

My shoulders slump. "I *am* limp celery."

"Is this about Duke and Liza?"

My head snaps up so fast that possibly I've given myself whiplash. "What?"

"Bridget. You forget I literally *live* here. I've noticed Liza with Duke around school. And I've noticed Liza *not* with you, and you two are usually attached at the hip."

I let the layers of shame envelop me, like I'm a fly and it's a Bridget Venus flytrap, an extra-malicious breed of the carnivorous plant. "It's terrible. *I'm* terrible. I mean . . . I thought he liked me, but I guess I was wrong, and now I want to be happy for Liza because I love her but I just . . . can't."

Piper lays a long, slender hand on my shoulder.

"And it gets worse. Ruby hates me, too. Because I'm *literally* the worst roommate ever."

Piper sighs. "I wondered when that whole thing would implode."

"You knew? Why didn't you say anything?"

"In my experience, these things are better left to unfold on their own."

"I feel like such an idiot." I cover my face with my hands. "About everything. And this stuff isn't even the worst part."

"What do you mean?"

"My dads just told me they can't afford for me to come back next semester. They were counting on me earning a music sponsorship, and I can't get one of those if I'm not onstage, and . . ." I trail off because my bottom lip's quaking too hard to speak.

Piper's arm comes around my back, pulling me to her. I try not to let it bother me that she has to be able to feel my shoulders shaking. After a while I use my hands to wipe wetness from my face. "How do I stop being limp celery?"

She smiles, a cross between sad and happy. One of those faces grown-ups make really well. "Well, all celery needs is to be dipped in a cup of water."

"Maybe I should go for a swim? Or take a long bath?"

She laughs. "Cheeky girl. But seriously: What do you need to do to nourish yourself?"

The obvious: eat something other than granola bars, peanut butter, and pizza. I don't think that fits the vibe Piper's going for, though. "I've been isolating myself for four days. It's depressing. I should go be around people again."

"Good idea. What else?"

I dig deep. What the hell else would nourish me?

"Maybe I need to find ways to be a better roommate for Ruby. Which I think means considering Ruby's feelings. Which probably means asking her about them sometimes." This makes me feel all squiggly inside, because it's just so damn *immediate* and Ruby is *scary*. Yet I also acknowledge it's probably the only way, unless Ruby and I keep this "you probably have leprosy" treatment of each other going for the next couple of months.

Last night I managed to ask her what kind of pizza she likes. Maybe I can build from that.

"Yep, good plan. Anything else? What do you want to do about Duke and Liza?"

"Avoid them until the end of time."

"And how's that going to work out?"

"It should be easy, given I'll be leaving in a couple of months and never coming back." My sobs threaten to return, and I end up stutter-gulping at the air.

"About the money part—let me do some digging around for you. I'm a whiz at finding obscure sources of financial aid."

A tiny sliver of hope shines through, like a new moon at the first sign of waxing. "Okay. Thank you."

"Now. About Liza and Duke," Piper prompts.

I grasp on to a deep breath, letting it fill my lungs until there's no more space in them, then breathe out, slowly, slowly. At the bottom of my breath, I find a pocket of resilience. "I can't change them. I'll have to change me. I can . . . be happy for them."

Piper flips her waves over her shoulder. "That's probably a good goal, but be patient with yourself. People don't lose something or someone they care about, then wake up the next day feeling fine. Let yourself grieve. You'll have to find room in yourself for lots of feels, feels that don't feel like they go together, inside of you all at once."

"That's deep, Piper."

"Well, I'm a trained helper, but I've also done a lot of therapy myself. Daddy issues," she says, smiling broadly.

A giggle escapes me, which I immediately regret. The last thing I want to do is offend Piper. But then Piper laughs, too, and a little bit of tension leaves my body.

I'll let my laughter *and* my pain carry me through the rest of this day, I suppose.

TWENTY-TWO

FOR THE NEXT COUPLE OF weeks, everything feels familiar but not, like the walls of my home are covered in fun-house mirrors.

I'm here at the academy, but not sure I'll be here much longer. Everything feels like it could all blow away with one stiff breeze. After the dads dropped their financial bomb, I realized I could sing my head off if I wanted. It wouldn't matter anymore. But that shred of hope in Piper finding me some financial aid buzzes in my chest, and I decide to hold to Octavia's humility challenge.

Liza's still Liza, but a different version. She smiles more, laughs more. For the first time, I realize she has a dimple—just one, on her left cheek. Her attachment to my hip is severed. She now splits her time between me, Duke, and dishwashing duty after supper, which is her dean/mother–induced punishment after the Drinking Incident.

And Duke isn't *my* Duke anymore. This is a tall order in terms of adjustment, because he's been *my* Duke Ericson for as long as I've known there was a Duke Ericson.

Max is around as much as he's always been, but he's weird, too. Not mean or anything, but it's like he's never quite all the way there, even when he's right in front of me. I have no idea what's going on with him, but I'm also not about to bring it up. I've had enough upheaval for the time being.

Lucky for me, preparation for *Holding Up the Ocean* (named after the first song Max and I wrote, which was wildly well received by our peers) recently went into full swing, and I've had my hands full. Just when I thought nothing could make my peers more neurotic than the graded solos, I got an effing rude awakening. Graded solo practices had *nothing* on prepping auditions for this musical.

Case in point: Amber, a sophomore. She's planning to try out for the part of Beth, June's youngest sister, who is a small part but is rumored to have a significant solo in the first major ensemble number. Currently, Amber sits on the floor of Triton 212. Crying. She just . . . collapsed, like someone punched her knees from the back, after she came in flat during the last note of her audition piece. And people say *I'm* dramatic.

"Amber, it'll be okay. C'mon, let's do it again."

"I can't!" She takes three tremulous breaths, her entire trunk shaking with sob aftershocks. "I'll never get that note. And my accent is all wrong for a Nebraska girl." Her native Boston accent erases her *r*'s and turns *a* into *ah*.

"Oh hush, your accent is cute and it's fine for this role. Now, let's try that last bit one more time. I know you can get it."

Her big doe eyes, bloodshot and red rimmed, look hopefully into mine. "You really think so?"

"Sure I do. Let's go."

I help her up off the floor, and we try the last page again. This time she hits that big note right in the middle and belts it out from her stomach like a pro. I knew she could.

I'm not sure when I moved into the role of unshakable cheerleader, but you know what? I don't hate it. I mean, *I* could have smashed that note the first time while doing a headstand, but other folx need more time and practice. Sometimes a little confidence boost. If the outcome's the same, what does it matter?

Ten minutes later Amber leaves, dry-eyed and with her groove back, thanking me profusely in Bostonian.

Liza's next. She hands me her music and heaves one of her signature sighs of martyrdom. "I'm trying out for Jeanie."

Another of June's sisters in the musical, a bit part. "Duh, Max and I wrote that role for you." I even gave the character Liza's middle name (almost).

She shrugs. "I don't even wanna do this, but you know Octavia. 'Oh daaahling, you *must* audition, or I'll spend your trust fund on Chanel.'"

We crack up together, and it feels good. Right. I've missed this easy talk, this stuff she says to me that is part of *our* language.

Yet what sits like a brick on my chest are the facts of Liza's current situation. Yeah, she's got an overbearing mom, but she's also dating the boy she was never into and got anyway. She's all set to be here at the academy *and* in the MFP. And now she's standing right here on the cusp of musical greatness, too. She could try out for any part in this musical—except for maybe June, she'd be a terrible June—and land it.

Worse, part of me wonders if Duke ever talked to her about that night after the bar, when I tucked him into bed—the night he thought I was her. Did she just go along with his version of events, knowing his after-hours caregiver had to be me? I don't think she'd do this, but then again, love makes us do weird things.

Why can't I hate her? *Why?* Lynch sophomore Bridget would have run away from Liza as fast as my long pasty legs could carry me. I would've never befriended someone so epically gifted in the first place, because the idea of anyone outshining me would have repelled me. But the Richard James version of Bridget *did* befriend Liza. Something about her called to me and I answered.

I'm still answering.

When the laughter dies down, her face goes dull and ashy. The dark side of the moon. "I really don't want to do this, B."

She's easily the best friend I've ever had. She's written me so many letters about her life, she's showed me her pain, she's let me in.

Though my old, every-girl-for-herself instincts say, *Run, save yourself,* I fistfight them back. Echoes of Piper's wisdom rattle around in my noggin: *Find room in yourself for lots of feels.* Love and jealousy and sadness and respect and sympathy and hope needle their way in and out of my heart, stretching it out and stitching it together with one long thread.

I stay put. I stand up and put my hand on Liza's. "I'll help you. We've got this."

Her tiny, grateful smile lets me know I've chosen wisely.

After we run through her tryout song a couple of times, Liza sits beside me and casually plunks out the treble line of "Heart and Soul," the song that unites piano players. Everyone who plays past a beginner's level knows it—literally, ask any pianist. I join in, carrying the bouncy bass line.

"Are we okay?" she asks, eyes on the keyboard.

How to answer, how to answer . . .

"Yeah. Why?"

"You've seemed off over the last couple of weeks. Ever since . . . that night we all went out."

I shrug without taking my hands off the keys. "Just been busy. Tryouts and all."

"Mmm. See, I was thinking maybe you had a little thing for Duke, with as much as you used to talk about him. Now you don't talk about him at all."

I do a glissando and shift into "Chopsticks." Liza follows.

"That's your domain now. Duke is, I mean."

I sneak a look over and find her wearing a bemused face. "Yeah. But did you want him to be yours?"

I don't want to lie. I don't want to tell the truth. Talking about this is the worst, yet *not* talking about it is also gross. Ugh. Life's a mess sometimes.

"I did have a crush on Duke, before I even really knew him. I'm over it."

Half-truths will have to suffice.

"Okay. Just . . ." She stops playing. "You're the closest friend I've ever had. I don't wanna mess that up."

I smile at her, and it's not forced. "You're not messing it up."

"Promise?"

We finish "Chopsticks" and I pick her hand up, make her lock pinkies with me. "Pinkie promise."

"That's so silly," she says, but she's grinning.

"No, you know what's silly? You were *so* not into Duke, and then you were."

"Hey." She shoves my arm and I tip over a little—not because her little push really moved me, but because Liza *moves* me. "Honestly, that's fair."

"I know."

She puts her hands back to the ivories, fingers meandering over random chords and scales. "He's not who I thought he was."

"Oh yeah?"

"You know how in his YouTube videos, and even sometimes in class or at lunch, he's got this . . . persona? Like he's trying to be an actor or a caricature of himself or something?"

I nod, because that's the Duke I know and love. Loved. Liked. Like. Something. And I know what she means about the persona, because there were times it cracked, in the practice room with me. I'd seen glimpses of the real Duke, but they were fleeting. Always fleeting.

"I *hated* that about him, you know? The mask, the facade. Years of being raised by an actress will do that to you." She purses her lips

208

and wrinkles her nose, like she's just eaten something sour. "But when he drops the act, when he's just being *him* . . . he's really something."

I love Duke's glitz, his sparkle. But Liza's telling me—and I'm starting to see myself, at times—that the glamour isn't Duke, at least not entirely. A brand-new thought dawns, settling on my shoulders with a thud. Maybe the truth is that I have no idea who this boy really is. The one I thought I loved.

"It's one of the reasons I liked you right away. You're nothing but you, all the time." Liza's eyes dart over at mine, almost shyly.

"Fair enough. And thank you." I'll have to remember, though: just because *I'm* real all the time doesn't mean everyone is.

"You want to know something funny?" Liza says this through a gentle laugh.

"Always."

"I think maybe I'm falling for that goofball." This dreamy look comes over her face, happiness and nausea jousting for room inside me as I watch her. But I find I've got space for it, all of it.

For the longest time I've believed that love was the most mysterious of all the mysteries, but I'm starting to think that maybe, it's friendship.

TWENTY-THREE

IT'S WEDNESDAY EVENING AND FOR the first time ever, I'm late for my standing theory session with Max. Don't get me wrong, I've fantasized about ditching. Hell, unless financial aid whiz Piper comes through for me, it's not like passing the test even matters anymore. But I promised Max I'd be there, and he's showed up for me week after week. I'm going to show up for him.

I'm late because goddamn Amber had *another* meltdown during solo practice. This time I had to coax her out of the corner, where she'd sat—nose pointed *into the wall*, mind you—to "punish myself for singing badly." Sad as I feel for her, all the king's horses and all the king's men wouldn't have been able to completely repair her shattered self-esteem, not this time. This whole "unrelenting optimist" gig is becoming sort of a pain in the ass.

Also, I'm starting to have some serious concerns about Amber's home life.

Max has asked me to meet him in another room today—Triton 310, which is called the music lab. Someone's playing piano in there when I arrive, two Heath bar Razzles in hand. Before I barge unceremoniously through the door to see who, I realize the most likely candidate is, of course, Max. I linger outside the threshold, ear to the door. He's playing something springy, waltzy, equal parts beautiful and wistful. And . . . he's *singing*. He's a tenor, clear and exquisite, really. Does he realize what a privilege he has, that he *can* sing, if he wants? And here he is, forgoing it.

I shove into the room. He stops abruptly, gawking at me with wide eyes from behind a piano.

Are his cheeks red? "You're late," he says.

"You're talented. What were you playing?"

"Nothing." Oh yeah, he's definitely flushing. I sort of love this.

"Well, it was obviously *something*. You had your hands on the keys and music was coming out of the back of the piano. You know, the little hammers were hitting the strings in a specific configuration—"

"It's just . . . this thing I wrote, that's all."

I come around the back of the piano to peer over his shoulder. "Can I see?"

He snaps his composition book shut and shoves loose sheets of staff paper inside. "No. It's time to get started. Past time, actually."

I *knew* he'd be extra righteous about me being late, even though I've *never* been late before. Dude has a total hard-on for theory. "Yeah, about that . . . Sorry. The student audition prep stuff is eating up all of my time. I got our Razzles, though."

211

He takes the cup of ice cream and licks an errant drip off the side of the cup, which makes me oddly tingly.

"B?"

"Hmm?" I yank my eyes away from the place where his tongue met plastic, now warm all over—and also mortified, because what the hell?

But Max is all hard edges, apparently still crabby about my lateness. "Focus. Let's get going."

The music lab is about twice the size of a practice room and packed full of stuff: two pianos, a keyboard wired up to a computer with a big monitor, percussion instruments, microphones on stands. We sit at stools pulled up to a small table, and I await my penance. But instead of the usual theory bullshit, he flips to the back of his beat-up composition book. "All songwriting today."

"Really?" My body yanks up from its slump, instantly energized by this development.

Max's cranky mood seems to turn itself around, too. "Really. I told the crew I'd put the finishing touches on what we've got for music, because we need to start rehearsing. And for that, we have to do auditions and casting."

"True story."

"Also, I'm supposed to ask: Will you be the pianist for the musical?"

"You're asking me? I don't have to try out?" *Is this even allowed for a non–MFP student?*

"Literally everyone I've talked to about the musical is in

agreement: we want you. Especially the Advanced Solo kids. They love you."

A very sunny, yellow glow hits me right in my middle. "Of course I'll play!" The enthusiasm in my voice is an exact match for what I feel. I'm *thrilled*. It's not an onstage role, but it's something. I guess I'll assume that if I'm allowed to accompany soloists, I'm allowed to do this.

Max's smile dominates. "Amazing, I'll let everyone know." From his composition book he grabs several loose sheets of paper—some filled-in staff paper, some blank sheets with words scrawled, several pieces of torn-out notebook paper—and spreads them all out on the table. "Okay, so now that you've agreed: here's the challenge. This is what we've got so far for music."

I survey the pile of mumbo jumbo in front of me. *"This?"*

"Yeah. Every musical starts somewhere, and this is ours. We've got five completed songs, stage directions, some written dialogue. It's all in here, it's just a mess."

I've never really considered how the sausage gets made when it comes to musicals, but here it is. Chaos strewn across a worn-out table. "What . . . do we *do* with this?"

"Well, if you're going to play, you need some music, right?"

My glowing heart sinks into a newly nervous stomach. Of *course* the score for our original work wouldn't just appear out of nowhere. "Oh, God. Do we need to write the sheet music?"

"That we do." Max grins, seeing that I'm catching up, but he also spies the grimace that's crawled across my face. "Don't worry. I know it looks daunting, but we've got this."

"Uh, maybe *you've* got this."

"No, *we've* got this. We're going to put all the theory you've been working on *and* all that talent you came with into practice."

I listen attentively as Max demonstrates the process by which we will (supposedly) conquer this. Even as my stomach sings its song of dread—*how will we ever get this done in any kind of reasonable timeline?*—I can't help but feel a lift in my chest, watching Max. His voice speeds up as he shows me how the keyboard inputs the notes, how to adjust the music in the program, eagerness bursting out of him with every new demonstration. His optimism settles under my skin, and we both glow with it, together.

"Okay, let's do it!"

Max's smile is so pure, it's almost distracting. He hands me what he has for the opener, one of the big ensemble pieces. "If we can get through 'Seven Sisters'—the most complicated song of the whole musical—we can get through anything."

Sitting next to me on the piano bench, Max plays through the chords, singing the melody line as "dah dah dah"—and again, I'm a little obsessed with his singing voice. "You've got some pretty pipes, Cuddlepuppy."

"I told you to never call me that," he says, but he's smiling as he marks up the staff in front of him.

"Ah, you said to never call you that at school. But it's just you and me in the ole music lab. Fair game."

His neck's gone as splotchy as ever, but he looks rather pleased. "I can live with that, Venus."

I put my hands on the keys and riff with the music he's just taught me, taking the chords and bending, twisting, breaking them up into new music. When we arrive at something that seems to work, Max sets me up on the keyboard wired into the computer, and we give it a go. It takes many fits and starts, and more than once I slam a fist into my thigh with frustration, but ninety minutes later we've got a rough draft of sheet music for "Seven Sisters."

"Perfect! Now we have something to give the orchestra kids. They need to write their own scores." Max hits a button and paper shoots out of a printer. Sheets and sheets of this original song, which I pick up and press to my face.

Do we have a lot of work ahead of us? Absolutely. And it will all be completely worth it. Because from nothing, now there is music. Is this how Dodge feels when his crops come shooting out of the ground every season? I never thought of that before. No wonder the land is precious, even beyond the monetary.

"Max. This is a miracle," I say, handing him the sheets.

He receives the pile like I'm handing him his firstborn, and then out of nowhere, his arms are around me. His body radiates excited heat, the music is still hot off the printer, and unbelievably, *this* kind of warm feels every bit as good as the glow of a spotlight at center stage.

TWENTY-FOUR

THE NEXT TWO WEEKS FLY by in a haze of chord progressions, lyrics, and piles upon piles of brand-new sheet music. Max and I meet in the music lab almost every night.

At one point in our third long night together, I slipped up. "How about this instead," I said, suggesting a slight melody change but singing it, thoughtlessly.

"Love that," he agreed, singing it to himself as he marked up the page. "Love your voice, too, for what it's worth." He didn't look at me, and I think that was an intentional move. All this time we've spent together has given way to him knowing my patterns, my quirks. He knows I like my coffee with one cream and two sugars, that I absolutely *hate* lint on clothing and attack it with fury (and I have, on his sweaters, on more than one occasion), that I like pineapple on my pizza, and that I've recently developed an aversion to peanut butter. And he knows that I don't sing, and further, he must have known that if he was going to comment on it, I was going to need a minute to process.

If there was ever a time to disclose my MFP secret *and* my humility goals to someone, it was then. But still, a couple of things held me back—fear that my confession would ruin everything I've built with Max, and a not-so-little chip on my shoulder otherwise known as pride. So instead of sparring back, I sat quietly next to him on the bench, speechless.

Max eased the silence with a gentle voice. "How about . . . in just this room . . . if I sing, you sing? And we don't tell anyone that we did. It'll make songwriting that much easier." Just like that, he handed me a gift. Freedom to be a little bit more me without having to explain why I'm not that way all the time.

"Deal," I said.

From that point on we sang as we worked, he in his perfect resonant tenor, I in the softer, singer-songwriter version of my soprano. Knowing that I got a chance to sing for at least a couple of hours every night made me crave the music-writing sessions even more. And seeing Max anywhere—in the halls, in the Rot, in classes—now sends me into autosmiles. Pavlov was on to something.

Last night we finished music for the song that will be the finale, "You Are My Home." Technically, the musical would be stronger if we had one more song, but no one had any great ideas and we all agreed to forge forward with what we had. Besides, our time is basically up—auditions are today, a Saturday morning. Instead of my customary laid-back morning in Hans's shop, I'm parked in the school auditorium behind the piano—and these tryouts are anything but relaxed. The auditorium crackles with tension and nerves, and even though I'm not the one trying out, the feels are catching. I pick at my cuticles, twirl my hair between solos.

In addition to the anxiety I've contracted from the hopefuls, not to mention the constant worry about my family's financial situation, I've got older emotional baggage weighing me down. Starting with the fact that this is the first time I've ever attended auditions and not been auditioning. Ever since I played Annie for the Athens Community Theatre at age seven, I've landed major parts in each summer's musical. I've been Mary Poppins, Dorothy of *The Wizard of Oz*, even Oliver in *Oliver!*—the only year I got to do drag.

There's a heaviness in knowing that if I could've earned the role of June, I very likely would have sung opposite Duke. The students would have to have their heads stuck straight up their asses to not cast him as the lead—not only because of his talent, but because of his notoriety.

Besides, as Max and I fussed with the songs, we more or less had Duke in mind for Socks.

I assume it's Duke's knowing he's a shoo-in that led him to practice very little—with me, at least. It was different during the one session he showed for. The clowning around and pseudo-heart-to-heart moments of last month's Duke-and-Bridget hang in the practice room, but they're ghosts now, things of the past. Now we practice, we troubleshoot, he leaves.

Duke's all business again this morning for his audition, yet as smooth and feline as ever as he strides to center stage of the auditorium. "Duke Ericson, for the part of Socks."

A panel of junior and senior students, Max among them, collectively smile and nod from their seats in the third row. Octavia's in the back of the house, apparently wearing her MFP chairperson hat today. She's as still as a mannequin, as if she's trying to go unnoticed, but we all know she's there. My piano is situated close to the edge of the stage, far from her but still close enough that I can see the light bouncing off her smooth auburn ponytail. One meticulously sculpted eyebrow lifts at its immaculate arch when she catches me staring at her. My stomach flips, but I smile demurely and turn my eyes back to my accompanist duties. A picture of humility.

Duke smiles and inclines his head my way, his gesture for me to start playing. Every performer has one, and Duke's is especially polished, impeccably suave.

He sings his audition piece—a song from *The Wedding Singer* musical—like he's been singing it for his whole life, probably because he has. He misses nothing. Even if he weren't Duke Ericson, he'd get any part he wanted.

A few auditions later, it's Amber's turn. She hits that big, troublesome note she's been worrying so hard-core about, and she beams at me. Anxiety's not the only thing catching in this room, because I grin back, pride for her exploding out of my chest and wrapping around my whole body. She worked so hard, and she deserves this moment. I so hope she gets the part she wants.

Liza's next. "Liza Lawless, singing for Jeanie."

Liza's effortlessly wonderful, of course, singing the solo "Hold On" from *The Secret Garden*, which I talked her into. It showcases all the best things about her voice.

One of the casting panelists speaks up. "Thanks, Liza. Are you sure you don't want to be considered for a bigger part, maybe Rosie or even June?"

"No, thank you," says Liza, stoic.

"Okay, thanks."

I dare to glance backward across the auditorium. Octavia's lips flatten into a thin line, which exaggerates the wrinkles around her mouth.

The June hopefuls of the day are lacking, but one of them is great: Danica Townsend, a senior who comes from somewhere in the Deep South and has this super-cute twang to her perfect-pitch voice, not to mention she's got a face made for the stage—huge eyes, big pretty mouth, naturally animated. The only strike against Danica is that she's constantly baked, and everyone knows it. Word on the street is that she does edibles rather than wreck her vocals with smoke—which proves her commitment to both weed and singing. Still, she's über-talented, and if Danica doesn't get cast as June, we're probably all going to need to dip into her stash of magic gummies.

The callbacks are posted just before dinner the next evening. I'm sitting at a table in the Rot with Max and Duke when Liza storms in, walking about two clicks faster than she ever does, eyebrows drawn together in a scary V. She slams her tray down on the table and sits heavily, glaring at her bowl of Corn Pops. She looks like some kind of dark magic enchantress, but now's not the time to tell her that.

"What's up?" says Duke, laying a hand between her shoulder blades, rubbing in circles. I try to tear my eyes away from the movement but find them stuck there.

Liza speaks through her teeth. "I got a callback."

"Isn't this a good thing?"

This is enough to deglue my eyes. I shoot Duke a withering look. He might be dating Liza now, but he doesn't know her like I know her.

"Who'd you get called back for?" I ask.

"They want me to sing for both Rosie and June," she says, slumping into her chair. "Even though I explicitly said no when they asked if I wanted to be considered."

I have to wonder what casting genius decided to go against the will of the dean's daughter.

Then again, this shady callback has Octavia written all over it. I cross my arms as I remember Octavia's face when Liza neglected to sing for a bigger part. Not just disappointed, but angry. Determined.

Duke's face brightens. "Hey, wait! If I get Socks, and you get June, we'll be an onstage couple *and* an offstage couple. That'd be fun, right?"

He *really* doesn't know her. Liza and I bestow upon him Twin Looks of Death. Max's eyes slide back and forth, like he's watching a sporting event.

"Not everyone loves theater the way *you* do, Duke." Liza grabs her stuff and leaves, dumping her entire tray of uneaten food into the trash can before bolting from the Rot.

"Nice work, man," I say, slurping down what's left of my soup so I can run after Liza.

"What? What'd I do?" His look of genuine confusion stomps on my sympathy button, but quickly, I remember Duke's feelings are no longer my problem. He'll have to figure this one out on his own.

Liza and I discuss two strategies for callbacks. One, she could sing so poorly that the committee has no choice but to demote her to chorus or remove her from consideration of casting entirely. This one is Liza's idea, and she's pretty wedded to it. I have to do some smooth talking to get her to consider option B—or, as I'm calling it, "Let's just make the most of this."

"But why, B? Why *should* I give a shit?" She tugs at her hair by its roots, and when she pulls her hands away, chunks stand straight up in places. It's the most disheveled I've ever seen her, and she still looks like a slightly rumpled princess. Snow White with Bedhead. Jasmine Gets a Bad Haircut.

"Okay, try this on for size. You've got a gift. For better or for worse, your voice is amazing and your range is incredible. Why not use it for the better, just this once?"

"But *why*?"

I glare at her. "Because some of us who would *love* to *can't*."

She has the grace to look moderately sheepish. "Fine. But I'm not doing this for me. I'm doing it for you."

"I'll take it. Let's go."

I make her run through the cuts that callbacks for her roles require, one of which is fairly challenging because it includes a high G sharp. Not that it's any problem for the daughter of Octavia Lawless, who nails it without effort.

About thirty minutes in I glance down at my phone, which is blowing up. Apparently Liza's not the only student who needs to run callback material with me. I spend the evening coordinating, practicing, and soothing frayed nerves in Triton 212 and then after that stay and finish up the homework and studying that needs to be done for my other classes.

Ruby's reading lamp is still on when I drag my tired shoulders in at one in the morning.

"Hey," she says, startling me.

"Hey," I reply, voice sounding as wrecked as I feel.

"You're out late."

"Yeah. Getting some schoolwork done. And *Holding Up the Ocean* callbacks are tomorrow and I was running the material with the hopefuls."

"All night?"

I yawn. "These divas have a lot of needs."

"You're a really dedicated accompanist."

Seabass let me know that I could set limits on my accompanist time and it wouldn't affect my grade, but these singers are counting on me. I won't let them down. Besides, I've grown to *like* my time with them, weirdly. "You know, I sort of am."

"You ever . . . accompany other types of musicians? Like

instrumental soloists?" She's scrolling through some feed on her phone, not looking at me as she talks.

"You asking for a friend?"

"There's this cellist I know. And her student accompanist kind of sucks."

"Tell your friend that after I get through these tryouts, I can help her out."

Ruby nods and sets her phone down on the table beside her, nestling deeper into her blankets. "Goodnight, Bridget."

It's the first time she's told me goodnight in . . . well, ever.

"Night, Ruby."

TWENTY-FIVE

CALLBACKS ARE RELATIVELY UNEVENTFUL, AND by uneventful, I mean a couple of performers had complete meltdowns after they sang, a boy vomited in a trash can offstage just before he went up, and two girls got into a henfight in the hallway while they awaited their turn to audition. Typical drama kid stuff.

Liza is cast as Rosie, which, the more I think about it, she's excellent for, even if we *did* write the smaller part of Jeanie for her. That dry, droll sense of humor, that constantly bored facial expression—these *are* Rosie as she is meant to be played, and they're Liza's jam, no acting required. Duke is Socks, as if there were ever any doubt.

Amber gets Beth, the part she wanted. After she reads the cast list, she finds me in the crowd and throws herself at me, squeezing me so hard my ribs pop. "Thank you thank you thank you! I couldn't have done it without you!" Well.

Sweet Southern pothead Danica is cast as June. She'll be great, even I have to admit it.

That precious evening time I've spent mostly in practice rooms for the past month becomes mine again—temporarily. I don't need to start showing up for rehearsals until the cast and crew have mostly worked out their lines and blocking, probably two weeks from now.

Since no one's prepping anything major at the moment, I'm surprised when my phone pings with a notification that someone has asked for a practice slot with me. Duke. My heart starts in with its habitual stutter-start-stutter, and then I remember. It settles back into a dull thud.

I meet Duke in a practice room on a Tuesday evening, just before supper. He hands me the score from *Holding Up the Ocean* with one hand. With the other hand he's pulling his ankle up to his rear, stretching his quads.

"About to go for a run there, killer?"

He mugs as he drops his ankle, then picks up the other one. "Naw. It's just my muscles get tight when I'm nervous."

"You? Nervous?"

"Yep, me. Nervous." Both feet now on the floor, he links his hands together behind his back and bends over, stretching his hands above his head.

"Why?"

"I don't know these songs. And Socks's range is higher than I'm used to."

"Okay, where do you want to start?"

He opens his music to "I Knew," the first big duet between June and Socks. I give him a little lead-in, but Socks has the starting line.

"No," I say, cutting the music. "Listen, it's like this." I play the intro again, humming Socks's part, then nod to him to try again. He gets it this time but then doesn't pause long enough for June's midsong interjections.

Duke scrubs his hand down his cheeks in frustration. "This would be a lot easier if I had a June in here. Any chance you wanna sing?"

Do I wanna sing? Ha. And yet, I won't. This isn't a safe zone, like what I have with Max.

He gently elbows me in the ribs. This would have set me on fire a few weeks ago, but now I know it's nothing. "C'mon, B. Your voice can't be that bad."

"Tell you what: I'll hum. Let's go."

With me humming June's lines, he's much better. We run the song a few times, and the reprise. After just twenty minutes of practice, he's already 100 percent improved from when we started. Quick learner.

After his final note in the reprise, his jaw goes slack—I didn't notice it'd been tight, but now that it's not, I see the difference. "Okay, I feel better about this whole Socks thing now. Thanks."

"Anytime."

He comes around the bench and scooches me over. Mindlessly, he starts playing the chord progression from Pachelbel's Canon in D.

"So, you're obviously Liza's best friend."

"Duh."

Long pause. "Does she talk about me?"

I refrain from rolling my eyes, and it's hard. "Sometimes."

"Good stuff?"

"Why do you ask?"

A few seconds of Canon variations tick by with no voice-over. But then: "Liza's kind of hard to read. Before that night we all went out, I really didn't think she was into me."

Welp, she might not be as hard to read as he thinks, because he got that one right. Not that I'm going to tell him that. I put my hands on the keys above Duke's and add some variations in the upper registers of the piano, like a descant.

"After she sang with me in the bar, I started to think maybe there was something there. But I wasn't sure until what happened in my room, after we got back to the dorm."

I halt in my variations, hands frozen. It's hard to move when there's ice water in your veins.

Duke keeps playing but looks over at me. "I figured she told you, since you two are so close. No?"

I shake my head, not trusting my voice.

"Hopefully telling you about this isn't a dick move. Remember how hammered I got at the bar that night? She took care of me, after you and Max left. Got me to my room, tucked me into bed. She . . . she sang to me." He stops playing and closes his eyes for longer than a blink before starting again. "It was intense. And sweet. I didn't know she had that kind of caring in her. I just wish I could've seen her face. It was dark, and my vision was all messed up from the damn liquor."

My whole body is cold, cold, cold. What's that they say about hypothermia—that it's a painless, peaceful death? I call bullshit, because this is about as painful as anything I've ever felt.

"See, I'm always surrounded by people, but I gotta level with you: sometimes I'm lonely. It's hard to know who likes me for me, ever since I started with the YouTube stuff. Seems like people wanna know Duke Ericson, music guy, not Duke Ericson, regular high school guy. That's why Max is still my right-hand man. He liked me before I was a *trend*."

I'm still in pain over his epic liquor-fueled mix-up, but I defrost myself enough to nod. Guy's baring his soul here; the least I can do is play along.

Also, I'm increasingly aware that I was one of the many who wanted to know Duke Ericson, music guy, without much thought to who he was before or who he'd want to be outside of that. A Duke groupie. Grossly shortsighted.

"And that's one of the things I like about Liza, too. I think she's into me for me."

I gain command of my vocal cords, because this is important. "You're right about that."

Duke's Canon variations get louder and more complicated, like his fingers are taking flight. "That's reassuring. I trust your opinion on this."

"I *am* the resident Liza expert."

"And the resident ass saver, with this accompanying stuff. Everyone's been raving about how much you've helped during this audition process and everything. You know that?"

My blood finally flows freely again, now back up to body

temperature. I'm thawed. No, more than that. I'm free. Free to build a me who's still valuable, separate from singing and separate from the idea of being Duke's girl. I wasn't meant for him. I really wasn't. I only wanted the facade. Liza wants the real deal.

The opportunities and options ahead of me are endless, and my heart soars as I consider this.

He sighs. "After the night Liza sang to me, I thought I'd know her voice anywhere. But then it sounded different the next day. Still awesome . . . but different. Maybe she's got a lullaby voice and performance voice?"

A few ice cubes rattle through me. If Duke heard me sing, would he realize I was the one in his room that night? And what would that mean for him? For Liza?

All the more reason to keep my voice on lockdown.

Maybe I'm not yet fully free, between this weirdness and my stupid money woes and not being a real MFP student.

But in a weird twist of irony, I still feel closer to freedom than ever before.

TWENTY-SIX

IT'S WEDNESDAY AND *I'M LOOKING* forward to my theory lesson. Because everything's still a little bit *Freaky Friday* / fun-house mirror in the Diza era. (BTW, Duke + Liza = *Diza*. Because the alternative is Liza + Duke = *Luke*, and that's stupid.)

The room's quiet from behind the closed door, so I let myself in. Max is absent, but his stuff isn't—his bag's on the table, guitar case on the floor, papers spread out all over the piano. I set our Mint Oreo Razzles aside and seat myself on the piano bench, idly playing chords and scales, when I notice Max's composition book is spread-eagle in front of me. He guards this thing with his life, snaps it shut every time I come near. Clearly, it's not something he likes to share with anyone. I train my eyes away from the pages, focusing on my nimble fingers across the ivory and black keys.

Despite myself, I catch a snippet of a line written across one open page: "The midnight sky swallows me whole."

God, that's good. The inside of Max's head must be a beautiful, terrifying place. I wonder what else he's written?

Soon the seed of my wonder grows into curiosity, and from there into impossible-to-tether full-on nosiness.

Oh, hell . . . how much harm can one tiny peek really cause? It comes from a place of wanting to understand Max better, right? And that's a good thing, trying to learn more about people—or so I've gathered. If it seems too personal, I'll set it down.

I flip to the beginning. On the first page, "Property of Maxwell Griffin," his phone number, and a reward offered if the notebook was ever found. Yeesh. Precious relic indeed.

The first few pages appear to be poems, written in a chicken-scratch hand, like he'd rushed to get the words out on the page. A few pages in, one of the poems is all marked up, struck through—just like the original copy of the song Max and I wrote. It's a draft version of something bigger and better, I'm guessing. The next page is a more polished version of the draft, Max's handwriting now blocky like an architect's, in straighter, neater lines, with chords above the words.

As I slow down to read more carefully, the peachy hair on my forearms stands straight up. Because by the end of every line, I know what the next line's going to be. I know this poem. This *song*. And as I read the next poem/song from draft form to finished product, my cheeks go numb. These words are as familiar to me as my own face in the mirror—which would inevitably be white with shock right now. An atom bomb of cold dread detonates in my stomach, sending an actual shiver rattling through me, and I wrap my arms around myself.

The door opens. "Oh, hi. On time today, I see."

I manage to lift my arm and wiggle my fingers at Max but can't muster a smile. My face is still frozen.

"What's the matter? You look like you've seen a ghost." His forehead crinkles with concern.

"That's hilarious, really. That choice of words. I think I'm looking at a ghost."

"What?"

"A ghost*writer*. You're Duke's ghostwriter."

He stops short between the door and the piano, now a pillar of salt on the tile floor. For a few seconds we blink at each other, our bodies otherwise still, and then as if someone offstage yells, "Simon says *move*," Max *moves*. In two steps he's to the piano, gathering up his book, his papers. Moving like the building's on fire.

Guilt gnaws at my stomach lining. I have supremely effed up. "Hey. Talk to me," I say, my voice shaking a little. I catch the sleeve of his hoodie between my fingers, but he yanks it away, nostrils flaring.

"How dare you look through my stuff? *Read my composition book?* What gives you the right?" He charges back to the other side of the room. Every *slap* and *bang* makes me flinch, as his notebooks, his book bag, all of his things are slammed into the table.

I plead with him over the top of the piano. "I'm so sorry. I . . . I don't know why I did that. I shouldn't have done it."

"No, you shouldn't have. You *really* shouldn't have." He's bent over, back to me, hands splayed out on the table. His shoulders heave with some big emotion; anger is my first guess. But when he sits down in the chair—more like falls down—he looks tired. Weary. Like an old man dressed in a young man's skin.

His words are gravelly. "You ever have to keep a secret that's so big, it could destroy someone if it got out?"

I hold my MFP secret close to the chest, but just for myself. Does this count? "Sort of."

"Well, that's what my world is like. Duke's the star, and I'm the unwitting silent sidekick."

My body finally starting to thaw, I join Max at the table. "You're like . . . Duke's Cyrano."

This earns me a tiny smile and one itty-bitty inch of dropped shoulder tension. "Guess that's one way of looking at it."

"How did this happen?"

"It's a long story."

I make a big show of getting my phone out of my pocket and looking at it. "You still owe me approximately fifty-five minutes."

"I don't *owe* you anything, technically."

"Okay, fine. But will you tell me if I admit I *want* to spend the next fifty-five minutes with you? Even if we don't work on theory or songs?"

He looks up at me through his eyelashes. "Why?"

"Because you're you." I say it without thinking, and I don't need to. It's true.

There are new-old things brewing in his sunflower eyes. Where there was anger just seconds ago, now there's softness. But also fear. What I'm asking him to share must be really hard for him. "C'mon, Max. It's only me," I say gently.

He speaks into his lap. "When I was ten, my family and I moved to a new neighborhood, which meant a new school. I was still an only child at that point, so I was on my own."

"I know what that's like, when it's you against the world. I'm an only child."

He gifts me with a smile that warms me from the inside out. "That makes me feel a little less alone."

"Anyway, go on."

"I was a small kid. Skinny, smart, big glasses, and all these freckles. Zero athletic bones in my body. I might as well have gone to school with 'Bully Me' screen-printed on my T-shirt."

I wince, and Max sees. "Yeah. It was bad. The first week, it was just childish insults, things like 'four eyes' and 'loser.' But day by day, the kids got meaner. They started calling me names not worth repeating. Names no one should be called."

I can imagine the names he means. My chest aches for him.

"By week two, this group of kids was jamming me into an empty locker every day. I went through three pairs of glasses in three weeks." His fists are so clenched that his knuckles go white. As if some power beyond my understanding is working on my behalf, I reach across the table and gently cover his fisted hand with mine. His head snaps up and stares at our tower of hands, but then his fist unravels. I break out in gooseflesh as his warm palm swallows up my cold—which makes no sense if he's warming me up, but then, what does anymore?

Max continues. "Week three at that school, everything changed. I was once again getting shoved inside a locker when this tall kid from the basketball team comes over and grabs one of the bullies by the front of his shirt. 'You sure you want to do that?' he said, and that group of boys went running down the hallway. They left me alone after that. See, Duke had that much clout *then*, even before he was Insta-famous. It's just something about him. It's like . . . he can control the energy in a room. I've seen it happen so many times."

"You and Duke have been friends for that long, huh?"

"Yeah. I mean, at first, I thought maybe he was just taking me on as a charity case or something. He was a jock back then, so I didn't get why he'd want to hang with me. But we were in chorus together, and band, and after a while it just . . . clicked. We were inseparable."

"Like salt and pepper shakers."

Max laughs. "Just like that."

"This is cute and all, but it still doesn't explain how the whole ghostwriting thing started."

"I'm getting to that. Patience, Venus."

"Not my strong suit."

"You don't say?" He squeezes my hand, and it's only then that I realize he's still got it. Would it be awkward to take it away now? I mean, how does a person do that? Snatch it back, abruptly? Slide it back, slowly? I remember I have an elastic on my wrist, and I bring both hands up to the nape of my neck to gather my curls into a loose side pony. Inconspicuous? I keep my eyes on Max's face as I fix my hair, but he gives nothing away.

"Duke and I did a lot of music stuff together. I got really good at piano and guitar, and he was really into singing and performing, so together, we were a hell of a duo. We won a lot of local music contests."

"And I haven't even seen you guys perform together once. Sad."

A cloud hovers over his face. "I was dating this guy sophomore year, Sam. He doesn't go here anymore. He's . . . hard to describe, but basically everything I'd ever wanted but had never believed I'd actually have. For five months, we were happy. And then we weren't. When we broke up, he told me he hated my voice and I sucked at guitar and the world would be a better place if my music wasn't a part of it."

"Holy crap."

"Yeah. My confidence has never been quite the same, and it wasn't that great to begin with. I got really depressed. The only thing I enjoyed other than sleeping was writing. I journaled, I wrote alternative histories in which I said really witty, cutting things to Sam instead of letting him shit all over me. And there was poetry. A lot of it was abysmal, but some of it turned out okay. Case in point, I wrote this poem about how Sam used to finish my sentences, and he'd always make the joke it was my 'sandwiches' he was finishing—you know, like that line in 'Frozen'?"

"Ohhh. 'Sandwiches' is about Sam."

"Correct."

"Wow. All this time, I've been wondering who broke Duke's heart, and all along it was your heart that bled for that song."

Max snorts. "Duke has a lot of good qualities, but heart-bleeding depth of emotion might not be one of them. He feels stuff, don't get me wrong . . . but not in the way that original music comes naturally from."

"Yeah, I could see that."

"But he's savvy enough to know a good thing when he hears it. I played 'Sandwiches' for him one night when we were jamming, and he fell for it. Asked if it was okay if he 'borrowed' it for our next competition. And then . . . well, the rest is history, I suppose."

"But you're not in any of the videos. It's all Duke and the piano and his songs. Your songs, I mean."

"He tried to get me to perform with him when he got big with 'Sandwiches' and the rest of the songs. I kept saying no. Eventually, he stopped asking. I wrote songs, he performed the songs, and that's just the way it's been."

I scrunch my nose. Something's rotten up in here. "But . . . that's not fair."

"Life's not fair."

Well, he's damn right about that. But I've never been one to just lie down and take it.

His vulnerability hangs between us like a kite. I'm holding the string, and his disclosure is the wind keeping it in the air. Maybe I need to take a turn, take some responsibility for keeping this kite aloft.

"Hey. So. I have a confession."

He leans forward. "Okay?"

I swallow hard and prepare to accept my fate, whatever that may be—I'm either severing or tightening my connection with Max, and I won't know which it is until I've just *said it*. My heart is a bass drum in my ears. "I'm not in the music focus program. Not technically. I didn't get in because my theory scores were too low."

His already big eyes go humongous. "What?"

"Yeah. And that means I'm not allowed to perform. When I got here, I asked to be reconsidered for the MFP. Octavia not only denied my request, but she also told me I needed to work on my humility."

Max's mouth falls open. "Wow."

"Yeah. So, to prove to her that I could, I don't sing at all. Ever. Except with you."

"Except with me."

"And it's meant everything to have that little piece of myself back. Singing is my whole life. Or was? I don't know for sure, but I *do* know that every time someone else gets to sing in class, or on stage, or in the Rot, I ache, because I want it to be me." I pause, swallow, soldier on. "You asked, before you told me about you and Duke, if I knew what it was like to keep secrets that held other's futures in the balance. That's my secret. But it's my own future that's at risk."

And I wait. Because what Max says next determines whether our shared path continues or stops cold. Can he still respect me, after knowing I've lied to him for months?

Max's voice drops to a whisper, and his eyes are just as soft. "Thank you for telling me that. But why? Why tell me?"

Relief floods my entire body as I drop my voice to match his level. "I figure I owed you a secret."

Max's face splits open a little bit as he reaches back across the table for my hand. This time when we touch, it's different. Loaded. Charged. Absolutely without my consent, my heart splutters and then expands, pushing its way into every rib. I have no idea what any of this means but lack the headspace to try to figure it out at the moment.

"We're going to make sure you pass that theory test for next year," he says, so earnestly that tears prick at my eyes.

If I'm here next year, I think but can't bring myself to say. *Please, Piper, do your financial aid magic.*

His thumb strokes the webbing between my thumb and index finger. "The world needs your voice."

As we sit in now semicomfortable silence, hands linked over the top of our practice room table, I think a thing, but I don't say it. *It needs yours, too.*

TWENTY-SEVEN

AT THE REQUEST OF BOTH Liza and Max, I start showing up for musical rehearsals half a week earlier than I was originally supposed to. I mean, why not? It's not like people who are *just accompanists* have anything else to work on, like studying for theory tests and tackling English papers on Nabokov and dominating trig. No big deal.

All testiness aside, it's nice to be valued.

The reason they asked is that they both, separately, mentioned that rehearsals weren't exactly the smooth sailing they'd all hoped for. Turns out the main cast member on the struggle bus is—wait for it—Duke. Liza's spared no details in the privacy of my room, away from prying ears and boyfriend egos. Ruby and I giggled as she parodied him singing his part from "Bill's Elegy" like she was a prepubescent boy with a voice that bends almost to a yodel. She's either the best girlfriend ever for not excluding Duke from the list of people she'd make fun of or the worst for being mercilessly critical of his attempts.

Truth is, I didn't believe the Duke situation could really be *that* bad. He seemed relatively prepared after our practice session, so I figured Liza was exaggerating for some laughs.

But no. It becomes obvious during my first rehearsal that Duke has rented out the penthouse of suck. He's missing cues, speaking out of turn, forgetting lines. At one point, he comes in completely *off-key*. I can't even fathom this. This is *Duke Ericson*. Duke effing Ericson. Witnessing his stage folly is like taking everything I thought I knew, dumping it on the floor, and doing the chicken dance on it.

And this is how he ends up in another extra practice session with me, late on a Thursday evening. I'm starting to think I should probably just move my bed directly into Triton 212. I wouldn't scoff at a water cooler. Maybe a little bucket, too, for bathroom situations.

He rolls in three minutes late and gifts me with his typical winning smile.

"You're late." Past Bridget would have felt a lot more sympathetic. But this is the post-Max-disclosure Bridget. The I-Know-What-You-Did-You-Big-Asshole Bridget.

"Aw, I'm always late, B. Forgive me?" He makes his eyes big and sad.

Though his puppy-dog face claws away at my resolve, I remind myself: *This is the boy who took another's work and passed it off as his own.* I shake my head, my attempt at shaking out cobwebs left behind by a starstruck girl. "Let's just get going."

He frowns but gets out his music. We work "Bill's Elegy" so

many times, I think I might lose my shit. You know when you say a word over and over until it loses all meaning? That's what this song has become. Those lines that were so hard to sit through before, about loss and saying goodbye to someone dear—which, at an earlier point, felt like an echo of what I felt for Duke—move nothing within me. My insides are as dull as unconditioned hair.

We finish the thing for the umpteenth time, and Duke stretches his arms. "Thanks, B. Hopefully I've got this more down pat now. Rehearsals have been rough."

One side of my mouth hitches. "You don't say."

He winces, shoving his music back into his bag. "By the way, did I miss something? You seem . . . different."

"Me? I'm fine."

"You sure?"

I don't owe this guy anything, but I owe Max everything. I take a deep breath and launch in. "Were you ever going to come clean about your songs?"

I'd assumed he would freeze or get pale or something, but there's no stutter in his movement, no change in his face. "What do you mean, come clean?"

"I mean, you've been doing all of these videos of you and your *original* music on YouTube, even with Blythe Rosen, and at no point did I offer up any credit for the writer of these songs."

Finally, I get a reaction—but it's not the one I was looking for. Duke *laughs*. His face is all jolly, shoulders loose and unconcerned. "Max never wanted any credit. That's not who he is." Duke throws his bag over his shoulder and relaxes back on one leg, channeling epic dude-bro proportions of chill and calm. Which only serves to piss me off more.

"You sure about that?"

"Look, go back and watch the videos. I never claimed I wrote the songs myself. I only said they're original."

"Hmph. Meanwhile, you reap all the benefits of the music and Max is invisible to the world."

"Hey look, I know Max better than anyone. If he wanted acknowledgment, he would've said something by now." Duke's tone is as affable as always, but his hand clenches tighter around the strap of his bag.

I cross my arms and glare.

"You think I should do something about this." Duke looks incredulous.

"I do."

"*What* do you think I should do?"

"I don't know."

He heaves a massive sigh and rakes one bent-fingered hand through his curly hair. It's the closest thing to a frustrated reaction I've seen out of him, and I get this weird thrill of excitement to see it. *Moi*, responsible for ruffling the unrufflable Duke Ericson? I hold myself back from striking a Rosie the Riveter pose.

"All right. If you think it's that important, I'll think of something."

And that's how you crack 'em, folx.

I'm in my room for once in my life when my phone starts blowing up.

Ruby hurls a pair of socks at me. We've been folding our laundry for the last half hour, chatting about her upcoming cello final, which is called a "jury" at music school. (I have a jury for piano lessons, too.) I've never taken an interest in Ruby's studies before, but *I'm making an effort*. Also, I'm her accompanist now, and she's a part of the orchestra pit for *Holding Up the Ocean*, so we have more to talk about these days.

The socks bounce off my voluminous chest. "Hey!" I protest, tossing the socks back at her.

She dodges my sock missile and rolls her eyes—but, like, affectionately. "Those are *your* socks, B. And are you gonna see what's going on with your phone?"

I've got a barrage of text messages and DMs in various apps, but at the top of the list is Liza. Fifteen unread messages. A cannonball drops through my middle and lands on my feet, which promptly start sweating. This much Liza commotion could *only* be bad, as she's about as enthusiastic and bubbly about good news as a Tibetan monk.

> Liza: OMG, did you see the thing on
> YouTube?
> Liza: B?
> Liza: BRIDGET VENUS BLOOM, ANSWER
> ME RIGHT NOW

And so on like this for another five messages, with increasing threat levels, until the last of them:

> Liza: I'm coming for you.

Just like a teen horror movie, the knocking starts at exactly the moment I finish reading the last message from Liza.

"Tell me you've seen it," she says, pushing into the room.

I grimace. "I haven't seen it."

She's already got whatever it is pulled up on her phone. "Get over here, then. You too," she says, gesturing for Ruby to join us on the bed. We huddle together around her phone, three little peas in an extra-long-twin pod.

The video starts with a close-up of Duke's face. "Hey, loyal fans," he says, issuing his signature blinding smile. This was the smile that did me in the first time I saw a Duke video. Now, I see it and feel a whole lot of nothing. Funny, how time and circumstance can change everything.

"I've had the time of my life making these YouTube videos, and it's humbling that so many of you love them. But there's one thing—you could call it a secret"—here, he leans into the camera and cups the side of his mouth with his hand, like he's really telling the viewer something in confidence—"I haven't told anyone. Until today."

A picture of two little kids flashes on-screen, one tall and curly headed, one small and impossibly freckled. Duke and Max, Duke's arm slung around Max's skinny shoulders.

Duke intones the voice-over. "This is me and my best friend, Maxwell Griffin, but you can call him Max."

Another photo, both of them a little taller, Max on guitar, Duke behind a keyboard. "Max and I started making music together when we were eleven years old. We covered a lot of old Queen and Journey songs, stuff we'd grown up listening to with our parents." A picture of Max and Duke wearing matching Bon Jovi shirts.

"Over the years, we fell into a groove of what music stuff we each did best. I was more of a singing guy, Max liked making up songs on his guitar."

A photo of both boys, a little younger than they are now, on a stage together, Max perched on a stool with his guitar, Duke in the foreground singing into a microphone.

"One day Max handed me a piece of paper with lines of scribbles and capital letters and he said, 'Play this.' At first I thought he'd lost his mind, but when I looked at the page closer, I realized it was a song." A shiver rolls through me as I realize I've seen the very page Duke speaks of.

Duke's video of "Sandwiches" starts. The music fades, with Duke's speaking voice mostly drowning out his singing. "This was the song that came from those scribbles. My buddy, Max Griffin, wrote 'Sandwiches,' and he wrote all of the other songs I've done for YouTube."

Back to just Duke's face, now as serious as a defendant awaiting his verdict. "I didn't give Max credit for the ghostwriting he's done for me. This might sound like a bad excuse, but I didn't think he wanted the attention. Recently, though, a friend reminded me that giving credit where credit is due is important. So, here's to Maxwell Griffin, songwriter extraordinaire!"

A black-and-white photo of Max, again seated on a stool, his leather jacket over a faded band T-shirt, flashes across the screen. His body arches over his guitar, but his eyes gleam up at the camera, the upward curve of his mouth mischievous, almost coy. I didn't know he had that in him. I wonder who was behind the camera the day that photo was snapped. Maybe Sam? Or maybe a hot music theory genius, because if there's anything that could get Max to look even remotely flirty, it'd involve theory.

Max's social media handles fade in at the bottom of the picture, where they remain as the final strains of "Sandwiches" die out.

Liza locks her phone and lets it fall into her lap. For a span of probably fifteen seconds, we sit in cinder-block silence.

Ruby speaks first. "Whoa."

"Yeah, whoa is right." Liza fiddles with the phone, tossing it up and down against her legs.

More Ruby. "That was either really stupid or really brave. Maybe both. I wonder what got into him?"

"Me." My voice catches in my throat, and I'm clearing it when Liza and Ruby, in stereo, say:

"What?"

"Me. The friend he mentioned, who said that giving credit where credit is due is important? That was me."

Ruby's got her eyebrows all out of order, in an expression I would title Dubious Lite, and Liza's face I would call What the Fuck.

I relay my discovery of Max's notebook, what I learned, and the confrontation I had with Duke about it.

Liza's hands grasp fistfuls of my comforter. "I can't believe Duke would do something like this."

"Honestly, he seemed to think Max was fine with the 'arrangement' they had." I draw the air quotes with force.

"How could he think that?" Liza's voice is climbing by octaves with every new statement, and I'm halfway afraid she's gonna shatter the one mirror still up in here—Ruby's, mounted inside the closet door.

"I don't know, but . . . just talk to him. Give him a chance to explain himself." I don't know who the hell I've become, giving up the guy I've liked forever, *then* trying to keep my best friend involved with him. Is this kind of behavior what it means to grow up? What's next, a 401(k)? Mortgage? Dentures?

"Yeah, I agree with Bridget. I mean, this is shocking for sure, but we don't really know the whole story. Better talk it through with Duke before making any conclusions." Ruby lays her hand on Liza's knee.

Liza's quiet, her head pointed toward her lap, hair hanging like curtains on either side of her face. Then she sniffles and her shoulders start trembling. Oh my God, the sky is falling. Liza's not a crier.

I pick up one of her hands, and she turns her big brown tear-soaked eyes toward me. "Is it wrong that I'm hurt? I feel like he lied to me."

"It's okay to feel hurt. Feelings are never wrong," I say, parroting words Dad has said to me so many times. I stroke my thumb across her soft hand. "All we're saying is, getting more info from Duke might help. And if what he tells you sucks, we'll totally help you TP his room and post ruinous videos of him on Insta."

We sit like that on my bed, Liza sardined between me and Ruby, until the crying stops, and all the while I wonder how I ever got so lucky as to have a friend who will let me be with her at her worst.

TWENTY-EIGHT

THE ROT IS A MOB scene on Monday morning. A clump of students is mutating around one of the tables like a big, cancerous cell. It's not until I'm well into the middle of the cafeteria that I realize it's Duke's table the horde has descended on. *My* table. But Duke's not even there.

The center of attention is Max.

But of course! Everyone's seen the video by now.

I don't even attempt to get to Max, but I do peer between busybodies as I pass. He looks about as excited as someone on the receiving end of an enema. He's gripping the table for dear life, jaw clenched solid. A short blond theater kid named Peony stands way too close to his face, and he nods mechanically at whatever she's saying, then squeezes out a pinched ambiguous grimace smile.

Huh. How is he not thrilled about hitting the fast track to stardom?

Maybe he's the kind of guy who's clammy with compliments. Seems the type, now that I think about it. I'm just getting seated when he bolts, cutting a straight line through the middle of the crowd.

Guess I'll check in with him later.

After class I hit the practice room for myself for once. I've got a piano seminar test coming up, and though I'm already competent enough with the material to do fine, I'm learning that a little extra practice never hurt anybody.

Triton 212 is open. I don't think anyone else even tries to use it anymore, given how often I'm in there. The room next door, however, is *quite* occupied. Loud, angry piano music rolls out like a tsunami, fantastic and lethal. Someone's playing one of the virtuoso Romantic-era composers—it's got to be Rachmaninoff or maybe Liszt—and they're doing the composer proud. I squint through the teeny crack left in the door.

The pianist's barely visible forehead is covered in freckles.

I've heard Max play before, but hearing *this* is an entirely different experience. A pleasurable ache grabs hold of my breastbone and squeezes, and everywhere, everywhere, I tingle, like my skin's covered in Pop Rocks. Maybe it's because I'm used to Max's folky-pop piano vibe, whereas *this* is all verve. Or maybe it's about that moment we shared at the end of our last tutoring hour, our hands twined together across the top of the table. Lately I'm seeing there's more to Max than sage, self-deprecation, and pretty

251

melodies. He is passion personified, and goddamn, it's sorta hot if I'm being honest.

He finishes the song with a series of big and impressive chords, and I'm so wowed by him and so overwhelmed with the full-body glow that the ground sways, just quickly. Two seconds of music-induced vertigo. I've never been more of a delicate flower than right effing now. Is this what smelling salts are for?

I take two deep breaths and the world rights itself, because of course it does. I push into Max's room, applauding with gusto, my face feeling like it does at the end of a really satisfying musical. My smile stretches so wide it hurts, but I can't stop it.

He rears up to his feet as I enter the room but then sits again, just as quickly. "You've got a knack for getting into other people's business, don't you."

I start to laugh, because I assume he's playing, we're joking around together, ha ha . . . but he's not looking at me. His eyes are focused straight ahead, at the music holder with no music on it.

Silence descends like summer damp, cloying and so thick, it's almost palpable.

"I'm sorry. I was just so impressed with your playing. You're really good. So, so good. And from memory, too? Wow." I take a tentative step forward.

"That's the thing, though: I wasn't performing for you, or for anyone. My music is for *me*." He speaks into the piano.

"Don't you care that you're gifted in a way that not many people are? Why would you hide that? It's such a waste."

"It's *not* a waste if I don't *need* the attention. If I'm getting enjoyment out of it, if it's serving the purpose I have for it, then why do I need to share it? Is it any less valid if I'm the only one who hears it?"

"Yes!"

"Just . . . take a beat, B. Think."

I smash my lips together and peer toward the sky, really trying. "I feel like we're getting into the 'if a tree falls in a forest and nobody hears it, does it make a sound' debate."

A smattering of humor crosses his face, but he quashes it. "Fair enough. I guess all I'm saying is that I'm happy with my music being just for me. And clearly, you don't get that."

"What's that supposed to mean?"

"What I mean is: Why in the hell did you tell Duke to give me credit for all those songs? Don't you know me at all?"

You know when your computer takes a shit and you get the blue screen of death? That's what happens to my brain. I can't form thoughts or words and certainly can't formulate a cogent response. What Max just said to me will not compute.

Finally, that's what I go with. Because I have nothing else. "I don't get what you mean."

Max growls. I'm serious, he *growls* like a wolf-man, a deep rattle in the back of his throat. It'd be funny if it wasn't so startling. "I don't *want* credit! I don't *want* notoriety, or accolades, or attention. I just want to make music, for the sake of music. Everything else is extraneous. And I thought you understood. I thought . . . I thought we were alike, in that way."

Me? Unassuming, seeking to blend in? When pigs write arias, Max Griffin. "Why did you think that?"

"Because it oozes out of you, all the time. Your face, your

presence, the very pores of your body, it all radiates music, music, music, and your passion for it. Especially when we're writing together—do you have any idea of what you look like, when you're composing? It's like you . . . *glow*. There's fire in your hands and eyes and words when you're making music. And to then learn you'd decided to stay at Richard James even though you didn't get into the MFP and aren't allowed to perform? I thought it meant your love for the craft, for the very essence of what music is, was bigger than your need to be seen."

I'm not sure if Max sees something in me that I can't or if he's missing this vital, central thing about me. He's making my whole world tilt on its axis, and it's unsettling to say the least.

"And . . . I know the level of your sacrifice. I *know*. I've heard you sing, and not just in the music lab with me. I heard you that night you helped Duke get home."

"What?" I squeak—I'm not in control, the words are just falling out of me. "How?"

"Top bunk."

My body goes rigid, from my toes to my bulging eyes. The blunt force of what he's just said demolishes me, like I'm lying in the road and his words are a Mack truck that drives over me, then reverses, then drives over again. He was in the room that night? That tender, private moment with Duke that I've since banished to a secret but sacred place in my heart was shared by another. Intruded upon.

In my stunned silence, Max pushes on. "It all happened so fast, and I didn't know how to tell you I was there, and then you were singing . . . and you've got the voice of a goddess or a siren or something, I don't know, but it was one of the loveliest things I've ever heard, and to know you aren't allowed to use that and stayed at Richard James anyway . . ."

My legs find a nearby chair, and I sit. "Why didn't you ever say anything about it?"

"I tried, the morning after it happened. We were interrupted. And then afterward I never found a good time to bring it up."

My body is still as my brain works overtime, trying to see the last few weeks through the lens of Max knowing what he knows. Finally, I'm able to distill the essence of my confusion enough to speak. "I still don't see how you and I are the same."

His eyes are sad and much, much too old to be in the vicinity of so much peach fuzz. "There were things I thought I knew about you that reminded me of me. First, that you'd do anything for the sake of music, and second, that you could put someone else's needs before yours."

"And now?"

His gaze skitters away. "And now, when it comes to the latter, I'm not so sure. Or maybe you only put Duke's needs first, no one else's."

Ouch.

There's a part of me that wants to stay and fight. I want to convince Max my heart was in the right place when I guilted Duke into giving him credit for his songwriting. But there's a bigger, louder, and I think righter piece of me that's screaming, *Intent doesn't matter. Not this time.*

And to be honest, I think I'm too hurt to fight. So hurt, that he would think I would do for Duke what I wouldn't do for him. A few weeks ago that was probably true, but now . . . it's far, far from it.

I make my sluggish legs take me to the threshold of the door. "I assume we're not on for tutoring this week."

"You'll be fine in theory class, and for next year's test, as long as you keep reviewing. The songwriting was extra." He speaks to the grainy console piano rather than to me. "I stopped billing the school for tutoring as soon as we started the songwriting stuff. Because it was maybe as much for me as for you."

That disclosure hits me in the face and in the heart. I want to ask more—why keep meeting with me for no money, *why* not work with someone who already knows how to write music—but wouldn't that be making everything about me, yet again? I need to let this be about Max, so I stay quiet for once in my life.

I think back to the day he said the world needed my voice. Does he still think that? Does he still want that for me?

And because I'm too scared to ask, and far too scared to answer the question myself, I nod and leave the room.

TWENTY-NINE

HANS IS SITTING CROSS-LEGGED ON the wood floor when I make the shop door jingle, the sun plunging down into the city skyline behind me. Towers of books box him in, though he's left a tiny opening in the front of the square.

"Athena! How unexpected!" He scratches his head. "It *is* Wednesday, isn't it?"

"Yeah, it's Wednesday."

At this time on a Wednesday I'm usually with Max, but since theory and songwriting with him have now gone the way of Freddie Mercury, I've got time on my hands. Idle time. Restless time.

I make a slow circle around the stacks of books, leaning in closer to check out some of the titles. *Emma. The Taming of the Shrew. Don Quixote.* Loads of classics, and many of the spines still looking tip-top.

"New stuff today?"

Hans runs a hand lovingly over his recent haul. "A collector died last week, and I acquired these at his estate sale. Beauties, they are, and many of them first editions."

"Amazing." I reach out to touch one but pull my hand back just in time, remembering I need to wear gloves to work with the books. Hans taught me a few weeks ago that acid from your skin can damage fragile, aged paper—and you can't know, until you open a book and check out its pages, which ones are most vulnerable.

Just like Max and his dislike for being seen. I didn't know that soft spot was there until I stuck my finger right into it.

Much as I want to play in the books with Hans, I don't want to make any more messes this week. "I'll tidy up." I grab the cleaning supplies and head back to the inventory, body on autopilot, as I've done this so many times now. My arm stops short as I come upon the shelf where the wooden owl has preened for the past several weeks. Hans must have moved him. Yet, as I work my way over shelves and tables, there's no sign of the owl.

"Hans?"

He peers up at me from his book fortress. "Yes, dear?"

"Did you sell the owl?"

"Indeed, the owl has found a home."

Something starts up in my chest—a little ache, a tiny fire. It's sadness, I suppose. I should be thrilled that someone purchased him, after all the hard work I did to show him off. But I'm not. I guess it's fair to say I'll miss that silly little guy.

I'm not sure what to say about that, so I only nod. "Care if I spend some time with the letters today?"

"Of course, of course. I left them under the counter for you."

Passively, I wonder why Hans doesn't have me wear gloves to look at the letters. The pages are no less precious than the prose in *Beowulf* or whatever. Despite the many pictures I've taken, Hans never questions my desire to keep physically touching the pages. I imagine he understands why. There's something about holding the actual documents that June and Socks created that's special, almost mystical. The yellowed paper and faded ink makes me feel closer to them, and maybe also closer to figuring out how love works. Clearly, I've still got a lot to learn.

In any case, my bare hands slide open the cedar box, itching for revelation—not only about love, but about music. We've fictionalized the June and Socks story and made it our own for the musical, but something still feels missing. I'm starting to think we need that sixth song, but I have no idea what it should be about.

Surely there's something song-worthy in these pages I haven't noticed before.

I get my first taste of a clue about fifteen minutes in, in a letter written by June.

Remember how I told you a few months ago that my mother seemed to doubt you and me? I was right, because last night she up and said, "June, are you sure you should be waiting for that boy?" And I said to her, "I'm absolutely sure. Because he makes me feel safe, and wanted, and like I'm the most interesting person in all the world." Ma smiled and said that sounded like love. So Ma's finally on our side.

June makes no reference to Socks's qualities—his kindness, good looks, or humor—though she talks about those in other letters. What she mentions specifically, when talking to her mother about the man she loves, is *how he makes her feel*. Safe. Wanted. Interesting. Huh. Love's a pretty hard thing to put into words, but that definition's not half-bad.

I feel safe, wanted, and interesting around my dads, and I know they love me. So the definition works there. I also feel those ways around Liza.

Did I ever feel any of those ways with Duke? It pains me to admit it, but if I'm being honest . . . no. I don't think Duke found me any more interesting than he did anyone else. And *never* did I feel safe. Not in a "he's a creeper" way, more like I was sitting on a bed of needles every time we were together. Ugh, why are the hindsight lenses always so much clearer than the in-the-moment ones?

Hans is up and shuffling over, peeling off his gloves as he nears. "Anything worth discussing today?"

I twist a curl around my index finger as I consider putting my heart out in the open, but after all, it *is* just Hans. "I'm trying to understand love. What makes someone fall in love with someone?"

"Ah." Hans strokes his chin. "That is a most complicated question."

"Tell me about it."

"Is this for you, or for a song?" His eyes twinkle a little.

"Both."

"Ah. Did the letters provide any answers?"

"A few, and also more questions. June says she knows Socks is the one for her because of how he makes her feel: safe, wanted, and interesting. But is that the only way people feel around each other when they're in love?" I prop my elbows up on the counter and plunk my head into my hands.

"What do you think?"

"Do you always answer questions with questions?"

Hans smiles and says nothing. He can be seriously coy for an old guy.

"I guess what I imagine is . . . maybe there are many ways people feel when they're in love. Happy, and excited, and maybe . . . nervous?" The ways I felt about Duke. Before I'd ever even *met* Duke. And then around him, in real life.

Hans nods.

"But I'm thinking maybe you could feel all of those ways on a first date, too, and not be in love with the person. Like, I can be excited to go get a piece of pizza with somebody but not be ready to tie the knot with that person."

More nodding from the peanut gallery.

"So maybe excited and happy and nervous is part of love, maybe the very beginning part. And . . . the stuff June said, feeling safe and wanted and interesting, maybe that comes a little later. I'm not gonna lie, I'd never thought of any of this before, but it sounds important for love. Love beyond a crush. Real love."

Nervous, excited—that was as far as things ever got with Duke. Nothing deeper. Nothing more valuable. I was in like with him, never in love with him. And honestly, that's a little startling.

"Wise conclusion, Athena."

Yeah, I *am* pretty wise. So wise, in fact, there's another windstorm of an idea swirling in my cranium. I scrunch my forehead all up because I'm having a hard time putting words to it. Things are shifting, transforming, little origami cranes of new ideas, trying to take flight even through the storm in my mind.

It's inspiration, of course. Because it's me.

"Maybe love at first sight is kind of bullshit."

"Say more."

"Well, let's take Socks and June. They meet. They really like each other's company, and June feels safe and wanted and interesting and Socks seems to feel the same. *But*, where the love really grows is through the letters. He asked her to wait, and she does, but if they hadn't corresponded all that time, told each other their life stories . . . and *proved* their dedication to the relationship through all of that writing . . . would love have remained? Would it have deepened? Would she have waited?" I shake my head. "I kind of doubt it."

Hans's eyes crinkle at the corners, the perfect complement to his wide, warm smile.

"The letters were their way of showing up for each other when that was all they could do. Maybe part of love is showing up."

"I think you're starting to understand, my dear."

Ruby paces the hallway outside the auditorium, the click of her heels echoing off clean tile and eggshell walls.

"Hey. Ruby."

She glances over at me but keeps pacing.

"You're gonna be fine. You've got this. Seriously, you nailed the piece every time we practiced this week. Hell, even last week."

262

She flails her hand at me, too quick and floppy to be a proper wave. I'm not really sure what she means by it, but if I had to guess, I'd say, "Oh shoosh, I'll be nervous if I want to be nervous, and also I have no blood in my head right now because it's all in my limbs so please don't ask me to talk."

Just a guess.

So I let her pace and feel her feels, and I chill on one of the chairs that lines the hallway, scrolling through my social media feeds. Max has gained thousands of followers across platforms over the past week. Any other MFP kid would be thrilled. But of course, I have to come to the rescue of the one weird boy *in a music program* who *doesn't want attention for being good at music*, because *that's* a thing that makes sense.

Boys will probably be the death of me. What a stupid way to go, too.

Dr. Chen, the head strings professor, appears at the stage doors of the auditorium. "Ruby, we're ready for you."

Ruby's wide blue eyes dart to me, and I give her a double thumbs-up before throwing my arm around her shoulders and steering her toward her fate. On the threshold of where backstage meets visibility, I detach myself and face her. "You're gonna kill it."

She can't quite muster a smile but does pull herself up straight, like her spine's suddenly had a yardstick inserted into it. To my great surprise and even greater pleasure, she walks onto the stage like she owns the joint, face neutral, shoulders low. Impressive. I trail in well behind her and with far less presence and seat myself behind the piano.

"Ruby Deterding, sophomore, first-semester jury," she says

for the benefit of the audio equipment that will record her jury. She lowers herself gracefully into her chair, handling her cello like it's an extension of her body. First, she plays a series of scales she has prepped, and then, she tackles music the committee has selected for her to sight-read. The surreptitious glances among the jury panel tell me I'm not the only one who thinks Ruby's on fire.

Finally, her prepared solo. She looks up at me and nods. She has this way of closing her eyes—longer than a blink but not too long—that is elegance personified. It's my cue, so I start the accompaniment to her piece.

Ruby plays like her life depends on it. Truly, there are times during the solo I have a hard time focusing on being an accompanist, not a spectator. The deep, resonant thrums of Ruby's cello tap into a bone-level sanctum that I didn't know existed, and her music picks me up by my sternum and moves me. No, more than moves me—it *changes* me. By the end I have tears pooling and I don't even bother to blink them away. I know Ruby's accompaniment front to back; a little blurring around the edges of the paper won't hurt me.

"Thank you, Ruby. Lance, can you please cut the recording?"

"No problem. You're officially off the record, Dr. Chen," says—presumably—Lance from someplace offstage.

Dr. Chen walks up to the stage. Her eyes are too bright, and there's a ghost of a tear track on her right cheek. "Ruby. That was incredible. Your audition for the MFP was memorable, but that, my dear, was something else entirely. Well done, and welcome to the beginning of what I can only assume will be a very celebrated musical career." The two judges who remained back in the middle of the auditorium now stand. One of them shouts, "Brava!" and both applaud enthusiastically.

Ruby's cool stage presence slips away and her face splits open with pure joy.

Rarely does Ruby talk about past honors and awards, but I know after working with her, and especially after hearing her today, that they must have been aplenty. Ruby's not a shouter. She's stealthy, a whisperer of ideas and even quieter about herself.

And yet this quiet, unassuming wisp of a person can command the attention, respect, and even admiration of tough judges, who themselves are all seasoned string professionals.

I can't help but compare myself to her as a performer. I am a force, a juggernaut. If there's space to fill, I shout my way into every crevice, every nook and cranny. If there's praise up for grabs, I do my damnedest to snatch it. I am demanding in my pursuit of attention, always looking to take center stage.

Then there's Ruby.

She and I, we both work hard. We both *want this* thing— music—and we sweat and weep and bleed for it. And now I see that it sings in her every bit as much as it sings in me, though Ruby's way is quieter. She garners admiration and respect simply because she *is*. She doesn't need to be flashy, doesn't need to demand attention. She *commands* it.

And maybe . . . just maybe . . . I can, too.

THIRTY

"HEY, WATCH IT, HELICOPTER ARMS! You about took off my head!" With one hand on her popped hip and one eyebrow hitched so high it nestles into her hairline, I honestly can't tell if Amber's kidding around or seriously being mean.

Danica takes her for serious. "Ugh, I'm *sorry*, but if you'd get your blocking right it wouldn't *matter* what my arms were doing."

Amber adds the second hand to her other hip and glares. Oh. She *was* kidding, before. This is what she looks like when she's for real pissed.

I let my eyes fall closed, the beginnings of a tension headache needling my forehead. It's four days 'til opening night of *Holding Up the Ocean*, and while rehearsals are overall going okay, the pressure of being ready—and getting everything right—is getting under everyone's (rather thin) skins.

Amber and Danica both look to Duke, who's still acting as unofficial leader.

Which is awful, because he still sucks at leading.

"Umm. Amber, you, umm . . . I mean, Danica! I think you . . . ," he stammers, and tugs at his hair.

Liza steps up. "You're both right. Danica, bring your arm swinging down just a tad right there, and Amber, move your blocking about a foot to the left. Easy fix. Let's go." Which is in my opinion the perfect feedback, though I'm trying to leave the choreography to those who are doing it.

Currently, we're on our third run-through of "Seven Sisters." Pretty sure these zigzagging, catchy lines and tight harmonies are gonna haunt me in my dreams until the end of time.

I exchange an eye roll with Ruby, who's now in attendance at rehearsals along with the rest of the orchestra pit. Max is down there, too, on guitar, but whenever I look over at him he's got his nose buried in his music stand. It's hard to say whether that's just Max being Max or if he's intentionally avoiding eye contact with me, but I'd bet two opening-night-on-Broadway tickets it's the latter.

Liza's waiting for me at the door of the auditorium on my way out. As I predicted, she's a very good Rosie—not that I'm going to tell my musically apathetic best friend that. "Hungry?" she asks as she links her arm through mine.

"Hungry for a little silence." I massage my forehead with my free hand.

"Wanna eat off campus? Pizza? No. Wait. What about—"

"Oh, you know it."

About a month ago I took Liza to Hans's shop to meet him, and on the way back we stumbled upon a hole-in-the-wall falafel restaurant, Persian Palace, the doors of it covered in playbills and social justice organizational material and flyers for art exhibits. We had to go in, of course. What we found inside were snug low tables and dim lighting, worn carpet but spotless surfaces, and the friendliest, sweetest owners, Adnan and Sana, a young couple from Iran. Maybe it was because we were starving, or maybe it was because our expectations were high based on the ambience, but no matter what it was, Liza and I agreed it was the best damn food we'd had in weeks.

We've been back twice since.

And I know without asking: that's where we're going now.

Two hours later we traipse back to campus, stomachs full of chickpeas and tabbouleh and grape leaves and olives. Spirits renewed, energy replenished, and most important, headaches banished.

We open the doors to our hall and Piper's there, face in her phone. She looks up and relief floods her features. "Oh, thank goodness. Where have you girls been? Don't you ever check your phones?"

Liza and I have a policy of silencing our phones when we eat together. Now, however, we grab them out of our pockets with a breakneck speed that comes from hours of practice. "Why? What's going on?"

Piper opens her frowning mouth to speak, but Liza beats her to the punch. "Mom's called an emergency mandatory meeting for everyone involved with the musical. And it's starting in five minutes."

Nothing with "emergency mandatory" in the title ever bodes well.

Liza and I *run* to the auditorium—I'm not kidding, it's a dead sprint. I wished I'd opted for a sports bra this morning. All the heads in the room swivel to check us out as our panting bodies burst through the back entrance. We're the show before the show, the fate of latecomers for any performance. We grab seats at the rear of the hall just as the click of stiletto heels announces Octavia's presence, well before she's visible. A hush falls over us as the rhythmic footsteps fall louder, and Octavia appears at stage right, impeccably dressed in a smart black pencil skirt and white blouse. Does the woman ever shut off? Does she even own a pair of jeans, or—*gasp*—athleisure? I make a mental note to ask Liza.

She doesn't smile as she taps at the lone microphone on a stand at center stage. "Good evening, students. I regret to inform you that Danica Townsend and Chastity LeFevre were caught with marijuana in one of the dormitory bathrooms this evening. As all forms of drug use are expressly prohibited for Richard James students per the student code of conduct, they are suspended from all school activities until further notice."

The nervous murmuring starts, because our show is now down two major players. The loss of Danica is a crushing blow—and Chastity, a chorus member, was her understudy.

Octavia holds up one crimson-nailed hand. The whispers quiet as students turn their attention back to the stage. "As this is a student-led musical, you're now faced with the task of recasting and recalibrating. Choose wisely." And then she walks offstage— slowly, casually, like this is all just totally normal for her—and plants her ass in the back of the auditorium. She's going to revel in watching us flail.

Or maybe because she wants to exert some influence—as MFP chair or as Liza's mom.

Everyone looks, as they always do, to Duke. Max, who's sitting by him, elbows him in the ribs—hard. "Oh! Um, yeah. Okay, who has ideas?"

I put my head in my hands, because it's the only way to hide my massive and uncontrollable eye roll.

Amber stands up. "I think Liza should take over the role of June." As she sits back down, her eyes drift to where Octavia sits, and I realize that Amber's need for authority figure approval is *pathological*.

Liza rears up beside me, her mouth already open to protest, when Duke replies, "Oh yeah, great idea, Amber! Who's in favor?"

And of course because Duke endorsed this plan, everyone else will. And how could they not, with Octavia still in the room? Hands go up all around the auditorium, but not mine. And not Liza's. Liza has now slumped as far down in her seat as she can without her ass slipping off onto the floor.

"Great, whew, that was simple enough! Sydney, can you take Liza's place as Rosie?" Sydney Marks, the only sophomore in Advanced Solo class and a member of the chorus, nods so enthusiastically that I think her head might fly off her neck. "We can make a go of it with one less chorus member, I think. Everyone okay with that?" No one disagrees. "All right! Meeting's over!"

Max stands up. "Wait wait wait. We're going to need extra

practices to make this work, obviously. Double practice tomorrow, seven a.m. and six p.m."

There's a fair amount of grumbling and many weary shoulder slumps, but everyone must realize Max is right. This is a major, major change of plans, and we only have four days to pull it off.

Students file out, everyone side-eyeing us as they go. Liza hasn't moved so I sit tight, too, in solidarity. Duke tries to fist-bump her as he exits, but she shoots him a look so nasty he pulls his arm back and keeps walking. Max, who's with him, blows us off.

The last student's gone, and then it's just me and Liza. And Octavia, who's barreling at us like a hawk about to swoop in on field mice. But Liza darts quickly out of the row, black hair flying behind her like a cape. Within a foot of Octavia she stops and pulls herself out of her usual slouch, bringing herself to eye level with her mother. Some field mouse Liza makes.

"How could you?"

"Darling, what do you mean? I had nothing to do with Danica's poor choices."

"Oh, cut the crap. You knew—we *all* knew—Danica's a pothead. You can't tell me you didn't wait for this moment, this *exact moment*, to bust her."

"And pray tell, dear daughter, why I would intentionally pull the lead from my school's biggest public performance of the year? Doesn't that seem rather like self-sabotage to you?"

"Any other year, yes. But this year, no. You did it because you knew this gave me a shot at the lead, and *then* you stuck around to make sure that happened."

"How did my sitting quietly in the back *make* that happen?"

"You're the MFP chair *and* the dean! And you're my mom! Do you think the students are immune to that kind of influence?"

"Nonsense. You were chosen because you are an exceptionally talented singer."

Lila snorts. "When are you going to stop trying to live vicariously through me, Mom? *When?* When I was four, I thought maybe you'd stop when I went to kindergarten. And when I was ten, I hoped in middle school, you'd back off. But. You. Never. Did. And now here we are."

Octavia's shoulders seem to droop for a moment during Liza's tirade, but she pulls them back again and her chin with them. "Yes. Here we are. You will make a wonderful June."

"And you will never, *ever* make a good mother."

Liza whirls and runs up the stage stairs, disappearing behind the velvet curtain. Octavia, after shooting me one bold, unreadable look, clicks off in the other direction.

I find Liza backstage, where she's pretzeled up on a folding chair, crying into her knees.

"Hey," I say, kneading one of her shoulders.

"I can't do this. I really can't."

"That's what you said about being Rosie, too, remember? And look how well that's been going."

"Yes, but that was different. Much as I hate to admit it, I make a good Rosie. But me, as June? Have you ever heard of a worse choice for that role?" She turns her black-rimmed eyes up to mine to gauge my reaction, and I'm sure she can see the truth written on my face.

Liza as June is a terrible idea. June's defining characteristic is that she's bubbly. Perky. Indefatigable. Liza's about as naturally peppy as Eeyore, and while she's a decent actress, she's not *that* good.

"See! Even you agree."

I grimace. "It doesn't matter. You can do the part. I'll help you."

"Can you teach me to tap-dance in three days?" Her tone's sardonic. This is rhetorical.

I feel my jaw unhinge but can't help it. "You. Can't? Tap?" June and Socks have a major tap-dance bit in the musical.

She sniffles loudly and wipes her nose with her forearm. "I was trained years ago, but I'm, like, truly awful. I'm so bad Mom actually let me quit when I was eight, after the teacher strongly suggested that I stick with jazz."

Good. Lord.

"Okay, well, the tap dancing isn't essential. We'll figure out something else you can do during that part." Surely, we as a cast and crew can come up with something.

"This is gonna be a mess, B."

I squeeze her into my side, trying to offer her the comfort of touch, but say nothing.

Because this musical *really is* gonna be a mess, y'all.

THIRTY-ONE

THE NEXT DAY'S FIRST REHEARSAL is abysmal in every way. Liza's jittery and sulky, the antithesis of June. Worse yet, even though I know she knows the part well enough, she misses half her cues.

It's a nightmare. You can see it on the faces of the rest of the cast.

At the mid-rehearsal break, Duke mutters something in Liza's ear, and though I'm sure it was meant to be positive and encouraging, Liza bolts away like he's full of the plague, spitting, "Easy for you to say," over her shoulder like it's venom.

Though we desperately need the rehearsal time, Duke wraps practice a half hour early. "Let's pick up tonight, an hour earlier than planned, okay, folx?" He plasters a smile on his face, but it doesn't reach his panicked eyes.

"Bring your dinners with you," adds Max, and the entire cast and crew groans.

I offer to stay after rehearsal to help Liza work through some blocking and dance, and she reluctantly accepts. Duke also offers his help, but Liza shoos him away. She's wanted nothing to do with him since he basically volunteered her for the role, which for Liza was like being drawn out of the lottery for *The Hunger Games*. The opening song has a complicated dance number that I picked up on quickly, but Liza hasn't. I'm demonstrating a shuffle ball change for the fourth time (Liza wasn't kidding about sucking at tap) when her face undergoes a very weird, extremely unexpected transformation. Bye-bye, disgust; hello, hope.

"Bridget. *You* should be June."

I snort. "C'mon, Liza, you know I can't."

"I know you're not *technically* allowed to perform. And I don't know what would happen to you if you did this. But . . . just look at yourself. You *are* June."

What she's saying isn't fully registering. She of all people knows how doggedly I've stuck to my humility plan and that I'm still holding on to hope that Piper makes a financial miracle happen so I can come back next year. I know my chances are slim, but still, I can't just throw them away.

As if she's read my mind, she continues, "Like I said . . . I realize what I'm asking is a huge gamble. Maybe Mom would see this and kick you out of Richard James immediately. I don't know. But what if this is your moment to prove you deserve to be a part of the program? Save the school musical from certain disaster? How could the staff expel someone who'd done that?"

I cock my head to the side and push my lips together, considering. It's a decent point.

"And I will also admit I'm being kind of selfish here because, babe, I can't do this part. There is no version of me, not even me with a happier childhood, not even me on a caffeine bender, not even ideal me in a parallel universe where unicorns are real, who could pull off the role of June as we need her to be. You know it, and I know it, and *now* everyone else knows it, but no one will say it. If you take this on, you're not just doing it for the school . . . but for me. Because I will fail. In front of . . . everyone." Liza does her Liza thing, where she slouches to take up less space. Like she'd disappear if she could. I consider how awful a feeling it must be for her to perform at all, given that she truly would prefer to not be seen. But to perform and to flub, making a spectacle of herself? Liza's worst nightmare. It has to be.

A couple of months ago, I would have absolutely pounced on this opportunity without a hesitation, without a doubt. But something's shifted in me, and now I feel a vague sense of disappointment in being asked to perform onstage. I cowrote many of these songs. I wrote almost all of the piano accompaniment, and I was so looking forward to playing that part—the show's backbone, rather than the big hair. I've learned I can shine even when I'm not the center of attention, and being part of something bigger than me feels amazing.

I'm about to say no when I look back up at Liza's sad but hopeful face. I remember how even before she knew me, she saved me from failing in front of our entire theory class. And she's been there for me every single day since. Refusing to help her now would feel not only wrong, but cruel. So I find myself saying, "Can I take a few minutes to mull this over? It's kind of a lot."

"I mean, sure. You're the one with the power here, B."

From the back of the auditorium, I fire off a text, then dig the heels of my palms into my eyes. *Think, Bloom.* (Adios, mascara.)

Maybe motivation matters. Maybe—because this isn't really *about* me, it's about Liza—I'm still being true to these new ideas, these things I'm working on. Would saying yes to the role of June be putting someone else's needs before mine, the very thing Max doubts I can do? And would saying yes be a version of showing up for someone, like Socks and June did because they loved each other?

My phone rattles. A response to my question, which had been:

> Me: Hey, did you ever happen to figure out
> any financial help options for me for next
> year?

> Piper: I turned over every rock I could
> think to, but as far as I can tell there's
> nothing available for you this year. I'm so
> sorry. Maybe your dads could take out a
> loan?

I cringe at the thought. I won't ask them to. And they are *not* selling any more farmland on my behalf. I'll suck up my pride and finish my high school career in Lynch, where I can sing to my heart's content, but still no one will *see* me. Not the real me, the me I am now.

I exhale in a whoosh, breathless with the force of my realization. The me I am now wants to help the people I love, even at a great risk to her own dreams. And why not go out with a bang while I'm at it? With my decision firmly made, I stride toward Liza and the first and last performance I'll ever have as a Richard James Academy student.

Within thirty minutes, we are a party of fifteen. Liza's called in the entire cast, which makes sense, but then Ruby and her friend Lily arrive and I haven't the foggiest idea why. Max walks in last. Upon his entrance, all the hair on my arms stands straight up. I didn't expect him to be here for this, as he's not a cast member.

Liza's left her slouch backstage and now stands tall at the front. "Thanks, everyone, for coming back. After today's rehearsal, I think we can all agree that something has to change if we want this year's show to be a success. We need to make some important calls, and fast."

The group collectively nods, and Liza continues. "So. After much consideration, I'm stepping down as June. Sorry, Sydney, but I'm holding on to my role as Rosie."

Sydney looks crestfallen but nods.

Duke pipes up. "Wait, okay. Hold on. You're stepping down. Who's stepping up?"

Liza sweeps her arm toward me. "Bridget."

Cue the record-scratching sound that happens in old sitcoms, to mark a "Whaaaatttt?" moment.

Duke pulls a dubious face. "Huh. Well, that should really be a great show, given that Bloom doesn't sing."

"And that's where you're wrong. Max, would you mind?" She gestures at the piano, and suddenly it makes sense why Max is here. "Let's try 'I Knew.'"

Max plays the short intro, quiet and plaintive. My heart thumps like a subwoofer, because after all these long months, finally, *finally* I get to do the thing I love most in the world. When my cue arrives, I've already drawn my deep, steady breath, and the notes careen out of my mouth, my vocal cords fist-pumping their triumph. Deep contentment settles over me, even over my jackhammering heart.

I close my eyes and sing the story of June's love for Socks, which came so quick and certain that it scared her. A past me would have been thinking of Duke to find the feels to channel into this. But current me is thinking about Liza and about music. Things I actually love.

And there's grief in this song, about finding the one but having to quickly say goodbye to him. Those emotions are easy to find, too. Participating in this musical is the end of my yearslong dream; my Richard James swan song.

But Liza's worth it. My peers are worth it. My dads, too.

And *goddamn*, it feels amazing to sing.

The faces of my audience are so comical that I'd probably bust out laughing, if I had any space left for other feelings. Mouths hang open in disbelief and shock; Duke's face is lit up, full of joy and wonder and . . . something else. Please baby Jesus don't let it be recognition.

Even Max's stony face, the only part of him I can see behind the piano, has gone soft around the edges. He's not surprised, and he's not smiling. But he *is* looking at me, and he's not pissed. That's a start.

I sing through to the duet portion with Duke, which flows

seamlessly—even the dialogue in the middle. Liza motions for Max to keep playing, into "Holding Up the Ocean," which starts with Rosie. Liza sings it through; she really is a perfect Rosie. I hadn't realized how much I'd longed to be able to sing with my best friend, and the sheer satisfaction of it slides something home inside of me. The other singers chime in when they should, handling the random speaking parts and singing the chorus parts all throughout.

We wrap the song and everyone cheers. The auditorium hums with an energy so immediate, I almost feel like I can touch it. And I *know* I'm not the only one who notices. This is a group that gels. We're equipped for a killer performance.

Duke looks at me like he's never seen me before. *Or* possibly like some fuzzy memories are finally making sense.

Shit shit shit.

Duke croaks, "Bloom. You . . . you're—"

"Enormously talented, yes." Max cuts him off.

I flash Max a look of sheer gratitude. Did he also realize Duke was about to make a very poorly timed realization about a certain drunken night?

Jake (Bill, in the musical) grasps me by the shoulders. "You can sing! But . . . why haven't you? Before now?"

"Friends, it's a long story that I'll tell you some other time. For now, let's just get to work."

The group climbs up onto the stage, ready to practice. God bless them, every one of them. I'm about to join them up there when an unwelcome realization rips through my middle, so big that my knees go out. I sink into a cushy auditorium seat. "Liza. Wait. Small problem. Actually, huge problem."

"I take it you got to the part where you realized Danica's wardrobe won't work for you."

I nod into my lap. Danica's a size six at most. I am decidedly not. "Yep. That's exactly the part I'd gotten to."

"I'm already a step ahead of you. That's why Ruby and Lily are here." Liza gets their attention and gestures them over.

"What?"

"Lily's on the crew—she's the head of costume design."

"And Ruby's with me," adds Lily. "She's got a great eye for aesthetics."

What? She does? My brain will need a hot minute to figure *that* one out, but that's a problem for another day. For now I focus on Ruby and me, on the same team. Again. Who would've thought?

"B, I had no idea. I mean, your drunk singing was pretty good, but this . . ." Ruby's face is two saucers floating on ashy cream. She looks like she's seen a Bridget-size ghost.

"I'm sorry I kept it from you. Thanks for being here."

I turn to Lily, who's appraising my body in a way that might make me feel squirmy under other circumstances, but seriously, who's got time for self-consciousness? She whips out a tailor's tape. "Raise your arms, please." Lily swiftly takes a series of measurements, spouting numbers for Ruby to record.

Once satisfied with her data, she gives Liza a nod. "We've got this. Let's go make a battle plan," Lily says to Ruby, and the two of them head for the door. I take a moment to let myself feel absolutely awful for my not-so-gracious judgments of Ruby and Lily earlier in the year.

Fortunately, guilt is another thing I have no time for. I need every emotional and physical resource for practice. With Max sitting in as the new pianist, we run each song twice and many of the dance numbers several times—I mean, sure, I'm a quick study and light on my feet, but learning many weeks' worth of moves in a few days is a tall order. Still, I'm not too shabby, given this is my first night.

It doesn't go unnoticed. "How in the hell did you pick up these dance routines so quickly? I've been working at them for weeks," says Duke after we finish "Seven Sisters."

I shrug. "I'm a good dancer. And I work hard."

Duke shakes his head. "You're a regular ingenue. And your singing voice is so . . . familiar to me, somehow. Isn't that strange?"

"Huh. Yeah. That's super-weird." I turn my now super-sweaty body away, hoping that's enough to make him drop the subject.

Liza claps her hands to call everyone to attention. "Okay, folx, let's do 'I Knew' again. We're clunky and need to run the footwork a few more times."

I know she means "B is clunky," and I love her for not saying it like that.

We call it a night at two in the morning. I lie in bed, exhausted yet wide-awake. Excited as I am to finally get my two hours of stardom, sheer terror courses just underneath. For at least a half hour I let various outcome scenarios play out like mini-movies in my mind's eye. Octavia, thrusting her scarlet-tipped index finger at me, singing, "You're out," in her magnificent, terrifying stage voice. Seabass throwing victorious fists into the air when our company brings down the house on opening night. My dads beaming with pride as the show ends, faces falling when I greet them later with my room in boxes, ready for the long car ride back to Lynch. Eventually my dads turn into clowns, Octavia a Gorgon, and those are the last thoughts I have before my tired body tugs me down into the solace of dreamless sleep.

THIRTY-TWO

THE NEXT TWO DAYS ARE a flurry of clandestine rehearsals and slapdash fittings. Liza somehow keeps faculty away from the auditorium, probably because she hauled Duke, Mr. Charisma himself, with her to talk to Seabass and Octavia about a "need for privacy to boost team solidarity and confidence." Per Liza's report, Duke did his thing and charmed the pants off them, and their request for closed rehearsals was granted.

Watching Liza direct, correct, encourage, and inspire the rest of the cast is remarkable, especially given her general tendency to blend in. She's ten times the leader Duke is.

Duke's much better as a helper. He patiently stays right with me during every rehearsal, never complaining, even when I need to run the same set of lines five, six, seven times before I've got them. I'm realizing it wasn't only sheer dumb luck and natural talent that catapulted Duke into Insta-fame—he works for what he's got, alone and with others. And if there's one thing being at Richard James has taught me, it's that you can have loads of natural intelligence and talent, but even then, you've still got to put in the time. You've gotta play the scales until they're muscle memory. Run the flash cards until you've memorized every bone in the human body (which I did, a few days ago). Everyone here works so, so hard.

Another thing I've learned—people can surprise you. Case in point: Ruby. "Arms up, B," she says as she pins the back of the white blouse currently draped on my body. Lily's standing back, surveying her progress.

"Yeah, that's better. We'll just take it in that much," mumbles Lily, her mouth full of straight pins.

These girls have spent hours and hours over the past two days crafting a wardrobe for my curvier-than-Danica June. It's now Friday morning, and dress rehearsal is this evening at the off-campus theater the academy uses for major productions. Richard James excuses all MFP students completely on dress rehearsal day, that's how big of a deal the musical is. As for me, I'm basically skipping school, but what does it matter at this point?

This is my third fitting session with Lily and Ruby. Thankfully, they've about got the costuming whipped. "We'll have the last adjustments done well ahead of dress rehearsal tonight."

"Thank you, Ruby. Seriously. Thank you."

She waves me off, but her tiny smile lights up her whole face.

I start the aimless journey back to my room. We agreed, as a cast, that we couldn't possibly rehearse any more today, so that's out. I could do homework, but like I can focus. (Also, like it matters now.) My dads aren't coming in until tonight. Liza's going out to lunch with Duke's parents; Ruby's sewing something for me.

My feet point me toward the only place I can think of to go: When in Rome. When I arrive, Hans is sitting on his stool and staring into space, which throws me. In his native environment, he's a man of agency—always organizing, writing, polishing—but it's not "busy" movement. Hans's actions are all done with intent; he doesn't waste energy, but also, he doesn't waste time. Hans is the embodiment of mindfulness, if my psychology class definition can be trusted.

So my guess is that even as he sits, he sits with purpose. What looks to an outsider like a zone-out is likely to be something meaningful to Hans.

And I'm about to find out if I'm right about that. "Morning, Hans," I say as I come behind the counter.

"Athena! Happy Dress Rehearsal Day!"

"Thank you!"

"You will make a quintessential June. Rather perfect part for you, if I say so myself."

I stop in my tracks. "Wait. How did you know I'm playing June now?"

"A little bird might have told me."

A little raven-winged bird. "Ah."

"Now, be patient with me for a moment, Athena. I shall return." Hans bustles into the back room, reappearing a few minutes later with a tray holding various things. A kettle of tea. A plate of

286

scones. Two small boxes, gift wrapped in gold filigree paper. One single pink rose.

"I hoped you would stop in. A special tea for you in honor of all of your hard work!"

Tears rush into my ducts. "This is too much."

"No. It is just enough." He hands me the plate of pastries. "Here, let's eat, and then we'll get to the gifts."

With gratitude I demolish a scone, washed down with jasmine silver needle. Its heady florals anchor me to safety, because that's what this tea means to me now—comfort and something like *home*. As soon as I swallow my last bite, Hans holds out the smaller of the wrapped packages. "For you."

I generally get annoyed with those people who say shit like "Oh, this paper is too pretty to tear!" and then more or less unfold the paper that covers their presents. Yet here I am, enamored of the gold filigree wrapping and working to cause as little damage to it as possible. Under the last layer of paper is a white jewelry box. I snap it open and gasp.

"Do you like it?" Hans's eyes gleam with the mischief of a much younger person.

"Like it? I lo—" I cut myself off. "Yes, I like it very much." Because inside the box is the abalone necklace I admired on the day it came in, the shell still burning raucous shades of turquoise and indigo.

"Here, let me," says Hans as I struggle with the clasp. He stands behind me and fastens the necklace, the shell pendant shining like blue flames against my breastbone.

"Thank you. So much. It's gorgeous."

I'm surprised at the heft of the second package. When I see what's inside, I immediately start crying. The owl, *my owl*. "I thought you said he found a home?" I say, sniffling.

Hans hands me the handkerchief he keeps in his pocket. "He did. I knew his home was with you."

I wipe my nose and clutch the owl like a child snuggling a stuffed toy, so grateful for its presence.

"Athena. Do you love him?"

"Who?"

Hans sits quietly, elbows on his knees.

"Oh, the owl?" Well, do I? I consider. Week after week, though I could have paid attention to any trinket in the store—including items a lot more physically appealing or valuable than this homely wood-carved bird—I kept coming back to the owl. Something about him made me feel happy. So I put him on display, because I wanted him to be . . . loved. Loved like I love him.

"Yes, Hans. I love him."

Hans leans back in his seat, eyes sparkling in satisfaction. "That's what I thought you'd say. Your fondness seemed only to grow over time."

I finger the shell around my neck. "But why give me this, then, since you know I can't possibly love it?"

"To help you remember the difference."

Remember the difference. I'm tempted to ask him what he means, but so quickly I'm impressed with my own brain, I get there.

It's okay to like pretty things. Look at Hans and his shop,

full of the beautiful, the ornate, the precious, and yet he'd never admit to *loving* most of the items he stocks. The iridescent abalone I hold between my finger and thumb is stunning; who wouldn't like it? My other hand still curves around the owl, which for reasons I don't fully understand makes me feel calm and warm. Now the necklace and the owl are both mine, but still—there's a difference between the pretty things you like having around and the things you love.

I leave Hans's shop with a stomach full of scones, bag heavy with my owl, head stuffed with questions and answers. Even my hands bear extra—the pink rose, Hans informs me, is to deliver to Liza in honor of opening night. Always the gentleman, that Hans.

My heart bulges more than a little, gratitude spilling out of its seams. I'm grateful for Hans and his eternal patience and thoughtfulness. For Liza, because she came up with a genius—if incredibly risky—plan. For Ruby, coming through for me in my hour of need.

For Max. He gave me the gift of songwriting—his, mine. Ours. We're going to see the fruits of our labor play out onstage tonight, and I can't even imagine what that's going to set loose in me. Maybe someday, if he ever talks to me again, I'll be able to ask Max what it's like for him.

Hell, today I'm even able to find gratitude for Duke. He's been a gracious leading man to my leading lady, and he makes my best friend happy.

I'm going home after this semester, maybe even after tonight.

But I'll go home with so much more than I came with, and I'm *not* talking about my new antique goods.

I come up on a CVS, and with gratitude singing in exactly the way my voice hasn't been allowed to, I'm struck with an idea. Inspiration! My exploding heart and I duck into the drugstore.

An hour later, alone in my room, I fetch a few mirrors out of my closet. Out of my satchel, I grab the photos I printed at CVS. Pictures from my phone, from throughout my time at Richard James. Here's one of me and Ruby on our first day, snapped by Piper at our beginning-of-the-year floor meeting. Our smiles are strained, and we have no idea what's ahead of us. And here's another of us, from last night, Ruby holding the blouse to my body, pins in her hands and mouth, me crossing my eyes with my tongue out. Our new comfort level radiates out of that second picture, and my heart smiles to see it.

There's a selfie of me and Duke that we snapped after a solo rehearsal. And one of Hans, writing in his archaic ledger, a sunbeam lighting up only half his face. And one just of Max, which I snuck one day when I crept into my theory lesson early. His profile: straight nose, square jaw, head leaned into the piano, face full of love. Because that's how Max looks when he plays, and it's kind of a beautiful thing.

There are a thousand selfies of me and Liza. And some other random shots from throughout the fall: my dads and me the day they dropped me off, my owl (*my* owl!) on display at When in Rome, Adnan and Sana from the falafel restaurant.

In each mirror, I make arrangements that display the memories, places, and people I've grown to care for, fastening photos to the glass with sticky tack (Google told me it was safe for the mirrors, I swear!). When I'm satisfied with my handiwork, I hang them all over my dresser, ready to come home with me when I leave.

And now I'll be able to keep both the pretty things *and* the things I love, all in one place.

THIRTY-THREE

DRESS REHEARSAL IS A CRAPSHOOT, and we all know it. Though Liza's ploy kept Seabass out of the other rehearsals, there's nothing we can do to keep him out of the Big Kahuna, *the last rehearsal*.

So, after tonight, the show will go on, or it won't.

"What do you think's gonna happen?" Duke says this casually as he tosses yet another kernel of popcorn into his wide mouth, feet propped up on the folding chair in front of him.

"How can you be so calm at a time like this?" I tug at the ends of my hair, then freeze, remembering this hair has been precisely styled and tugging could have disastrous consequences.

"You forget I'm a good actor, B. Honestly, on the inside, I look just like you do now. But I'm working hard to channel cool, for the good of the cause."

"And because it's part of your image," interjects Liza as she playfully ruffles his hair.

Duke grins at Liza as he twists a few tiny curls around his finger, setting them back into place. "*And* because it's part of my image."

"What if Octavia shows up?" I spit a fingernail, which I just chewed off, onto the backstage floor.

Liza wrinkles her nose. "You gotta stop that. But as for your question: I took care of Mom. Remember?"

Liza realized keeping her mother away from dress rehearsal was paramount to our plan having a chance—because while Seabass *might* sanction the show with me as June, Octavia most definitely will not. So, Liza got in touch with her aunt Margo, who, weirdly, has both a great relationship with Liza and holds sway with the all-powerful Octavia. "Mom can't say no to Margo, and Margo insisted they meet for dinner tonight. Mom won't miss it."

"You'd better be right."

"I'm right."

Liza, like Duke, is bordering on infuriatingly calm, but as I force myself to heave and blow out yet another giant breath, I remind myself Liza's got the emotional range of a goldfish. This is normal for her.

The rest of the cast is comfortingly anxious. I see a fair amount of pacing among those standing, knee bouncing among those sitting, and muttering across the board. So at least I'm not alone.

Max's head pokes through the stage door. "Seabass is here. You all ready?"

"As we'll ever be," replies Duke.

I'm already in my starting place onstage when a voice tugs at my back. "Hey, Venus."

"Freddie?" I say it hopefully, like I'm also asking, *Can we be okay?*

"Break a leg." His glimmer of a smile feels like sunshine on my face.

The curtain rolls open. The auditorium is cavernous, seemingly endless, complete with balconies and box seats. The Chicago Arts Theater, where this production will open tomorrow, is much bigger, much fancier—just *more* everything than the in-house Richard James auditorium.

I try to look out into the seats for Seabass, but the stage lights are too bright. A barbell of disappointment and fear wedges itself between my ribs. I hadn't realized how much I'd counted on being able to see Seabass's face, to get a sense of his reaction.

But there's nothing I can do about that now. The stage lights are the stage lights, and they're there for a reason—to showcase me.

And I'm gonna do them justice.

The music starts and off we go. The whole first act goes off with very little problem. I forget one line, but Jake whispers it to me and I recover quickly. Two minor glitches: my magnet-fastened dress (an ingenious invention that allows me to quickly change outfits, onstage, during the first song) falls off a little during the very beginning of the show; and later, I pick up a banana instead of the telephone I'm supposed to be talking into. I improvise, pretending to be so flustered as June that it was a character error, not an actor flub. I hear laughing from the orchestra pit when I do so . . . and maybe, just maybe, from the audience?

At the end of the first act, the cast bustles around backstage, changing clothes and finding props, as the crew readies the set changes onstage, just like we would during a real performance. In the midst of this frenetic activity, Seabass appears.

And we collectively freeze, like we're all on a movie screen and someone pushed pause.

"Well. That was . . . a surprise." For once in his life, he's mum, face smooth and neutral. I can't get a read on him.

Liza takes one brave step forward. "For the record, this was my idea. I would've been a really, really bad June. Bridget is the only person at this school up to the task of playing the lead under such short notice."

My eyes drop to my toes. High praise from my best friend, but that's just it, she's my best friend and probably more than a little biased. Would the profs, who know the ins and outs of all the talent at this school, agree with her?

"I wish you'd come to me first. To discuss this. Bridget has never even performed or workshopped with us in class." Seabass is still unreadable. He turns and gives me a noncreepy once-over. Like he is *seeing* me for the first time. "Why *haven't* we heard you sing, Bridget?"

Didn't realize I was going to have to go all the way public with my secret, but I don't see any way around it. They'll probably all hate me now—a talented liar is *still* a liar. But I suppose it doesn't matter. Even if there are salty feelings about me, I won't be around to hear them come next semester.

I swallow deeply and clear my throat. "I'm not in the MFP. My audition was good enough, but my theory scores were too low to be admitted. So, I'm not allowed to perform this year. And . . . it was strongly suggested that I stick to learning theory and work on being more humble. By Dean Lawless. So, I chose not to sing. At all."

I hear the dull roar of my peers' whispers behind me but keep my eyes trained on Seabass. His left brow arches gracefully. "You completely gave up singing just to prove a point?"

I grimace. When he says it like *that*, it doesn't sound so great. "I guess so."

"What a curious decision." Seabass shakes his head and scrunches up his brow, clearly thinking hard. "You're not allowed to perform. And yet here you *are*, performing. In the most public, most prestigious ensemble Richard James puts on."

"I know. Dean Lawless is going to see this as defiance, and I suppose it kind of is. But . . ." I stumble, unsure of my words. How do I explain the way my heart has shifted, that performance doesn't *mean* what it used to for me? And will that even make a difference? "I think the challenge actually worked. When I left singing out of my life, I made room for other things. I learned I really like accompanying, and supporting other singers—and I think I'm good at it. I also learned how to write music, which has maybe been the best thing that's ever happened to me. Performance is one thing, but creating original music is . . ." I glance at Max, whose eyes are big and full of something I can't decipher, but it isn't anger. "Songwriting is *everything*. And that's just it—I cowrote most of these songs, I know them inside and out, not just their lyrics but how they *feel* and why. I was so pumped to be the pianist for this show, and to watch what I'd written play out from offstage—but then Liza needed me. And Liza's more important to me than even music."

My voice cracks at the last of this, surprising even me. Liza grabs my hand. Seabass glances back at the cast that stands behind me. I brace myself for sneers and crinkled noses, but when I turn around, that's not what's there. My peers are nodding, smiling. Amber's crying and fist-pumping the air; she'd make a great GIF. The relief in my veins is heavy, but not like an anvil—like an anchor.

I'll forever remember this moment. I'll remember I made the right choice for the people I love most.

But I owe them just a little bit more. My chest aches as I prepare to push the words out. "There's one other thing you should all know. I'm not coming back next semester."

Liza's grip on my hand tightens. I'd told her about my family's dicey financial situation, but I hadn't told her the latest. "What?"

"My family was banking on me getting a music sponsorship to keep paying for tuition. And since I'm not in the MFP, I can't get one of those. There aren't any other financial options for me. I'm going home—tomorrow if Dean Lawless makes me, or at the end of the semester." My voice wobbles through the entirety of my confession.

Liza starts sniffling, and then I do, too, and then she's folding me into her arms. Pretty soon the entire cast is wrapped around us, forming a giant ball of theater angst. It also feels like support, though. Maybe a little like love, if my newest understanding of love is close to right.

The ball disperses. Duke looks like his puppy has died. Max won't look at me at all.

"I'm sorry to hear this, Bridget. I think Richard James will be saying goodbye to someone with enormous promise."

"Thank you," I manage.

"But, as they say in our business, the show must go on. And since she agrees to this in the spirit of informed consent, it'll go on with Bridget."

The cast and crew go up in whoops and applause, and my entire body erupts in excited, grateful heat.

"Now on to act two! Show me what you've got." Seabass throws us a wink as he sashays off the stage.

Act two runs smoothly. We are, miraculously, ready for opening night. Seabass approaches the stage as we end the final number, applauding, face beaming. "Excellent, excellent! Who took the lead on the rehearsals?"

We all gesture to Liza, who promptly goes pink.

"Ms. Lawless, you might have a future in directing."

Liza's face goes thoughtful. "Huh. Well. Hmm." Apparently, this bit of feedback short-circuited her brain, but she bounces back quickly. "Speaking of, team. Four o'clock sharp tomorrow for hair, makeup, and warm-ups."

My stomach flips and flops.

Tomorrow, the day my dream comes true.

Tomorrow, the day it dies.

THIRTY-FOUR

TOMORROW BECOMES TODAY AT 12:01 A.M.

Obviously, I can't sleep.

Ruby, with no such qualms, slumbers peacefully. The smell of cheese from the pizza we ordered earlier still lingers in the room, as do the words she said when I admitted I was scared. "You've got this, B. No matter what. You've got a great future ahead of you, even if it's not here. I'll miss you a ton, though."

My owl perches happily on my dresser, facing me. I grab my phone off its charger, snap a picture of him, and open a text message with the picture attached.

Me: This guy is mine now. What should I name him?

I wait, wondering if he'll text me back at all.

CPuppy: Mercury, obviously. You know . . . maybe Venus needs a Mercury to keep her company.

I smile and squeeze the phone to my chest for a second before responding.

Me: Actually, that's perfect. Mercury the Owl.

I don't expect him to say more—he hasn't had much to say to me lately. But then my phone lights up again.

CPuppy: You ready for tomorrow?

Me: Yes. No. I don't know.

CPuppy: I know you're going to kill the performance. I have zero worries about that.

Me: . . . "about that"? Do you have worries?

CPuppy: I'm worried about what life at Richard James will be like without you.

And this, from Max, sets something loose in my chest. It's achy, but also it's . . . something else. Something good. And it's a big step for him to say this, given how much I hurt him.

Me: Me too. I'll miss you.

And I lay the phone down, realizing that I'd just sent a very honest text. When I leave Richard James behind, I'll miss school, and Chicago, and Hans. And Liza . . . I'm going to bawl my eyes out over saying goodbye to Liza (and I might actually just try to stuff her into my luggage). Yet one of the best things about the past few weeks has been writing my own music, and not just for the sake of the music—though that's certainly huge—but for the sake of who I've been writing with. Evenings with Max in Triton 212 became a happy space for me, a place where I just *was*. I could be saucy and kind of a dick that day, and Max would take it all in stride. I'd show up jittery due to caffeine overload or nerves, and Max would still listen to every one of my rambling stories. I never felt like too much with him.

Max made me feel safe. Wanted. Interesting.

Oh.

Oh, *shit.*

I rear up and my phone flies from my chest onto the floor, where it bounces on my rug one, two, three times before landing faceup. My text exchange with Max lights the whole room.

Max is my Socks.

Max is the book I didn't open with white gloves. I didn't think to handle him carefully, to open his pages to check his vulnerability. Instead I touched him with bare hands. While that was satisfying for me, I hurt him.

And Max is the unassuming owl, the one I went back to week after week. The owl I wanted to find happiness so much that I put him on display—before realizing he didn't need to be universally admired to be special. Before realizing he belonged with me. The owl I love.

Max.

"B? You okay?" Ruby sits up in bed, looking bleary. Part of me wants to share my revelation with her, but the bigger part of me knows that wouldn't be right. I've just barely shared it with *me.*

I gulp. "Yep, fine," I croak. "Hey, I'm going to go out for a little."

"Out? It's late. We've got a show tomorrow!"

"I know, but I can't sleep. I'm just going to the practice rooms. I'll be back in an hour."

As she slides back under her blankets, I grab for the notebook on my bedside table, slide on my slippers, and head to the music lab. There's a new song in my heart and no time like the present to commit it to paper.

There are three things about opening night I'm especially looking forward to.

The first is Persian food. Liza and I have been planning the cast and crew party for weeks, and what more fitting place for it than Persian Palace? Thrilled as I will be to stuff my face with falafel, what will taste even better is being included. Back in the day, I thought I didn't get invited to cast parties because people were intimidated by my talent. I now realize I didn't get invited to things because I was kind of a shitty person.

Second, the *drama*, and I don't just mean onstage. I went all in on shock factor and chose not to tell my dads I'm now playing June; they still think I'm playing piano in the orchestra pit. Seeing their faces after the show will be a fantastic moment—which may or may not end with me immediately getting kicked out of school, but details, details.

Third, did I mention the *drama*? Because I've just thrown a musical theater Hail Mary, one the rest of the cast and crew have yet to learn about. Here's to hoping it lands.

The cast and crew gather earlier than we'd planned—three p.m.—because I texted at three a.m. to ask if we could. Troopers, all of them. When we're all assembled, I pass around copies of the song I managed to write and score in the wee hours of the morning. "I know this is way last minute, but can we add this song? It's a simple duet, just June and Socks, and it's short. It would go second to last, before the finale song. If you all agree, we'll do it with piano alone, with Duke and me on stools so we can read the words from music stands. No blocking or choreography."

The cast stick their noses into the papers and read what I've got. Max mouths the words to himself as he pores over his sheet. My hands go damp, wondering if he sees the meaning behind the meaning. Yet then he moves to the piano to start plunking around with chords, because of course he would. The show is *tonight*, for God's sake.

Liza waves her sheet around. "This is great! I mean . . . it's super last minute, but if it's just you and Duke, I think it's okay?" She looks to Duke for affirmation, who shoots a thumbs-up.

"And it'll get us to six songs, which is what Seabass always says is the magic number for these musicals," Duke adds.

"Okay, then. Duke and B, you work this up with Max." She turns to the rest of the group. "We'll throw in this song after 'Bill's Elegy' and those talking scenes, but before we launch the finale. Got it?" Liza surveys the group, who look mostly relieved, probably because they don't have to do anything extra. Everyone disperses to backstage or elsewhere, and Liza leans to talk into my ear. "I've gotta go calm Amber down. She's losing her shit. Any words of wisdom?"

"Just keep reminding her that she can do this, you're super-proud

303

of her, and even if things go spectacularly wrong tonight, she's not a failure. That always seems to help."

Liza salutes. "I'm on it."

From the sound of it, Max has already mastered my song. He plays the melody for Duke, who catches on quickly. We write a few lines of dialogue for transitioning in and out of the music, and within an hour, it's all golden. Touchdown on the Hail Mary.

All except: I don't think Max sees *why* I wrote this song. He's still playing the piano, so nose-deep into making sure he has the music just right that I'm sure he hasn't truly taken in the lyrics.

Feverishly, I grab a copy of the song that another cast member left behind and scribble six words on its backside. Yes, they're barely legible, but they'll have to do, because I don't think I've got the moxie to write them again. I fold the page in half, write a three-letter name on the outside, leave it nonchalantly on Max's piano, and bolt.

I'm already halfway out of the room when the piano music stops. "Hey, Bridget, you dropped a page!"

But I pretend not to hear him, which is almost not a lie, with the blood pumping so loud and hot in my ears. Instead I walk straight out of the room, because if I've learned anything about Max in the past couple of weeks, it's that he does *not* love an audience.

At quarter 'til seven, everyone—cast, crew, orchestra pit—gathers backstage. I am crossing and recrossing my legs at a frantic pace, whatever foot's on the ground tapping at the exact tempo of "Seven Sisters."

304

Liza squats down in front of me, pressing her hands into my knees. Her hair is drawn back severely, horn-rimmed glasses sitting atop her elfin nose, and she's wearing the bland navy blues and grays of Rosie. She looks like a nerdy supermodel. "You nervous?"

"Duh."

"Don't be. You were made for this part."

She can't know *all* the things I'm nervous about because I haven't told her the Max stuff yet. Still, I throw my arms around her neck, and she loses balance and lurches into me. The chair I'm sitting on tilts onto its back legs and we almost topple ass over teakettle. But Liza is graceful and I have good reflexes, so we manage to stay upright, though we do not avoid catching a serious case of the giggles.

Max isn't backstage before the show, so I have no idea how he's feeling about the note I left. I still kind of can't believe I wrote it, but what's done is done. And what's a few more nerves on top of opening night jitters?

At showtime, all eyes shift to Liza. At first she looks uncertain, like she wants to shuck her skin and run right outta here. But then her shoulders rise and fall, and she lifts her chin. Willing to be seen. Willing to take charge. "Okay, folx. I know this was a risky move, and still kinda is." She glances at me. "But look what we achieved together! Even though it's been stressful, and I'm going to sleep for a week straight after this, these past four days have been some of the most fun I've ever had prepping for a musical."

The group speaks their agreement, enthusiastic smiling and head bobbing all around. Amber throws up her hands and shouts an "Amen," apparently completely recovered from her earlier meltdown. That girl is the hottest mess of unpredictability I've ever seen. And I'm me, so that's saying something.

"So let's go get 'em, team. We earned it."

As I walk out onstage, I think of my mother. If what Dodge says is true, she would have *killed* for this opportunity. *I hope you're proud of me, wherever you are*, I think, and I blow a kiss to the sky like I do before every performance.

In the two or three minutes of tense but quiet time before the curtain opens, I stand still, eyes closed, and do my other pre-musical ritual. It's not enough for me to act like June, I must *become* June. I imagine myself breathing in the essence of the character even as I breathe out my own needs, desires, personality. *I'm June. I'm June.*

The curtain opens and I'm June.

Except shades and shimmers of Bridget keep peeking through, and not in reference to Duke, my leading man. Yes, he pulls off every note, every longing, wistful stage glance, every move. And like before, my heart bursts for him, but not in the *way* of before. Now, I'm happy to watch my friend—who I thought I loved but never actually did—succeed. Duke is my abalone necklace, shiny and beautiful and absolutely worth having in my life, even if not in the way I'd originally thought.

The time comes for my last-minute add of a song, "Safe, Wanted, Interesting." I sing it to the orchestra pit, searching for the boy behind the piano. All I can see is his hair and freckled forehead behind the top of the baby grand, but it's enough. He's here, he's listening, and he knows what it means—because my note had said, "I wrote this song for you."

As the last scene pulls to a close and the cast makes its curtain call, my thirst to see him is finally slaked. He's stepped out from behind the piano to applaud with the crowd, and as I take front and center for the cheers, whistles, and bravas that are just for me, the lead, the *lead in the Richard James musical*, the only thing I can focus on is his face, radiating happiness and warmth and joy. For me. With me.

Even though I betrayed his trust and put him on a kind of display he never wanted for himself, he's happy for me.

I've dreamed of this moment for years. Standing at center stage in *this* auditorium, soaking in the approval and enthusiasm of *this* crowd. And still, none of it lives up to the way I felt when I was writing music with Max.

I'm lost inside a tangle of manly arms when Octavia finds me. My dads pull back to gape at her, Dad looking especially gooey and starstruck. Does nothing I've told them about meanie dean of students Octavia matter?

Maybe not, when faced with a Broadway star you've been gaga over for years.

"Oh. Um. Dean Lawless, these are my dads, Chad and Dodge. Dads, this is Dean Lawless." Obviously.

Dad juts his hand out to shake Octavia's, with too much gusto. "It's a pleasure," he says, continuing to look hugely douchey.

Dodge is a little more even-keeled, thank effing God, and shakes Octavia's hand wordlessly.

"The pleasure is mine," Octavia says, bringing out the ole Tony Award–winning charm by way of her dimpled cheeks. "Ms. Bloom, a word?"

I follow her backstage and into a wing we weren't allowed to use—personal dressing rooms, like the ones Broadway stars set up camp in when they do a long-running show. This one sports a little gold plaque, "The Octavia Lawless Room." Figures.

"Have a seat," she says as she lowers herself onto a chic gray armchair. I choose a perch on the white sofa across from her.

I'm starting to hyperventilate. I've never had a panic attack before, but the moment just before you get officially kicked out of your dream school is probably a good time for your first one, right? A wave of dizziness sweeps over me, threatening to knock me over.

"Breathe, Ms. Bloom."

"Easier said than done," I choke out, then put my head between my knees, which is something I've seen people do on TV. It sort of counteracts the head rush but does nothing for my dignity.

"Would it help if I told you I'm not expelling you?"

I sit up so fast that peach-tinted stars twinkle in front of my vision. "Wait, what?"

"I'm not expelling you."

I blink at her before putting my head right back where it was, because a new wave of dizzy is sweeping over. "That should be the best news of my life, because I want to be here more than anything in the world. Especially now that I understand what music means to me. Not performance. *Music.* But I have to leave at semester, anyway."

"Whyever would you say that?"

"My family can't afford the tuition. No sponsorship." I think back on how I begged my dads to sell more land. No, not begged. I *expected* them to do it for me. This time I consider what that would cost them, in all the ways, and I just *can't*. The guilt of making life any harder for my dads than it already is—it's too much. "But I won't ask my dads to go into debt for me."

I try sitting up again, this time at a more reasonable speed. When I do, I see Octavia's face is . . . soft? Compassionate? She doesn't even look like herself with those kinds of expressions on her face. "A sponsor has already stepped forward for you after tonight's performance. Didn't you think that was a possibility? That as soon as you stepped onstage, a patron might take an interest in you?"

I might pass out. What is Octavia even *saying* to me right now? "No. I hadn't even considered that. I was fully planning to leave at semester."

"Well. Wonders never cease."

I cringe. "I sort of don't want to know, but I have to ask. What do you mean?"

"Ms. Bloom, please forgive my bluntness, but when you entered this school you were self-absorbed to the point of myopic. I let you take on the role of student accompanist because I knew it would be the perfect test for you."

"Of my humility."

"That, and your dedication to music. I have to admit I thought you'd fail. But never once did I hear you complain, though I think accompanying was mostly thankless work for you. I saw you helping others, cheerleading others. Focusing on people *other than yourself*. The girl who sits across from me today is not the girl who stood in my office at the start of this semester, demanding to be seen."

I swallow twice, hard, and finally I just embrace the lump in my throat and let it do its work. Tears push out of my burning eyes and run down over my trembling lips.

Octavia continues. "Once upon a time there was a Broadway diva who could sing like a bird but who was notoriously hard to work with. Too sure of herself, not able to work as part of a team. Directors admired her talent but didn't cast her because of her reputation. She struggled, for years, to figure this all out before she learned how to—as the kids say—not be a dick."

I wipe my nose with my hand, like the class act I am.

Octavia smiles as she hands me a tissue. "I wanted a better fate for you, Bridget, and now I think maybe you'll have it. Do you think you can pass the theory test now?"

I nod.

"If you pass, the committee will let you officially into the music focus program at semester—I'll make sure of it. This would give you access to the sponsorship money."

I am full-on *bawling*, but that's just how it is. There's no holding back the force of this emotion. I'm not expelled. I don't have to leave. I'm *staying* at Richard James.

Just then, the door bursts open, Liza flying in behind it. She takes one look at the puddle that my face has become and starts bellowing. "Let her at least stay 'til the end of the year! The whole recasting thing was my idea! She did it for me!"

Octavia, either ever-the-actress or ever-the-unfazable, merely crosses her arms, no change of facial expression whatsoever. "Yes, I thought the operation smacked of Liza Lawless. Covert, reckless, and exactly the opposite of what I'd instructed . . . yet impeccably done. Your brand indeed, daughter of mine."

Liza cocks her head at her mother and squints, looking at Octavia like she's never seen her before. "Impeccably done?"

"Well, yes, Bridget did a marvelous job. As I knew she would."

"As you knew she would?"

"Liza, did you think that something as big as a change in the lead for the musical could happen at *my* school and I wouldn't somehow find out about it?"

"Well . . . yes." Liza's arms go floppy and she swings them side to side, a childlike motion. I've never seen her do it. Is this what Freud meant when he talked about regression?

Octavia laughs. I've only ever heard her laugh onstage, and her real laugh is different. Less round, less loud, but more joyful. Prettier. "I have eyes everywhere at this place, Liza. But once I heard of your recasting plan, I thought it was possibly a grand idea. I decided I'd let it play out."

Liza and I must look like twin jack-o'-lanterns, carved into perpetual states of shock. With every passing word from Octavia, I'm further convinced I may never be able to pull my mouth shut again.

"Is Bridget expelled?"

"No."

Liza's face lights up. "Am I?"

"Also no."

Ah, so Liza had another motivation for playing this risky game of casting musical chairs. She'd planned to fall on her sword, in the hope that Octavia would have no choice but to boot her. Liza's face falls, landing in an even more sullen expression than her typical.

"No, I won't kick you out for doing something that was truly in the best interests of your school. Also, Liza Jean, even though you went rogue, it was one of the first times in your life I saw you *try*."

"I try at lots of things, just not the things you want me to."

The two of them—like two points in a time continuum, Liza a younger, surlier version of Octavia—play tug-of-war with their eyes.

Finally, Octavia breaks. Her perpetually ramrod-straight posture relaxes, shoulders curling in toward each other. "I know I've been rigid. But I've decided I'm willing to compromise."

If Liza were a dog, her ears would have perked up right then. "Compromise?"

"If you *keep trying* in the MFP for the rest of this year, like you did for this musical, next year I'll let you audition for the visual arts program, if you still want to. Or you can be a gen ed student and take all kinds of classes, to see what you like best."

"Really?" Liza sniffles.

"Yes, really."

There's a pause as Liza stands wary, sizing her mother up.

312

Trying to gauge her genuineness, I think. Yet then Octavia holds her arms out and the expression on her face is one I can only describe as *Please.*

Liza moves at a pace just shy of a run and dives into her mother's waiting arms. "I'm sorry I'm so stubborn," says Liza's muffled voice.

Octavia strokes Liza's hair as Liza sobs into the shoulder of what is probably an Armani dress. "You come by it honestly, darling."

Eventually, Liza turns back to me. "I'm so glad you're not expelled. I get you for another month, at least."

I manage to smile, though my chin is quivering with leftover sobs. "I'm staying. I got a sponsor. And your mom's letting me into the MFP if I can pass the theory test."

She grabs my arms, just like I've done to her with my big feels so many times. And ouch, does it fricking hurt. "Are you serious?" she screeches in a very un-Liza-like way.

"As a heart attack. Which I'm about to have."

And then we're hugging and then we're jumping up and down together, because this is possibly the best day two people have ever had, ever, in the history of the world.

"Your sponsor stuck around for you to meet, if you'd care to, Bridget," says Octavia.

I probably look like a drag queen who walked through a car wash, with my stage makeup smeared all over my blotchy post-cry face, but I don't care. I *need* to hug this person and tell them how much this means to me. "I'd *love* that."

Octavia leaves for a moment, then steps back in, holding the door open for my sponsor.

He wears a dapper three-piece suit and carries a bowler hat in his hands. His pants are maybe slightly too short; below them are loafers with no socks. And his unruly, fluffy white hair gives the impression of a man who's just stepped in from a tornado.

A fresh round of sobs starts up as Hans puts his arms around me.

THIRTY-FIVE

HUMMUS AND PITA ARE INSANELY delicious when served with a side of unexpected and very sweet relief. My body's simultaneously light and floaty while also heavy with exhaustion, and the only thing I can think to do given this odd state of affairs is *be*. Soak in the moment. Lock it into memory.

The whole gang's here: the cast, the crew, and whoever's family felt like joining. Ruby's parents didn't come, so my dads and I invite her to sit with us. Maybe it's postshow adrenaline or the coffee she's guzzling, or maybe it's just that hypnotic quality my good-listener dads tend to have on others, but she's really sharing. I learn more about her life in ninety minutes than I'd learned in the past month. In a moment when it's just the two of us—the dads have left to fawn over *casually dressed* Octavia—she makes the biggest self-disclosure yet. "I don't really get along with my parents.

That's why I used to be so salty when you'd talk with yours every Sunday. Jealousy."

"Oh. Wow. I'm sorry, Ruby. I didn't realize."

"Yeah. I'm just . . . not who Mom and Dad want me to be. But I'm working on being okay with that."

My heart squeezes for her. "Good for you."

"You're lucky. Your dads clearly love you just the way you are."

I smile. "In other good news, I can tell they love you just the way you are, too."

Her face lights up like Rockefeller Center.

I keep trying to catch Max's eye across the party room, but no dice. One minute, he's doing some kind of complicated bro hand-shake with Duke. The next, he's in deep conversation with some kids from the orchestra pit. It's very unclear as to whether he is accidentally or intentionally avoiding me.

I'm looking for Max yet again when another boy nudges my shoulder. "Bloom," Duke says, his face weirdly serious.

"Yeah?"

"C'mere a minute."

He leads me over to a quieter part of the establishment, near the restrooms. I'm about to ask if he whisks all the girls away to the toilet area when he says, "I realized how I knew your voice. Your singing voice."

The joke turns to dust in my mouth. "Oh."

"Your face says it all. It *was* you in my room that night I got drunk. Not Liza."

"What can I say? You caught me, Delbert."

His look is way too intense for a night like tonight. "Why didn't you say anything?"

I give myself a few seconds to gather my thoughts. Weird. "By the time I learned you thought it was Liza who tucked you in that night, and *that* was why you went for her . . . it was too late. You two were dating, you're happy, and who was I to mess with that?"

He runs a hand down the back of his neck, making whooshing noises with the hair he's ruffling. "But did you . . . I mean . . . I didn't know you felt enough for me that you'd take care of me like that."

"It doesn't matter. It's in the past."

"All of it? Feelings and—"

"All of it."

And it's true. Whereas being anywhere in the vicinity of this boy used to make my knees go the way of Grandma Evelyn's Jell-O salad, I'm sturdy on my feet right now. No butterflies. No urge to twirl my hair. No nothing.

But across the room, someone starts plucking a guitar and I'm a live wire, from the unfortunate halo of frizz around the crown of my head to the very tips of my toenails. Because I'd know those plucks anywhere. Leaving Duke behind, I step back into the party room, where Max is sitting on a stool, guitar slung around his neck.

"Hey, all. I. Um." He tugs at his guitar strap and swallows so deeply I can see it, but he soldiers on. "I've been working on a song for the last few months, and this feels like the right time and place to share it, if that's all right with you."

Max. Is. Going. To. Play. And sing! In front of people! And he gave himself credit for what he wrote! My heart pumps with pride and gratitude and something else, something bigger than excitement and bigger even than a crush. Something so big that my chest swells and pushes water up into my tear ducts.

His song is pretty, waltz-y, a cross between a lullaby and a ballad, and hauntingly familiar. Even from the intro alone, I feel like I should know it—I've *heard* this before, but where? He starts singing in his gentle croon, about being swallowed by the midnight sky and a girl who is his beacon in the dark.

And then he drops the chorus. "But I orbit Venus. She's all I can see." He looks right at me as the lovely words push out of his lovely mouth.

My body breaks into head-to-toe goose bumps, followed by a massive head rush. *I've been working on a song for the last few months*, he said. It's then I remember where I've heard the song—weeks ago, when I caught Max playing piano before one of our first tutoring sessions. Even back then, he was working on this song.

I *need to touch him*, but I rein myself in, because also I want to fully immerse myself in this experience. At what other point in my life am I going to get to hear a love song, written for me, for the first time? Maybe never again, but it's happening now and I'm going to soak it up. I'm going to flash frame the way this feels in my body, in the very marrow of me.

The salty heat on my face as he finishes the song is welcome, but there's enough of it that I need to dig around in my purse for a tissue. When I pick my head back up, he's *right there*. Like, a foot away from me, in front of everyone. The gasp that leaves me, without permission, is embarrassingly loud and horror-movie-like.

On Broadway there'd be a big talking scene right here between the two love interests. He'd say something like, "Venus, it was always you," and I'd say, "I can't believe I couldn't see," and then there'd be a song, and *then*, we'd give the audience what they've been waiting all night for, the Big Kiss.

Fortunately this isn't Broadway, so I just lunge at him. His lips are softer, fuller than I expected, and his fingers tangle up in the hair at the base of my neck, where my curls are the curliest. Every surface of me is aflame.

The cast and crew go into a full-on studio-audience-worthy "Ooohhhh," along with assorted whoops and wolf whistles, but it's all muddied by the rush in my ears, in my hands, my feet, my everywhere. Somewhere off to the side, Liza deadpans, "Jeez, *finally*."

When we come up for air, he drags me to a private corner.

"You like the song," he whispers. His breath is like July summer on my earlobe.

I inhale sage and soap and exhale sheer joy. "I love the song," I say into his neck. And when I say *love*, I mean it; this song wasn't a fleeting tune I heard once and can discard without missing it. This will be a part of me forever. It has left me better than it found me— and so has Max. Because of that, I say the hard, important things that need to be said.

"I'm really sorry about what I did, convincing Duke to go public about your songs. You're so talented, *I* thought you deserved the credit, and *I* thought getting Duke to acknowledge you was the right thing to do. What I realize now is that I didn't ask what *you* wanted. I made assumptions. I leapt before looking. And . . . I'm trying harder to look, now. And ask. So anyway, I'm sorry."

"The unwanted attention has kinda sucked, I'm not gonna lie."

I flinch, but he squeezes my hand and continues. "But it's also given me the shove I needed to take credit for the things that are mine, and risk putting my voice back into the world."

"I'm so, so glad," I say, grinning and returning the hand squeeze.

"I'm sorry, too. For what I said in our last tutoring session. When you took over for Liza in the musical, I realized I was right about you the first time. You love music for the sake of it. But you love your friends most of all."

I must be glowing. I have to be. "Did you like my song, Max? The one I wrote for you?"

"Of course I did. It was incredible, B. Just like you."

He hitches my chin up with his fingers and I meet his eyes, un-flinching. If he wants to look, I'll let him look. This is me, mascara-streaked stage-makeup face and puffy eyes and all.

The sunflowers in his eyes are almost invisible because his pupils are so big right now. I once read that your pupils dilate when you look at something you're attracted to. "So we like each other's songs. That's a start. But do . . . do you like me?" he asks.

My heartbeat is hummingbird wings taking flight. "I more than like you."

He tastes like coffee and vanilla frosting.

And sage.

And the future.

THIRTY-SIX

REGARDLESS OF MY NEW, DEFINITELY-THIS-ERA'S-ZAC-EFRON paramour, I still have a bunch of tests on Friday. I spend almost all my free time studying in trusty old Triton 212, but now Max is usually there with me. He's taken to practicing for his senior performance—a capstone solo mini-concert that all senior MFP students have to do—while I study, which unexpectedly aids my focus and motivation. Social facilitation at work, if my psych textbook is right about anything.

Max is doing some piano pieces and some guitar pieces for his performance, because he's a musical genius. Today he's working on a Schumann piano piece, which gets a little better each time he plays it.

"Bravo!" I say, smiling up at him from the study table as he finishes.

"Eh. I'm still butchering the second-to-the-last line."

"Butchering? Nah, not even close."

"Sure you're not biased?"

I make an "oh no you didn't" face. "Hey, I'm into you, and I'm not *technically* an MFP student yet, but let's not forget that I'm still Bridget Venus Bloom, piano wonder and performance snob."

"Speaking of all of that—are you ready for your big test?"

Which big test? I want to say, but of course I know which one he's talking about. Between the musical, my massive academic course load, and the ample time spent admiring my new boyfriend's impeccable Grecian nose—not to mention his full lips, among other parts of him—I haven't really thought much about theory. Which is probably stupid, given that my whole future rides on it. "Umm . . . I think so."

"*You think so?* The test is next week!" He looks at me like I've confessed to murder. Within seconds he's rummaging through his bag, pulling out . . . oh no, not a review packet of doom.

"You made *another* theory packet? How? When? With what free time?"

He flushes. "Like I told you before, I think they're fun. Kind of a leisure activity for me, like pre-bedtime."

I goggle. "I can't believe I'm willingly in a relationship with you."

"You're doing that thing where you try to distract me. You're *very* good at it, but how about you work on the packet so we can keep all of this"—he gestures between him and me—"going next semester."

"Well, when you say it like that."

Pencil in hand, I sit in front of the thick stapled booklet of theory shit and prepare for disaster. Unlike before, this time Max pulls his chair around the table to sit right beside me.

"What're you doing?" I ask.

"I'm going to watch."

"For the love of Freddie Mercury. Do you get off on watching me do theory?" I cannot smother the giggle that's bubbling up.

I expect at least a blush, but all I get is words, balmy in my ear. "Wouldn't you like to know?"

My body automatically arches closer to his as I shiver from those words in my ear. He pushes my hair aside and nuzzles his face into the side of my neck, running his lips from my collarbone to the curve of my jaw. Oh, dear Lord, thank you for letting me suck at music theory.

A few minutes and two sets of swollen lips later, I pant at him, "And you accused *me* of being distracting."

He swallows heavily, pulling himself away. "You're right. My fault. Do the stupid packet."

Finally, I've found what it takes to get Max to see that these packets are the worst.

I get through the first page with little difficulty, the earlier lessons coming back to me without much effort. Yet by the end of the second page, I'm faltering, floundering, unsure of every answer. How did I convince myself I knew this stuff? I'm so going to fail.

Max moves his chair to ninety degrees from me.

"I was going to wait for another day to tell you this, but I really hate your shoes."

Wait. Hold the phone. I'm wearing my very favorite sling-back wedges, which were meticulously chosen after weeks of internet research and *then* waiting for them to go on sale.

"You. Hate. *These?*"

He shrugs. "Yeah. Just never liked them. Kind of tacky."

The roots of my hair are on fire—and I'm not talking about the color. "Well. You clearly lack taste. Now, if you'd please move around to *your* side of the table, I'm going to work on this *stupid* theory packet so I can stay here at this school with the boy who *hates my shoes.*" I hunch over the table and start scratching away at papers with my pencil.

Of *all* the things to say to me. We've been together for all of two days and he thinks he can just insult my wardrobe? And does he even know what he's talking about? Has he even looked at my feet? We've spent all of our time playing piano and kissing and laughing and talking—

"There. You see that?"

"See what?" I grumble, not looking up from my work.

"When you're angry, you can do theory."

My pencil freezes midway through drawing the second inversion of an E-major chord on the treble staff. "Wait, what?"

"This is the key to everything. To pass this theory test, all you have to do is get mad. I don't quite understand how, but anger unlocks your knowledge. I had a hunch and today seals the deal."

I throw down my pencil and lean back in my seat. "Huh."

He's completely right. When I'm mad I get into a head-space of "well, I'll show him," and the spite becomes brain fuel.

Malice-induced confidence. It's the same thing that got me into my whole "no singing ever, I'll show Octavia how humble I can be" mess. Not to *mention* the "I need to shout my face off onstage because I'm pissed my mom never got to and my bio dad didn't care about me." Effing great.

But seriously. Effing great!

"Do you really hate these shoes?"

"Of course I don't. I know they're your favorites. And they make your legs look even longer than they already are."

I lean in to kiss him.

The boy's got taste after all.

The promise of falafel and feta cheese is the only thing getting me through this night. That, and my friends.

Because tonight I find out if I'm officially an MFP student or officially on my way home.

During lunchtime at the Rot, Piper tracked me down and handed me an unmarked envelope, which we both knew held the results of my theory retake exam. "Good luck," she said, her midnight eyes sparkling with hope. And even though a part of me wanted to rip the thing open right there, so I could just *know* already, a bigger part of me didn't want to do it alone. Good news or bad, I wanted my people around me. So I rallied the troops, and here we are back at Persian Palace, awaiting our food and my fate.

The envelope sits in the middle of the table, like an off-limits exhibit. Or like a bomb.

"Well. Are you ready?" says Ruby, her eyes sympathetic.

"Yes. No," I say. My palms are sweating, and of course so are my stupid feet. I can never get through anything nerve-racking without destroying my socks.

"We love you, no matter what," Liza reminds me. She's got her hair pulled away from her face, which seems like a metaphor for how she is lately. So much more willing to be seen.

I honestly could throw up, but I don't want to wreck Persian food for me and everyone else at this table forever. So, because it's better than hurling, I grab the envelope and unceremoniously rip it open.

As soon as I read the results, the sheet falls from my shaking hands to the table.

Max, who's sitting close enough to read them, nudges my leg with his. Our eyes lock and I'm not sure whose are wetter, his or mine.

"Well? What the hell does it say?" demands Liza, angling to grab the letter for herself before I snatch it away.

"I didn't test into beginning theory," I say, and everyone's faces fall.

I save them. "I tested into intermediate. I passed. I'm in."

The table gets *very loud* for the next few seconds, so much that Sana pokes her head out from the back. "Everything okay?" she says, because she's too nice to say, "Shut the hell up, you fools."

I make the "quieter" sign with my hands, one that all music students know. "All okay, Sana."

Duke raises his Diet Coke. "To Bloom, Richard James's next Broadway star!"

"To B!" says the group, and we clink our plastic glasses together over the top of the table.

I smile and turn all shades of red.

"I knew you could do it," Max whispers, close to my ear.

"Because of you," I whisper back, and our kiss is soft and feels like gratitude.

"Oh come *on*, you two. Get a room already." Liza feigns exasperation, but I think she left all her best acting juice out on the stage. It's clear she's dying of happiness for me.

Duke snorts. "Oh, they've got a room. Triton 212's got steam pouring out from under the door every night now, or so I hear."

Everyone hoots and teases, but I let them. I'm happy. Max is happy. And besides, Duke's right about the fireworks going off in Triton 212.

"B, this means you can sign up for interterm now! More time with meeeee," says Liza, doing the cabbage patch with just her arms. MFP students are allowed to sign up for a three-week intensive that happens between first- and second-semester classes.

"What's everyone taking?" asks Ruby, reaching for one of the pitas that just arrived. "I think I'm going to try that jazz-singing one. Get outside of my comfort zone a little." Because apparently "instrumentalist" is *not* an all-inclusive term. Thank goodness for Ruby and the way she helps me redefine "truth."

Liza's wearing her usual nonchalant face, but it's lit up underneath, like she's full of a new kind of energy. "Me too. I mean, getting out of the comfort zone. I'm taking Music Leadership Seminar." She's *excited* about music leadership. What is this day?

Duke swallows a mouthful of grape leaves. "I'm taking the singer-songwriter class. Because, you know, I figured I should learn to write some of my own stuff, now that my ghostwriter's all famous and stuff." Max's "I Orbit Venus" music video went viral within a matter of days, and now he's almost as in demand via the interwebs as Duke. "I figure you're doing singer-songwriter class, too, Max?" Duke holds a fist out.

Max does the obligatory bump but says, "I . . . er . . . well, I'm doing the advanced Broadway one. I figure it's time to come out of my shell." He glances over at me, looking embarrassed.

"That's amazing," I say, squeezing his hand.

"You think so?"

"Absolutely."

Liza slugs my arm. "What do you think *you'll* take for interterm?"

Million-dollar question.

The advanced Broadway course would mean six hours a day spent singing, dancing, learning another Broadway musical. Six hours a day with Max. Maybe we'd be cast across from each other; maybe I'd finally realize my goal of being in real-life love with my leading man.

It'd be a dream come true.

But it's an old dream, and now I've got some new ones. So quickly I don't think anyone will notice, I look toward the sky, to ask my mom's permission. And just like that, she gives it to me. It's okay to find new ways to shine.

"Advanced Broadway sounds awesome . . . but I think I'll take the singer-songwriter workshop."

"Really?" Max's eyes gleam, and I can see my reflection in them.

"Yeah. Turns out, not being able to sing showed me all the other things I love."

And I know, from the way he catches and holds my gaze, that Max understands the entirety of what I'm saying. He slides an arm around my back and holds me tight.

Liza plunks her drink down on the table. "Girl, I hate to say it, but you picked up a lot of stuff during your singing hiatus, didn't you."

I suppose I did. I know now I can tackle theory—when I get angry enough. I've become a boss accompanist. I've grown into a not-so-shitty roommate. Songwriting, self-awareness, and a place I belong—I found it all at exactly the point in my life at which I thought I'd lost everything.

"Yeah, I learned a lot. But at the risk of being corny—the very best things I picked up this semester were all of you."

The table goes up in both groans and awws. Duke clutches his chest like I've shot him in the heart. But under the table, Liza picks up my free hand and squeezes, and I know that's her way of saying, "I see you, B, and me too."

My other hand is still firmly in Max's. I lean over to him and whisper, "I've never felt more safe, wanted, or interesting."

He beams.

Joy looks amazing on him.

EPILOGUE

ONE SCHOOL MUSICAL, ONE ACED theory test, multiple relationship epiphanies, and six other course finals later (all As and one B—*suck it*, Richard James) and the semester comes to a screeching halt.

The Saturday after it all wraps up finds me at When in Rome. I have approximately six hours to kill before my flight to Nebraska departs O'Hare. I've said my temporary goodbyes to Ruby, Liza, Max, and co., with many promises to text and sing Christmas carols together via video chat. I'll see them in three weeks, when we're all back for interterm.

Hans and I are working our way through a tin of butter cookies, a pot of jasmine silver needle, and two hundred holiday cards, which the shop sends to regular customers and other dealers Hans maintains relationships with. I stuff, seal, and stamp; Hans hand addresses. A light dusting of snow, just barely enough to be visible, falls outside the big storefront window.

Hans lays one envelope aside and picks up another. "What's the first thing you will do when you get home to Lynch?"

"Kick off my shoes and dive headfirst into my comfy bed." Oh, how I've missed my pillow-top queen. Not even the best memory foam mattress covers can duplicate the effect on a dorm bed.

Hans chuckles. "That sounds delightful."

"Also, I'm going to ask my dads about their lives before me. I don't know a lot about that stuff, and now I'm curious." Because I've learned expressing interest in others is a bonding thing, and who better to bond with over my break than my favorite people?

"Astute, Athena. Look at you grow."

Many hours later we've finished the cards, half the tin of cookies, the whole pot of tea. We've also swept, dusted, rearranged, and trimmed the small Christmas tree near the shop window, as well as prepared a menorah right in the window itself. Hans is Jewish, he explains, but his wife was Christian so they celebrated both Christmas and Hanukkah for years.

It's nearly time for me to leave for the airport. I've been waiting for this moment. Out of my rolling suitcase by the door, I pull a flat wrapped parcel. "Happy holidays!" I say, handing it off to Hans.

"Athena. You shouldn't have."

"Of course I should have. This is *nothing* compared to what you've given me."

"I appreciate the gesture, of course. Yet, my dear . . ." His eyes go cloudy. "Do you understand that your presence here at my store, week after week, has been the best gift of all? You've brought youth and vibrance and . . . hope to this old lover of old things."

"Well . . ." I swallow heavily, and my vision's blurring around the edges. "You're welcome. Truly. And I'll keep giving that gift as long as I'm in Chicago. But still, open the present I *meant* to bring," I say, smiling a soggy smile.

Hans is one of those deliberate present unwrappers, but now, I get it. "Handmade wrap?"

"Liza." She'd covered craft paper with hand-drawn Christmas and Hanukkah motifs.

"Ah, I should have known. It's lovely."

"Just like Liza."

"Indeed." Gift now unwrapped, Hans picks his glasses up from the string around his neck and hangs them on his nose, all the better to see his present with.

Liza snapped a picture of Hans and me together on opening night, Hans in his three-piece suit, me still in my June costume. My face is a disaster of mascara and blush, but the joy underneath redeems the photo. I carefully chose an antique frame from another store several blocks away. I hope it isn't a party foul to buy something like this for Hans from another man's store.

He's blinking fast, too fast, as he continues to survey the picture. "This is . . . wonderful." His voice is thick.

Never one to miss out on an opportunity to hug, I step in and put my arms around Hans's delicate frame. "You're wonderful. Thank you for everything, Hans. I wouldn't have gotten through the semester without you. Let alone next semester!"

He clears his throat, which rumbles just near my ear. "Likewise, Athena."

I start back toward the door, but there's a question that's been eating at me. One that I'd asked before and Hans had said, "Wait. I'll tell you after the musical." The time had come.

"May I ask about June and Socks now? Do you know if they worked out in real life?" We'd written the musical as if they did, but the letters end upon Socks announcing he was on his way home from war.

"Yes, you may, and yes, they did. Socks had good instincts. They were married for over fifty years." Hans's beatific smile subtracts at least twenty years from his wrinkly face.

The relief I feel over a situation that has long since unfolded is both surprising and not. I'm so glad they made it work. "Wow, that's incredible. Did you know them?"

Hans touches the storefront window as he speaks, staring out into the snow. "In February of 1960 I was on military furlough. I didn't have a home to go to, so a friend of mine—Bill—let me tag along with him. He had a girl back in his Nebraska hometown, and this girl happened to have seven sisters. The first time I saw June, she was hanging clothes out to dry, her worn-out skirt flapping in a stiff wind and brick-red hair—like yours—blowing over her eyes. I walked out to help her. I asked so many questions that I earned myself a nickname—Socks, short for Socrates. Two days later, before I went overseas on tour, I proposed. And June was my girl for always, until she died last year. To this day, I maintain that I'm the luckiest man I've ever met."

"Holy. Shit. What? You're Socks? Socks is you?"

His eyes twinkle. "Indeed."

Something worse than the realization of obliviousness drops into my stomach. "Ugh, I'm sorry, Hans. I never asked your wife's name." Which of course would have been a giveaway.

I guess I'll be getting Socks to write *me* some metaphorical letters.

"Ah, it is okay, my dear. But now you see why I have rather a soft spot for Nebraska girls. I've met many who've passed through my store, and there's a solidness about you—something real, something authentic. Hold on to that, Athena. It was one of the very best things about my June."

This Nebraska girl arrived in Chicago, in the scorching August heat, an actress. Full of facades and one-liners.

I leave Hans's shop today, walking out into the fairy snow, something else. A songwriter. A friend. A girlfriend. Someone who understands love a little better.

Someone real.

Someone authentic.

I'm different and I'm the same.

You know, Venus *is* the brightest planet, but many celestial objects burn nearly as strong; so many luminous, sparkling miracles have a place in the vast, endless dark. What would a night sky be without the North Star, the Big Dipper, the Pleiades?

Perhaps Venus shining alone would still be beautiful.

But nowhere nearly as wondrous as an entire galaxy of stars.

I Orbit Venus

Music and Lyrics by Allison L. Bitz

Andante

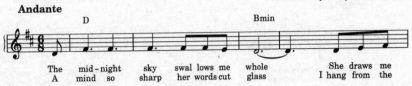

The mid-night sky swal-lows me whole She draws me
A mind so sharp her words cut glass I hang from the

in I am her moon My eyes are wide but I am
ends And ne-ver for-get Her laugh-ter's song Her hands spin

blind Anchors to home wiped out of sight
gold I'd wish three times for just one glance

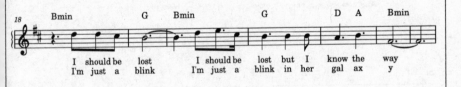

I should be lost I should be lost but I know the way
I'm just a blink I'm just a blink in her gal-ax-y

Cause I or-bit Ven - us And she's all I can see
But I or-bit Ven - us And she's all I can see

Sandwiches

AUTHOR'S NOTE

DEAR READER,

I wrote Bridget as a fat teen because I intimately know what that is like, and also because it was so incredibly important to me to create a fat character who knows her worth. To Bridget, her body just is. She is graceful and attractive and confident and talented *and* fat and exactly the girl I wish I would have seen that I absolutely *was* (hopefully minus Bridget's benign narcissism!), back in high school.

Bridget's mermaid costume story was directly inspired by something that really happened to me, but with the Bridget Bloom twist I think all people deserve. In my senior year, I wanted to be drum majorette. With my music prowess and leadership skills, I was uniquely qualified for the role—in all ways but size. At the time I attended my tiny rural school, the same pretty, white, size eight majorette dress had been worn for many years. I wore a size eighteen my senior year. When I was indeed chosen as the majorette, it wasn't without some hubbub. *How will she fit in the dress?* my peers and the interested adults said, with their eyes only, and in those humiliating moments I would have given *anything* to be perceived as less of a burden, less of a sideshow. Anything *but* stepping down from the role I knew I'd earned. Eventually my (extremely kind but working-with-a-shoestring-budget) teacher came up with a costuming solution. For next to nothing, one of the local moms crafted a knee-length black skirt I could wear with my usual band uniform top and a gold sequined cape that fastened to my shoulders. On marching days, I worked that cape for all it was worth, whirling it around and over my face as though I were the Phantom of the Opera. The laughter was a cover, of course, for the guilt and shame I carried due to my hometown's sidelong glances, taking in the size eighteen body at the end of a yearslong line of size eight majorettes. There was no pretty white dress for me. I was "other." And I wish no one ever had to feel these ways because of their body.

When Bridget needs a new mermaid costume for the Lynch high school musical, it just happens. It's all practicality; bodies simply come in many different sizes. There is no shaming via herself or via others. She wears the sparkly dad-crafted fin and conches with gusto and poise, and she makes no apologies. *This* is the world I want for fat teens, and better yet, I wish for a world where all schools have enough arts funding to enthusiastically shell out (see what I did there?) for mermaid costumes of any size.

Since my youth, I have lived in every clothes size between a six and a twenty. It is hard work to remember that I have exactly the same amount of worth at every size, because society is loud. *Take up less space*, say the masses, whose collective whisper is a roar. But I issue the charge: Take up *more* space, folx. Especially you, my ladies and femmes. Let your hair be big and your smile be bigger, and your ass, is that big, too? Good. Be vast. Be brilliant. Know that your worth as a human being is immutable.

I really could have used Bridget as an inspiration and a validation when I was younger, but since I didn't have her, I can only hope that she has helped you.

—ALLISON L. BITZ, AUTHOR

ACKNOWLEDGMENTS

WELL. THESE ACKNOWLEDGMENTS WERE LITERALLY years in the making and I'm a bit emotionally overwhelmed that I get to write them at all. My heart overflows.

First and absolutely most important, to Laura Taylor Namey and Joan F. Smith, my critique partners and two of the best friends anyone could ever ask for. At this point it's hard to remember a time I didn't talk to you every single day. Thank you for loving cheese (caprese for life!), for letting me be the Fireball to your Sancerre, and for never giving up on me. You have undoubtedly grown me in ways I know and in ways I'm sure I don't. I am forever grateful.

To Natascha Morris, who is my literary agent and my friend. You told me so many times that I was a *when* not an *if*, and your unshakable confidence in my work means more to me than I'll ever be able to tell you. Thank you for fiercely championing me and Bridget.

To Erika DiPasquale, my editor, for choosing Bridget and loving her as much as I do. Your vision for this book amazes me again and again. Every time I hear from you, I think, *I am the luckiest.* Thank you also for being my NYC concierge, especially the part where you made a special trip into the city so we could meet. (See? I'm the luckiest.) Next time I will drink less coffee.

To the entire team at HarperCollins, thank you for fighting for Bridget and for taking care of me during the publication process. Special thanks to Megan Ilnitzki for being an early reader and supporter of Bridget, to managing editors Mikayla Lawrence and Gwen Morton, to production managers Annabelle Sinoff and Nicole Moulaison, to designers Laura Mock and Joel Tippie, and also to Audrey Diestelkamp, Taylan Salvati, Patty Rosati's team, Andrea Pappenheimer's team, Caitlin Garing's team, and everyone else who had a hand in making Bridget sparkle!

To my cover artist, Mallory Heyer—thank you for capturing the essence of Bridget in visual form! I have the close-up of Bridget's sweet, saucy face printed out and proudly displayed in my office, and don't you think that's exactly how B would want it?

The manuscript for *The Unstoppable Bridget Bloom* had many readers over many years. Thank you to Ambriah Underwood and a second anonymous sensitivity reader—your careful work was much appreciated. Thank you to Michelle Hazen, Emily E. Dickson, and Linnea Schiff, who read early versions. Brett Hall and Nicole Lozano—thank you for being my trusted beta readers and cheerleaders, every single time. John Rundall, thank you for reading all my stuff, even the terrible stuff right off my computer screen, and for keeping me sane. I also vote you Most Likely to Lose at Cribbage.

So many villages sustain me! My Twitter and beyond writing community, including but not limited to Lynn Painter, Dante Medema, Kelly DeVos, Deborah Crossland, and everyone on Team Nat—thank you for being there. My psychologist group, without whom I could *not* have weathered pandemic-era mental health provision (let alone writing!): Drs. Megan Watson, Chelsi Davis, Gina Furr, and Nichole Shada. Thank you for keeping me alive. (And here's a shout-out to my own therapist—thanks, Lindsey!) My friends, particularly Janelle Jenniges, Jena Johnson, Amanda Johnson, Alex Krejci, and Kami Kobza—thank you for believing in me, asking questions about the process, and celebrating with me. To the Mill coffee shops in Lincoln—thank you for the light, the background noise, the caffeine, and the chance encounters.

It's maybe weird to write an acknowledgment to my clients, but I'm going to. Thank you, clients, for continuing to trust me with your hearts and hurts. I work for you, but you give me hope, and without hope, I could not write.

To my family, who has given me both roots and wings. Alan and Shari Michl—I've always said I got the most extreme parts of both of you, and lucky me, you love me anyway. Thank you for caring for me at my best and at my worst, *even* when I'm hungry. (*Do something!*) To Nate, Abby, and Cason Michl, for food and warmth and hugs. My extended family and my in-laws (Margaret Bitz, Paula Brown and co., Lois Relys, so many others)—I am grateful for every one of you. Thank you for being in my life. (And I miss you, Jim.) To my late grandpas, Richard Michl and Richard "Nick" Nicholas—I named the whole school after you. I imagine somehow you know this and are laughing over a drink together, *We are in a children's book, what a world*. I wish I could hug you both one more time. To my grandmas: Doris Nicholas, Evelyn Michl, and Carol Michl—you are all in these pages, just like you are all in *me*.

Last and not least—more like the grand finale, my loves—the people who make my house a home and make that home somewhere I can create. Jonah Bitz, thank you for making me belly laugh every single day. Evie Bitz, your smile and your nurturing spirit bring me so much joy. You two are my greatest accomplishments and always will be. And to James "Jeb" Bitz—there would be no books without you. You have provided space for me to be unapologetically myself. Thank you for growing up with me, for patience on the nights my brain was fried, for being the person I go to with every hurt and every triumph, and for loving me with an open hand.

I have to mention Maple Moo, the dog who greets me every day (multiple times a day) as if she hasn't seen me in years, even if I haven't left the house. It makes a girl feel good, you know? Rosie Cotton, our hot mess dog, and Willy and Teddy (cats)—you guys are all right, too, I guess.

Though I tried my best here, I'm positive I forgot to credit someone or a few someones. (Hellooooo, anxiety, my steadfast friend!) If you are that someone, forgive me.

Finally, to you, reader—you made it all the way through these sappy acknowledgments? I am impressed. Thank you for picking up this copy of *The Unstoppable Bridget Bloom*, whether in hard copy, in ebook, in audiobook, or from your library. You are why I write! And if you happen to be making any of your own music with the sheet music / chords / lyrics included in this book, please, please share with me!